New Carthage

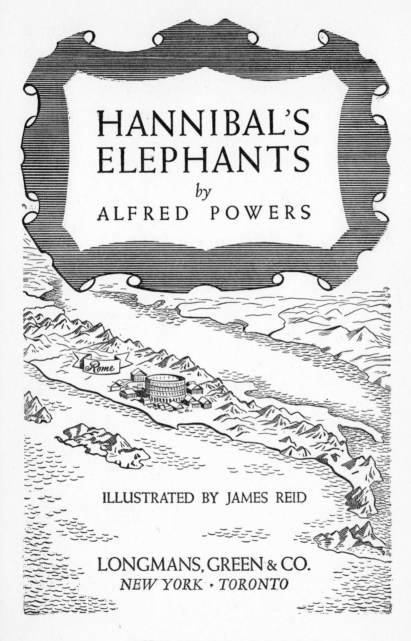

HANNIBAL'S ELEPHANTS

by

ALFRED POWERS

ILLUSTRATED BY JAMES REID

LONGMANS, GREEN & CO.
NEW YORK · TORONTO

LONGMANS, GREEN AND CO., INC.
55 FIFTH AVENUE, NEW YORK 3

LONGMANS, GREEN AND CO. LTD.
OF PATERNOSTER ROW
43 ALBERT DRIVE, LONDON. S.W. 19
NICOL ROAD, BOMBAY
17 CHITTARANJAN AVENUE, CALCUTTA
36A MOUNT ROAD, MADRAS

LONGMANS, GREEN AND CO.
215 VICTORIA STREET, TORONTO 1

20006
2/5/48

HANNIBAL'S ELEPHANTS

COPYRIGHT · 1944
BY ALFRED POWERS

PUBLISHED SIMULTANEOUSLY IN THE DOMINION OF CANADA
BY LONGMANS, GREEN AND CO., TORONTO

First Edition October 1944
Reprinted November 1946

PRINTED IN THE UNITED STATES OF AMERICA
MONTAUK BOOK MFG. CO., INC., NEW YORK

ILLUSTRATIONS

ONE

I, AGENOR THE CARTHAGINIAN, WRITE THIS, I, AGENOR OF THE Elephants. I set down this account of my days with the great Hannibal. When I am through writing, I shall hide it from the Romans deep in the catacombs of Carthage.

I begin with a May evening at sunset. Scarbas stood gloomily with me in front of Old Anak.

Along the Spanish rivulets the bushes were heavy with bloom and scent. A salty breath came up from the Mediterranean. Around us was the musk of the elephants. These three fragrances met and mixed deliciously in my nostrils. I, Agenor the Carthaginian, sniffed the delight of it in the camp of Hannibal at New Carthage in Spain, in the Year of the World 3786.

A debate that night was to decide whether or not the fighting tuskers would be taken on the long march to conquer Rome.

"I feel it in my bones," said Scarbas, "I feel it in my bones like a great ache that the elephants will be left behind. The debate can mean naught but damage. I mistrust the mouthings of these rhetoricians, this Gillimas and this Misdes. They will prattle out of their books against elephants in war. Hannibal will believe, and the generals, and the army. So, Agenor, set not your heart on going, unless you practice enough with the bow to become an archer. Then you can leave Scarbas behind, and Old Anak, and Little Enoch, and all the rest."

"No," I cried, "I will never leave you. But you will go, the elephants will go. Nothing has been decided yet."

Scarbas, an old Carthaginian of woeful countenance, was headkeeper of Hannibal's elephants. I, a stripling of thirteen, was his assistant. He had rescued me from peevish, nagging Morbal, in charge of the three hundred heavy-eating idlers in the stables at Carthage. There I had waited on Morbal more than I had on the elephants.

As we talked, the rosy sunset added a slight flush to the ivory of Anak's tusks, each of which weighed almost as much as I did. His trunk swung over us and between us, and hovered about us, and curled ticklishly under our chins, and rested on the crowns of our bare heads so we could feel the suction of it in our hair. His place was at the beginning of the herd that stood picketed in a long row. The open ground in front of him, more than our tent, served us as headquarters. Here, after several minutes of the darkest forebodings, Scarbas clutched at the thought of an intervening fate to keep Hannibal from going to Rome without us.

"The same fate, Agenor," he said, "that saved him twice before when he was nearly lost to the Carthaginians."

"How was he nearly lost twice?" I asked.

"Through the Carthaginians themselves. In both cases they almost gave him up to death. The first time was when he was a small boy. A hundred sons of noble families were sacrificed to Moloch. Hannibal was ordered to be one of them, and a priest of Moloch came to fetch him."

"How did he escape, Scarbas? How did Hannibal escape?"

"Hamilcar, his father, dressed up a slave boy in fine clothes and wept over him in pretended grief. The priest didn't know the real lad he was after had a bulging forehead. So it was the slave boy who rolled down the sloping, outstretched arms of the great, brazen idol of Moloch into the fire, and Hannibal lived."

"And the second time, Scarbas?"

"That is what caused the war. Rome and Carthage were at peace. Then Hannibal besieged and took Saguntum—"

"I know," I interrupted, "we were there with all the elephants—"

"And this," continued Scarbas, "threw the Romans into a great rage. They claimed Saguntum was a Roman city even though it was in Spain and straightway sent ambassadors to Carthage. They demanded the guilty general. They demanded Hannibal."

"But Carthage would never give him up," I cried. "The Senate would never think of giving him up to the Romans to do with as they pleased."

"Yes, to their shame, Agenor, they did think of it. The Senators were afraid of Rome. Besides, there were men in Carthage jealous of Hannibal. General Gisbo of the Purple Band belongs to the powerful party of big slave-owners and rich merchants who did not want him as leader. The Roman ambassadors were kept waiting for an answer until one of them impatiently stood before the Senate. He held out a fold of his toga as a woman holds out her apron with vegetables in it.

"'I have here peace or war,' he said. 'You can take either. Which will it be?'

"This insolence was too much even for the cowardly Senators who came to their senses. 'Whichever you please,' they answered.

" 'I give you war, then,' said the Roman.

"Now they will have Hannibal in Rome, but not in the way they expected. He had won. Hannibal had won. A second time fate had protected him. It may do so a third time, saving to him the elephants."

But Scarbas was only talking to prop his dismal spirits. Soon all his forebodings returned.

"Agenor," he said, "I have served under three supreme commanders—Hamilcar, Hasdrubal, Hannibal—and now I am to be left behind. Always before, I have known as many battle secrets as General Hanno, General Mago, General Maharbal, General Barmocarus, General Samnis, even proud General Gisbo. Now, when Hannibal plans with them how the great army will fight next day, there will be no talk of elephants and what Scarbas will make them do."

I, Agenor, did not share his fears because I knew the world could not move without Scarbas and the elephants. Hannibal told Scarbas. Scarbas told the drivers. The drivers told the elephants. And so upon the battlefield great Hannibal's thoughts would come to life and reality in the movements and perfection of these immense creatures. Sometimes far in the night Scarbas would wake up and see the supreme commander in his tent.

"Tell me, Scarbas," he would ask, "suppose the elephants are on our right, and we want them to go forward diagonally against the enemy's right, will they do it, or must we have them go straight ahead against the enemy's left?"

"They will go diagonally, sir, if you wish it," Scarbas would answer. "You can depend upon it."

I gazed up at Old Anak. Ten feet high he was. His small, piglike eyes had looked upon a warring world for eighty-seven years. He had fought Romans in Sicily, Romans in Carthage, Romans in Spain, and—soon it would be—Romans in Rome.

About this last, Scarbas was so doubtful that he set up his wailings again: "These rhetoricians, this Gillimas, this Misdes, what do they know about elephants? In their books they will find mean things to prove elephants are not good in battle and cannot cross mountains. The army will go to Rome and we will be left behind. Hannibal will need us and we will not be there to help."

As officers and men began to pass by on their way to the place of debate, it seemed to him they were going forward to certain condemnation of the elephants.

General Hanno, General Samnis, and General Barmocarus walked past, and with them was Hannibal. The generals were talking but Hannibal was silent and in deep thought, and he took no notice of us. This was the last straw for poor Scarbas. He now considered himself utterly forsaken and the elephants completely discarded.

"He knows," declared Scarbas, "he knows they are going to be left behind. And he doesn't want to make us feel bad by telling us."

"No, Scarbas, he doesn't know. No one knows in advance how a debate will turn out."

A group of soldiers went by, singing a song which some camp poet had roughly put together in rhyme and some camp musician had as roughly given a tune:

Across the Alps and Apennines,
In battles far from home,
His elephants lunge at trembling lines—
When Hannibal conquers Rome.

"Hear that?" I demanded. "Hear that, Scarbas?"

"It's only a song. It means nothing."

The men moved on, and their cadenced footfalls served somewhat as the accompaniment of a drum. A second stanza of their song came back to us:

His elephants large,
With tusks they charge,
They gore to death
And tramp out breath—
When Hannibal conquers Rome.

"Scarbas, did you also hear that?"

"I heard."

"My bones are beginning to tell me things too. They tell me the debate will end in our favor."

"You can't count anything on what a song says," persisted Scarbas.

General Mago, Hannibal's younger brother, and General Maharbal, the great cavalry leader, passed along a few yards away and called out greetings not only to us but to Old Anak.

Soon afterward came General Gisbo, walking with a group of lesser officers of the Purple Band. He wore his red cloak and his shining helmet and his six rings on his left-hand fingers, one each on the index and little finger and two each on the others. These stood for six important campaigns he had been through. He was tall and stiffly straight. At his side was a short Spanish sword in a scabbard studded with gems. In his right hand he carried a light club about a yard long, with which he flicked off leaves or the heads of plants or tapped on the ground or drew figures in the dust.

He stopped in front of us. The other officers left him there. "You look downhearted, Scarbas," he remarked. "I suppose you realize that there is little chance of the elephants being taken on this long march of a thousand miles. You should feel relieved at not having to expose the animals to the rigors of crossing three high, snowy mountain ranges which would surely kill them."

"It has not been decided yet, sir, that the elephants will not go," replied Scarbas, concealing his heavy doubts with dignity.

"Only an encumbrance. The forty-three elephants could be nothing else. Any idea of taking them is absurd."

"We would take only thirty-seven, sir. Three have young calves."

"The same thing. Imagine starting out on the longest and hardest military march of the world loaded down at every turn with thirty-seven elephants."

"Formerly, sir, you were not so much opposed to them."

I thought Gisbo's straight, rigid frame jerked into sudden, tenser rigidity. For a long moment he stood studying the unhappy face of the old elephant keeper.

"What do you mean?" he asked quietly, slowly.

"You did not object to elephants on campaigns against the barbarians in the days when Hasdrubal was supreme commander—before he was killed by the Spanish slave."

The tightness went out of Gisbo's shoulders and neck and face. He smiled a natural, easy smile, free of the control that usually characterized his every expression.

"That was different, Scarbas, from this great march," he

explained. "The animals are often valuable in war. I favored their use against the barbarians."

"I wish, sir, you favored them now," said Scarbas, less tense himself from the kinder tone.

Gisbo made no further response. His side had been toward Old Anak. He now faced the big elephant. "Anak," he asked, "do you recognize me?"

Old Anak's trunk dropped close to the ground and curved inward toward himself and it was perfectly still. In this position he looked out of his two small eyes at Gisbo, who now took one step toward him and repeated:

"Anak, do you recognize me? Do you recognize me as a friend?"

I could see that Scarbas was flattered by this neighborly attention to the elephant from the great general of the Purple Band.

To me it had curiously the appearance of being a challenge, a test of the elephant's memory of something which only those two had known. I felt it was for this exchange with Old Anak he had really stopped rather than for any polite gibes at Scarbas. I thought I saw relief upon his face when the big animal remained immovable. He took another step forward. These overtures of good will pleased Scarbas, and their passive acceptance by Old Anak pleased him.

The elephant's trunk very slowly began to move. It lifted and uncurled and reached forward. The end of it went over Gisbo's left shoulder like a great hook. If this had been a swift movement, I would have known it was hostile. If there had been an instantaneous, violent pull forward I would have recognized it for the death grasp I had seen upon battlefields. Though I cannot be sure, I believe it was a friendly gesture, an active response to the overtures of good will. No time was given by Gisbo for me to know the certainty of it. With his staff, he gave two hard, quick blows, and his shoulder was released.

"Anak!" called Scarbas in sharp command, and the elephant's actions were no longer his own.

"The ill-mannered beast with his dirty trunk!" exclaimed Gisbo.

"I am sorry, sir," said Scarbas. "He only wanted to be friendly."

"I do not like the familiarity of such a gross creature," declared Gisbo. "His filthy snout, his foul breath!"

Scarbas and I thought an elephant's breath pleasant, with the purity of a warmed breeze, tinctured but mildly with agreeable flavors, as it passed back and forth through its long, clean channel—not offensive like a camel's. But we smelled things as rough men smell them.

"He will apologize for his manners, sir," said Scarbas to Gisbo. "Down, Anak!" he commanded the elephant. "Down in humility!"

The elephant's legs crumpled and folded to let the great body down flat upon the ground, with his trunk stretched out over the earth in front of him, much in the posture of a remorseful dog. There he lay, all the groveling bulk of him, in abject apology to Gisbo. As he looked at this man before whom he was prostrated, he trumpeted once, sharply, resentfully.

"Up!" called Scarbas.

"All is well," said Gisbo. "The incident is forgotten. I will ask the boy to brush the shoulder of my cloak."

He gave a little shake of adjustment and started away. He had taken only two steps when Old Anak's trunk was thrust suddenly in front of his knees, like an unexpected barrier across a pathway. Gisbo tripped and fell forward, his staff dropping, with both outspread hands breaking his fall upon the dusty earth.

"Anak, down! Down in humility!" In that position Old Anak remained the rest of the time while we brushed Gisbo and brought water and towels for his hands, and said our apologies over and over. As he left, I thought he wore an aspect of concern that would not be wholly accounted for by the actual affront he had received.

"He irritates the elephant," said Scarbas. "He seems to do it on purpose. Old Anak only. Never the others."

"Why does he do it?"

"I do not know. He only began it after the death of the Supreme Commander Hasdrubal."

Men continued to pass on their way to the debate.

"Is it not time for you to go?" I asked Scarbas.

"You go in my place, Agenor," he suggested. "To hear the mean things this Misdes will say against elephants is more than I can stand. You have good ears. Listen to all and come back to me and tell me when it is decided. You can ride Little Enoch and sit upon him while you listen. It will enable you to see all and to hear all."

I went down near the foot of the line and mounted the half-grown elephant to follow the scattered groups of men to the place of the debate. It was a kind of natural amphitheatre. Its sloping walls were covered with officers and soldiers sitting upon the ground. At a camp table in the center were the two debaters and General Hanno, the chairman. Torches burned here and there. Additional light was afforded by the moon and many stars.

Little Enoch stopped at the upper and outer edge of the big saucer, with soldiers everywhere before me and below me too thick to get through. I did not intend to stay so far back but to join the inner edge of listeners.

"Officers and men," I called, "make way for the elephant!"

As I proceeded, men slid out of the way to the right and left. One of these, where I stopped at last, was Hannibal, who immediately re-established himself with his back leaning against the right foreleg of Little Enoch.

A soldier rose and beat upon a big sheet of metal with an iron club, which made an awful clangor. The din fell upon my ears like a blow. The little elephant must have been equally jarred, for his enormous flaps were nervous and twitching. As the sound died away, General Hanno stood up.

"Officers and Soldiers of Carthage," he said, "we now begin a debate on the value of elephants in war. This will decide whether we are to take the Carthaginian herd across the Pyrenees, the Alps, the Apennines to Rome. Gillimas will uphold the affirmative, Misdes the negative. These two young men, trained in Hippomedon's School of Rhetoric at Carthage, will depend wholly upon cool, calm reason. Neither of them, they tell me, has ever ridden an elephant."

Everybody laughed at this, including the rhetoricians themselves. I thought they ought to have been ashamed. I, Agenor, sitting astride Little Enoch's neck, wondered why the great Hannibal and his chief captains should come out to listen to such an ignorant pair.

"We will open with the record of Alexander the Great," announced General Hanno. "Gillimas, are you ready?"

"Ready, sir," he responded.

As he stood up, I saw he was about six feet tall, but stooped at the shoulders, in contrast to the soldierly straightness of General Hanno. And he blinked. I thought to myself that he had always used his eyes too much and his muscles not enough.

As soon as Gillimas had made his point, Misdes jumped up. He was small and quick and dark and, though only a young man, he was half bald already.

"Honorable Chairman," he began, "when King Darius fought Alexander at the Battle of Arbela, he had six hundred thousand men. How many elephants did he have—how many do you say?" He pointed his index finger at me. "You, the boy there on the elephant!" he called out.

"Yes, sir," I replied. "My name is Agenor."

"Well, Agenor, did you make a guess?"

"Yes, sir, to myself I did, but I expect it's wrong."

"What is it?"

"Two hundred and fifty-eight, sir."

"How did you get such an exact number, Agenor?"

"Well, we have a hundred thousand troops and forty-three elephants. King Darius with six hundred thousand men ought to have had six times as many. That would be two hundred and fifty-eight. But I'm afraid it isn't enough."

"On the contrary, Agenor, I'm afraid it's too many. He had fifteen. Think of it, fifteen!"

When the use of Persian elephants against Alexander had been fully debated, the result was two points for the affirmative, three for the negative. During a short recess, the officers and men began to talk to one another, all except Hannibal. He seemed to be in deep thought and no one ventured to interrupt him. He continued to lean against Little Enoch's leg, which must have become cramped from time to time, for during the debate it had been lifted up occasionally as if to get relief from the pressure of the great commander's back. Hannibal had taken off his helmet and laid it beside him. I could look down at his young and handsome head pondering grand thoughts. My pulses leaped with pride and gladness that I was a Carthaginian like him.

General Gisbo and General Maharbal were sitting close together. They stood up to stretch their legs. Gisbo, only a few steps distant, looked at me and his glance was not friendly. He took out a handkerchief and put it to his delicate nose.

"I smell elephant," he said. "I prefer their military history to their fragrance."

If this was a hint that I could leave with Little Enoch during the recess period and not come back, I ignored it.

Hannibal, still silently wrapped in his contemplation, probably did not hear. He, the one most closely inhaling Little Enoch's scents, would not have missed the slur upon his own low taste in smells.

Harshly, deafeningly, the soldier hit the sheet of metal with his iron club. It was time again for the debate, and General Hanno, the chairman, began: "We shall now take up the record of the Syrian kings, then that of Pyrrhus, and finally that of the Carthaginians. Proceed, Gillimas."

"Worthy Judge," said Gillimas, lifting up his stooped figure to speak, "we now come to battles of elephant against elephant, forehead to forehead, pushing, goring, parrying, tusks entangled and jammed, the ground underfoot all encrimsoned and sodden . . ."

I no longer wondered why Hannibal and his great captains should listen to Gillimas and Misdes. It seemed to me now there was naught about elephants they had not learned. I forgot the stoop of the one, the baldness of the other. I wanted to be like them, to know all things as these rhetoricians did.

They spoke alternately, back and forth, until they came to the wars of the Carthaginians against the Romans.

"Respected Judge," began Misdes, "in Sicily the Romans captured one hundred and twenty Carthaginian elephants and took them to march in the general's triumphal procession at Rome. The huge beasts made a long, black section of that parade, stretching a quarter of a mile from the biggest one in front to the smallest one at the end, trunk holding tail, as they walked with stately slowness through the alien streets, along the Sacred Way, between crowded lines of the populace. Then what did the Romans do? They led the elephants to the Roman Circus and there, in sight of the cheering multitude, killed every one of them. That place was to be drenched many times with the blood of gladiators, but never was it to receive such red rivulets as now flowed out over the drinking earth. The captive Carthaginian drivers stood sickened, but only huzzas came from the throats of the Romans. It is a point, sir, that I offer with horror."

General Hanno, saying never a word, wrote down the score slowly. After the voice of Misdes ceased, a special hush lay upon the assembly.

I looked down at Hannibal. He was gripping his hands. I knew, we all knew, that as a boy of nine he had sworn eternal hatred of Rome. Those clenched fingers were not thickly encircled with rings like Gisbo's. He wore only one ring, and the gem of this was a little vial of poison, an escaping drink . . . the Romans would never have Hannibal abject and alive.

The debate was at an end. The two orators shook hands with each other, which was about the fifth time they had done so. General Hanno added up the points and announced:

"This debate has considered the value of elephants in wars over a period of no less than ninety-three years. As long-lived as elephants are, no little calf at the beginning of this period would normally have been living as an aged tusker at the end of it. I count up ten points for the affirmative, ten for the negative. Officers and Soldiers of Carthage, the debate has resulted in a tie."

A tie! My pulses leaped quick and cold in the panic of dismay as to what would happen to Scarbas, to the elephants, and to me. I, Agenor, wanted to do nothing so much at that moment as to go to Scarbas as fast as the legs of Little Enoch would carry me, bearing these dark tidings of a tie so portentous for us.

I leaned over and called down to the supreme commander: "Sir, if convenient for you, I wish to take away the elephant."

Absent-mindedly, Hannibal moved forward to free Little Enoch's leg. He said nothing; he did not thank me; he was deep in thought.

I looked behind me. "Officers and Soldiers," I requested, "if you will be so good as to make a passage, I will back out the elephant."

As soon as we were clear of the men, I turned Little Enoch around, head forward, and urged him on in the moonlight with all possible speed toward the elephant pickets and Scarbas.

TWO

As I came in sight of Scarbas, he was squatting on the ground in front of Old Anak with his chin upon his hands. When he saw me hurrying toward him, he stood up. Still sitting astride the neck of Little Enoch, with no more than three cubits of moonlight between us, I looked down into his dismal face, its swarthy, weathered contours softened, and the tragedy upon it softened too, but not concealed, by the luminous Spanish evening. But there was hope, a tiny spark of it, in his breast, and a great eagerness in his voice.

"Tell me, Agenor, tell me quick!" I hesitated, gazing at him in compassion for what I had to say and seeking a merciful way to say it, for I was still under the spell of gracious speech and wanted not to use blunt words. "Ah," he said resignedly, "you do not need to tell me. Those idle talkers condemned us. The decision was against the elephants."

"It was a tie, Scarbas. Not for the elephants, not against them, the same for both sides. Perchance the elephants were good in one battle but always there was another battle where they were not good."

The unhappy face of Scarbas twisted and his jaws worked in his effort to make head or tail of this impossible decision. "A tie," he muttered. "Ah, how much we suffer from these

16

bookish debaters! A tie, do you not see, Agenor, that such a thing is unworkable in case of the elephants? By the honest terms of a tie, we cannot go, we cannot be left behind. Did they say, then, what is to become of us?"

"No, Scarbas, they did not say, but they could send us to Carthage."

"Agenor, what is this I hear? Did they say they would send us to Carthage and you have not told me?"

"No, no, Scarbas. They didn't mention it. I was just answering you, just something I thought of."

"Carthage—would they do that?" murmured the old man dismally. "There with Morbal, mean, bossy, old Morbal, head-keeper of the three hundred elephants in the triple walls. Agenor, is there a chance, tell me, do you think there's a chance of this happening? I do not like Morbal, and Morbal does not like me, and he would be over me and he would be over you. We would never be happy again with our own elephants and with Hannibal who lets us manage them as we think best, as long as they do what he wants them to in battle. No, Agenor, anything but that, anything but going back to Carthage to be under Morbal. Why did not the great Hannibal himself decide what was to be done with us? This Gillimas and this Misdes, how long have they worked with elephants? Where did they learn about elephants? Did they work under Morbal?"

"No, I don't think they even know Morbal."

"That is good," said Scarbas, with lessened prejudice. "Who trained them, then?"

"They have never ridden on an elephant. General Hanno said so, and they didn't deny it."

"By the fires of Moloch," cried Scarbas, "what are you telling me? Old Anak here who can do all things when I speak to him, and many things when you command him, what would he be with this Gillimas, this Misdes—he would be nothing, no more useful than a great boulder on a hillside. And these two are the ones who say that Old Anak and the whole herd cannot go to Rome—ignorant men given the power to do all this mischief, ignorant, pernicious men."

"Scarbas, if you had heard them, you would not call them ignorant. They know the most about elephants of any two men in all the world."

"Agenor, hold your tongue! I will not hear such insults. Morbal and Scarbas are the two men who know the most about elephants in all the world. I do not like Morbal and he does not like me, but he knows about elephants. We fought, Morbal and I, with Hamilcar in Sicily, we fought with him against the mercenaries, and Old Anak was with us. Morbal stayed at Carthage, and Old Anak was with me still, carrying the boy Hannibal day after day upon his back, when I went that far distance with Hamilcar along the African shore to cross at the Pillars of Hercules. Was it not I who had charge of the elephants, and was not Old Anak always with me, when I fought with Hamilcar in Spain, and with Hasdrubal after he died, and with the great Hannibal after Hasdrubal died? I first, and next Morbal, we know the most about elephants."

I should have stopped, but I was only a boy of thirteen, obstinate in my opinions and filled, I suppose, with the spirit of argument from having just listened to so much debate.

"Yes, Scarbas, you know much, and Morbal knows much, but you know only what happened to yourselves. Gillimas and Misdes know what happened in all battles and all wars. Not you and Morbal but Gillimas and Misdes know the most about elephants."

"You insulting whelp!" he shouted. "A demon has possessed you. The debate has ruined you. I take you and cherish you like a son and train you as carefully as I would train a young elephant, and you talk to me so, and insult me, and say I do not know about elephants."

"Gillimas and Misdes," I said, "did not lose their tempers when they disagreed, but shook hands five times. They use reason in an argument, not anger like you do, Scarbas."

"You impudent, ungrateful son of my adoption, you add to my sadness. Get out of my sight. Take Little Enoch to his mother. Look after the calves. Leave me, for it was an unhappy day when I took you in as a son. Leave, I say! Get out of my sight!"

Little Enoch, big, lubberly fellow that he was, received joyful greetings and many caresses from his mother. The elephants were chained to their stakes in a long line. At the head of the line was Old Anak, whom I had just left. At the foot of it were the three cow-elephants with young calves. Next to them was the mother of Little Enoch, and then Little Enoch himself, still in many ways enough of a baby to have a place at the nursery end of the pickets where he was a happy companion of the very small ones. These youngsters wanted to play with me now; they were ready for frisking and games. But I was not in the mood. Two or three times I rather sternly placed the three alongside their mothers and gave them increasingly sharp raps with my elephant staff.

Then I sat down in front of the cow-elephant at the very end. Directly above was the big Spanish moon and all the countless stars. I could look along that moonlit line in front of the elephants and dimly see Scarbas in his accustomed position when sad or thoughtful—squatted in front of Old Anak with his chin upon his hands.

The man and his adopted son, after their quarrel, thus sat upon the ground far apart from each other, one in what I knew was rapidly cooling anger, the other in repentance. Somehow this evening I felt more regret than usual for what had happened between us. The debate had indeed changed me, as Scarbas had said, but not in the way he believed. It opened my mind to a degree it had never been opened before. It gave me my first full glimpse of the immeasurable capacity of man's thoughts compared with his limited body.

I waited a while and as I waited I heard the clangor of the iron club banging upon the iron sheet. I judged this was the signal for everyone to leave the place of debate, and it seemed to me that the meeting had been overly protracted. Soldiers and minor officers soon began to pass by on the way to their billets. I decided it was safe by now to rejoin Scarbas.

As I approached him he was in the same posture under the waving trunk of Old Anak, only now his face was completely buried in his hands as though he were asleep. Before I arrived, a tall man came up and stopped in front of him, without saying anything. It was Hannibal.

I shouted as I hurried forward: "Scarbas, attention!"

He jumped to his feet and saluted. "Forgive me, sir, I was not aware of your presence, with men passing all the time."

"Great heavens, Scarbas," exclaimed Hannibal, "that face, so tragic, so long! It is a face for a funeral. Has an elephant died?"

"Worse, sir. They are not to go with you to conquer Rome."

"And, my disconsolate Scarbas, who told you all this?"

"Agenor said the debate was a tie."

Hannibal reached out and took hold of the turned-down corners of the elephant keeper's mouth, and turned them up. "Now," he said, "that is more suitable for what I am to tell you. Agenor left too soon. The debate was thrown open to general discussion. A soldier, just a man of the ranks he was, jumped to his feet and here is what he said: 'By the fires of Moloch, worthy chairman, these young rhetoricians have had their eyes glued on the distant past so they couldn't see recent things. Does it mean naught that a great nation like Carthage has stalls in its triple walls for three hundred war elephants? Have you forgotten what Hasdrubal did with elephants in Spain? Have you forgotten what Hannibal did with them on the Tagus?' That is what the soldier said. Scarbas, do you remember the Tagus? Do you remember it, Scarbas?"

"Ah, yes, sir, when the barbarians were crossing the river and the elephants picked them up, and then slung them back, limp and lifeless as scarecrows, into the river, and Old Anak, all by himself, splashed the Tagus forty-eight times that afternoon with his throwings."

"And, Scarbas," Hannibal went on in glad recital, "another common soldier got up and asked if Alexander and Pyrrhus were to be counted and Hannibal was to be left out, and he said, by the scorched sands of the desert, he didn't think much of a debate that did that. And so it went on, Scarbas, until the affirmative had six points ahead. What pleased me most was that all of them spoke up for the affirmative, none for the negative. You see, Scarbas, the army wants the elephants along. I meant all the time that they should go. But I prefer to have these things come from the army itself, whenever possible, rather than from the commander. A man carries out his own will, or what he thinks is his own, with more zeal than another's. I would have found a way, Scarbas, never doubt it; but now, better still, the troops have ordered the elephants to go."

Old Scarbas stood in complete adoration before that twenty-nine-year-old man.

The great Hannibal turned to me: "I came by to stop Scarbas from worrying, and also to thank you, Agenor, for the comfort of Little Enoch's leg this evening. By the way, Scarbas, this lad has a good thirteen-year-old head and a ready, unembarrassed tongue, but he must still learn not to give up too soon, as he did over the tied debate. Shall we make him head elephant keeper of the three calves too young to go, and their mothers, and perchance also Little Enoch?"

My heart went faint. In the moment of supreme happiness for Scarbas, here I was cast down to the lowest depths. If Scarbas was still angry with me and did not come to my defense, I was doomed to be left behind as nursemaid at New Carthage in Spain and never cross the Alps and never ride Little Enoch through the gates of Rome.

"Little Enoch, sir, is now big enough to make a serviceable war elephant."

My dark outlook did not improve. Not a word about me, just about Little Enoch. Now I wouldn't even have him, just those three frisky, irritating calves, and their foolish, affectionate mothers.

"Then, Agenor," said Hannibal to me, "it looks as if you will have only six elephants to look after in New Carthage. The three calves will give you excellent practice as a trainer."

Was I indeed no longer like a son to Scarbas? Had he entirely forsaken me?

"The boy, sir, is my chief assistant. One of the older men can be left to look after the three cow-elephants and their young calves. I fought many years with your father. I am not so young any more. I use Agenor for my legs and sometimes, when he is sensible, for my head. It would be well, sir, for him to go along."

"By the fires of Moloch, so he shall," declared Hannibal. "Did I not live with my father in camp from the time I was nine?"

"Oh, thank you, sir," I said. "You will never regret it."

Just then Gisbo came by, giving no greeting to Scarbas or to me, but saluting Hannibal: "An interesting debate, sir, but the negative overlooked several weighty arguments against taking the animals. Adapted to warm climates, they will have to climb three snowy mountain ranges. Prodigious eaters, they will have to be fed when often there will be too little subsistence for horses and men. They will delay the march. They will complicate the crossing of streams. And one of them, sir, has become so old and ill-tempered that he is dangerous."

During the latter part of his talk, his movements had taken him under the waving trunk of Old Anak, and this was passing back and forth very closely over Gisbo's head. As he ceased speaking, he swung his club in a sharp blow upon the offending trunk. "Keep your slobbering snout and foul breath out of my face!" he shouted.

The features of Scarbas, as I could see in the moonlight, worked in anger. Hannibal's own countenance grew stern, and I thought he would speak in rebuke, but he refrained.

"I bid you good evening, sir," said Gisbo. He had not gone three steps before Old Anak's extended trunk took a corner of the cloak in its grasp. Gisbo was brought up short, the brooch that had clasped the cloak at his throat gave way, and the garment was swung free in the air by Old Anak.

Gisbo drew his sword. I thought for a moment that he would cut off the elephant's trunk at one angry blow. But he had the self-control, in the presence of the supreme commander, to return this to its scabbard. Instead, he took his stick and hit the trunk such a blow that I winced in sympathetic pain and Old Anak dropped the cloak. While Gisbo was stooping to pick it up, Old Anak swung at him and knocked him down, flat upon the earth, so that we were afraid the breath was dashed out of him. Soon he rose, but for the first moments on his feet he stood groggily. Scarbas took Old Anak in immediate charge, but this time did not order him to grovel before his assailant. I picked up and dusted the cloak and handed it to Gisbo. With great dignity and without a word to me, he threw the rich garment over his shoulders and held it, in place of its broken clasp, with the fingers of his left hand.

"The supreme commander has seen for himself the dangerous temper of the beast. Good evening, sir." He walked away, very erect and straight and soldierly, as if nothing had happened.

The look upon Scarbas' face was now one of concern for the reputation of Old Anak.

"Let's see," observed Hannibal, "Old Anak is now eighty-six. Is it not so?"

"He is eighty-seven, sir."

"Perhaps we should leave him behind with the mothers

I thought he would cut off the elephant's trunk

and the calves. I do not like the irritability and savagery he
showed just now."

"Forgive me for speaking, sir. But there is no kinder elephant, no more obedient one, none that would be greater in
war. Did he not fight for your father in Sicily and against the
mercenaries? Did he not fight many times in Spain for him?
Did he not fight for your brother-in-law, Hasdrubal, when he
was supreme commander? Has he not fought valiantly for you,
O Hannibal? If you value, sir, the work of the whole herd in
battle, you will consent that he shall go. He is not ill-tempered,
he is not dangerous. It is only that he has met with many
indignities and has suffered much irritation from General
Gisbo. It even seems, sir, that he wishes to provoke the elephant to some act that will brand him as dangerous. Old
Anak returns General Gisbo's hostility, and the reasons for
this, beyond the irritations and indignities, I do not know of a
certainty, and you can bear witness that I never come to you
with suspicions and surmises."

The old man stopped suddenly. He bit his lips as if he would
recall those last words. "Oh, forgive me, sir," he said.

Hannibal looked at him searchingly for a moment. What
was the seed of Old Anak's hate for Gisbo? That is what I
was wondering. Hannibal was much quicker and keener than
I. Was he wondering the same?

"In this army," said Hannibal very solemnly, "there can
be no justification of a dumb brute's hate of a human being.
Its very existence condemns it. It gives the power of punish-
ment and retribution to an unreasoning creature."

"This I know, sir," answered Scarbas. "If you will approve
Old Anak's going, I will be sponsor of his good behavior."

"Very well," agreed Hannibal. "You are the chief elephant

keeper and it is not for me to say which elephants to take and which to leave. I shall hold you responsible, Scarbas."

He told us good night and walked away. We watched him as long as we could see him in the moonlight.

"Scarbas," I asked, "what happened once to make Old Anak hate Gisbo?"

"You're but a boy, Agenor. I tell all the things I know only to Hannibal. Even to him I do not tell an old man's efforts to find out what an elephant remembers."

"But, Scarbas, you think you know something?"

"It is time for sleep, Agenor. Let us to our tent."

THREE

AFTER GOING TO BED MY EYES HAD BEEN LATE IN CLOSING. SO
the next morning they were reluctant to open. I rubbed them
to give them a clearer view of Scarbas standing beside my
pallet. His face had taken on its accustomed melancholy, but
this was belied by a voice that was happy and eager.

"Up, Agenor, to breakfast and to work. A great honor has
come to the elephants."

"I know," I said. "They're going with Hannibal to Rome."

"That's justice," Scarbas corrected me. "No more. The honor
is, if you will get up and about, you can distribute the notices
to the army. It's usually the work of a man on a horse. But you
can do it today on Little Enoch."

"What notices?" I asked.

"That the army is marching to Rome."

"Doesn't everybody except the Romans know it already?"

"True enough, but there must be notices for all that."

"Where do I get them?"

"At the tent of Gillimas and Misdes."

You may be sure, I lost no time. I bolted my breakfast,
mounted astride the neck of the young elephant, and was on
my way, feeling intoxicated with importance.

Gillimas and Misdes occupied the same tent. Other smaller

28

tents belonged to them, where scribes and clerks were copying and writing. There were tables, and papyrus rolls, and a general quantity of paper work that surprised me. Gillimas, seeing my surprise, said: "Hiserbal, show the boy the elephant roll."

I went into this tent, where the slim, weak-eyed clerk took out a list, from among others stretching on and on for what seemed cubits and cubits. He found the elephant roll and located it for me with his finger. "Elephants" was the big heading. Then came "Scarbas, headkeeper," and I was right under him, "Agenor, assistant." After the names of the drivers and others who worked around the herd, it said "Elephants" again, but not written so big this time. Here were the names of the elephants themselves, beginning with Old Anak, still put down as eighty-six, though his eighty-seventh birthday had been three weeks back. I told Hiserbal and he corrected it, and said for me to bring the ages up to date for any others which had had recent birthdays.

All those killed along the Tagus or at the siege of Saguntum had lines through their names and each time out at the margin was the word "dead." The twenty-one which Hannibal's older brother had, and was going to keep in his army to protect Spain while we were gone, carried check marks after them and the letters "tr," which meant transferred, as Hiserbal explained.

Our forty-three were all listed, with not a one of them missing, not even the three calves. After Old Anak came Zain who was seventy-one and surnamed Ear Flapper; Harab, surnamed Broken Tusk; Bolobo, surnamed the Thunderer; Sapor, surnamed Old Ivory Spear; Yenbo, surnamed the Roman Crusher. So the list went on, with ages and surnames. Fourth from the

end was Little Enoch. At the very end were the three calves:
Ziglag, Scaliger, and Sophonisba.

The scribes and clerks must have had cramped fingers from
all the writing they had turned out. There were one hundred
notices for me to take about, five to Hannibal himself, seven to
General Hanno for the Numidians, four to General Mago, five
to General Maharbal, three to General Gisbo, two to General
Samnis, one to Scarbas, and so on. I read what it said:

ORDER TO THE ARMY OF CARTHAGE

All Officers and Men Take Notice: On May 30, in the Year of
the World 3786, the army of 90,000 infantry, 12,000 cavalry, and 37
elephants will begin its march from New Carthage, across the
Pyrenees in Spain, up the Rhone, across the Alps, into Italy, across
the Apennines, to Rome. There will be adventure, victories, conquest
of a hated nation, rich spoils, and glory. Let all parts of the army
be made ready—the Purple Band, the Numidian horsemen, the
elephants, the Spanish foot, the Libyan bowmen, the Balearic
slingers, the African spearmen, all units whatsoever of the cavalry,
the infantry, the artillery, together with the commissariat, the baggage animals, the patrols, supplies, equipment, treasury, and gifts
for the barbarians and Gauls en route. Let preparations begin at
once. Detailed directions for the order of the march will be issued
in a later bulletin.

Hannibal,
Supreme Commander.

Still under the spell of my mind's awakening, I drank in the
formal language as one would swallow a delicious liquid.

"How beautiful," I exclaimed, "how beautiful are the things
Hannibal says in writing!"

Both Gillimas and Misdes laughed.

"Oh, Agenor of the Elephants," said Misdes, "what would

I not give to have your fresh and illusioned spirit! Do you think Hannibal wrote that? He called Gillimas to his tent and said: 'The army leaves for Rome on the thirtieth of May. You and Misdes get out the orders.' We do this sort of thing all the time, Agenor. That's what the Old Man's got us for."

"Why do you call him Old Man?"

"If a commander were not the Old Man to his troops, he would wonder what was the matter," said Misdes. "Gods, demigods, great men, generals, are never young, Agenor. One of them could be as beardless as yourself and he would still be referred to as the Old Man."

"I would like to work here," I said. "You know everything."

"Heaven forbid that you should be an army scribe," answered Gillimas sadly, looking down at me. "We indeed know everything and we know nothing. In our tents is the name of every Balearic slinger; we know the twin brothers, Yud and Dor, who never miss a bull's-eye or an enemy's skull; we even know that when they were small their mother put their breakfast of bread on a high limb and they couldn't get it till they knocked it down; things like that are at the end of our tongues; but if we tried to use a slingshot, we couldn't hit the side of a stable. We keep minute information on the elephants, as you have seen, but we never ride an elephant. Others are in the thick of battle; we are far behind the lines keeping books. We write all the time about glorious deeds and never perform any. We write all the time about excitement and never have any."

Going about through the great camp, seeing the men, hearing the tumult of their activities, was a new experience and a new adventure for me. My world had been mostly the world of the elephants.

In my rounds, I came upon fifteen men at some kind of practice and stopped to watch them. Eight of these carried a platform that had two poles running out from each end, one pole to two shoulders. On the platform was an elephant howdah; of four men in the howdah, one, acting as driver, carried an elephant staff. Of the other three, one was an archer, one a spearman, and one a slinger. Two slingers were in the sidelines looking on. The platform carried by the eight men was supposed to be an elephant; the four men in the howdah were supposed to be the fighters on his back and a battle to be going on. The maneuvers were under the direction of the fifteenth man, a sergeant, who certainly had no mercy upon the eight carriers.

"Double time, run!" he yelled, and they sped along. The driver dropped to his knees to be out of the way. The spearman threw his spear and bobbed down. The archer shot his arrow and instantly crouched. In the clearance, the slinger swung his slingshot around his head and let a stone go. Spear, arrow, and stone, all shot forth in quick succession. Three thuds, spaced almost as close as three hammer blows of a carpenter, sounded against a board about a foot square, centered with a black circle, that was fastened to a tree some distance off. The stern sergeant went over to this target to see which of the three projectiles had done the most damage and had hit within the black circle.

Then the sergeant took out the bowman and put in his place one of the slingers from the sidelines. Now the spearman threw, and, as he and the driver swiftly squatted, first one then the other slinger let go, so close together that one thud hardly quit jarring your ears before the second came.

The sergeant again examined the target. "That's better," he said.

The spearman was taken out of the howdah, and a third slinger was put in. The driver was stationary on his knees. The three slingers crouched on their heels. One rose in a twinkling, hurled his stone, and dodged down as the second sprang up, it seemed, with the stone circling his head—to be followed as quickly by the third. Then all three repeating, until a dozen stones bombarded the target, the board resounding as if a man stood there hitting it twelve times with a hammer.

"Why don't you use a real elephant?" I asked the sergeant, with the officiousness of a boy. "Scarbas would let you have one, maybe Old Anak."

"That will come later," replied the sergeant shortly. "Now, men, try again."

I could see how the four in the howdah might be having a good time. It was different with the poor fellows who carried it. I felt sorry for them, but the rough sergeant didn't seem to care. "Double quick, run!" he kept yelling. Once, when they did not get into high speed fast enough to suit him, he cried out, "Halt!" Then he walked up to them. "You heard the command, or didn't you? Now get some action into your legs. Double quick, run!"

They practiced again while I watched. Then, at last, the sergeant allowed them to rest. The three slingers grouped themselves about him. "When we get to Rome, we're going to use slingers in the howdahs. In the debate last night, always it was spearmen and bowmen the elephants carried. Hannibal wants slingers tried out. You had all better be good and it had better succeed. We'll give him a demonstration tomorrow."

"Will you use Yud and Dor when Hannibal is watching?" asked one of the slingers.

"No, nothing like that," answered the sergeant. "He knows Yud and Dor couldn't miss a target if they tried. He doesn't want to demonstrate champions; not enough of them; Yud and Dor can't work from thirty-seven elephants. He wants to see what ordinary slingers can do."

I bethought me of my duty with the notices and perforce had to tear myself away from the entertainment of this furious drill.

When I came to the quarters of the Purple Band and started through the avenue of tents, I saw a big, red one far ahead of me. Two guards in red cloaks stepped athwart my path and crossed spears in front of Little Enoch.

"Give the password," one of them demanded.

"Give what?" I asked.

"The password. Nobody but a Purple Bandsman can get through without it."

"I don't know it," I explained. "Nobody told me I had to have it. I have notices from Hannibal. Will you take the three for General Gisbo, then, and give them to him?"

"Can't leave my post and we're not notice distributors. You'll have to get the password."

"Where can I get it?"

"Who sent you?"

"Gillimas and Misdes."

"Go get it from them."

It was a considerable way back to their tents. When I got there, Gillimas and Misdes were both absent. I asked the young, weak-eyed clerk, Hiserbal, for it. He gave it to me with this

remark, "That Purple Band crowd can stand more on techni-
calities than any other outfit in the army."

When I returned, the crossed spears again went up in front
of Little Enoch. "Give the password," ordered the same guardsman, as though he had never seen me before.

"A thousand miles to Rome."

I kicked Little Enoch with my heels as a sign for him to
start, but the crossed spears still held him back. "You can go,
but not the elephant. Leave him here. Proceed afoot."

Now, I had taught Little Enoch to stand still, as a well-
trained horse will do, while I was absent on an errand. But
he was only a young elephant, and fifteen minutes was about
as long as he could be depended upon. After that, he was
likely to think I had departed for good, and go back to the
other elephants. I now dismounted and left him. The two
guardsmen resumed their pacing back and forth, very stiff and
erect, with their spears held just so, as oblivious of the elephant
as if he did not exist.

At the big, red tent, as I looked through the open flap, I saw
General Gisbo. An orderly took the three notices, thanked me
courteously enough, and dismissed me.

As I approached the end of the avenue, I saw that Little
Enoch was no longer there.

"Did you men scare the elephant?" I asked.

The two guardsmen, walking their beats very stiff and correct, with their spears at a precise angle, vouchsafed no reply.

I still had a handful of notices to distribute. I hesitated between my duty to them and finding little Enoch. He would
simply go back to the elephant pickets, but on his way he
might run against the guy ropes of tents or eat food that

tempted him or knock over supplies in crowding through or otherwise do an amount of damage, for he was still too young to be fully trained.

I went ahead with the notices afoot. When this work was done, I returned to Old Anak's place in the picket line. Scarbas, seeing me approach on my own two legs, with only a single notice in my hand now, the one for him, walked out several steps to meet me.

"Where's Little Enoch? What did you do with him?"

"Isn't he here yet?"

"No," announced Scarbas. "Did you turn him loose to come back by himself? That was a foolish thing to do. He may get into all sorts of mischief and further discredit the elephants."

I told him what had happened, and he was very angry.

"Another malicious trick!" he exclaimed. "The Purple Band guardsmen deliberately pricked him with their spears."

I found Little Enoch in the camp of the Numidian cavalry, eating hay with their horses. Several Numidians were gathered about him in friendly fashion. They liked elephants. Little Enoch had shaken up two or three tents and had enraged one cook by eating a whole tubful of vegetables, but no serious complaints came to us.

FOUR

It was a great spectacle that Hannibal's army made, as it set out on the morning of May 30, in the Year of the World 3876. There were one hundred and two thousand men and twelve thousand cavalry horses, besides thousands of baggage animals, and thirty-seven elephants. That multitude of men and beasts and carts made a marching line over forty miles long.

The elephants led the way. Scarbas was mounted on Old Anak at the very front. I was on Little Enoch at the rear of the entire herd. Little Enoch's mother was up close to Scarbas, far away and out of his sight. Scarbas meant to wean him from her as completely as possible. I did not ride Little Enoch all the time, or even half the time, since he was only part-grown and just the fifteen miles he had to walk was a pretty good day's work for him. Sometimes Scarbas let me ride Old Anak up front.

Then, as we climbed a hill, I could look back upon the men and animals following us as far as the eye could see, until they were lost in the dust and the distance.

Immediately behind us were the Purple Band cavalry and behind them the Purple Band infantry, and I must admit they made a glorious sight. There were about a hundred white horses in front, then many black ones all together, then bay ones and dun ones, and other groups of different colors. The riders had shining helmets and red plumes and all of them wore scarlet cloaks. At the head of this splendid column rode Gisbo on a white horse, sitting in his saddle as straight and erect as he stood upon the ground, and never sagging the whole day long.

Behind the Purple Band, and in great contrast to them, were the Numidian cavalry. Their desert ponies had neither saddles nor bridles. Each man wore nothing but a leopard skin, sometimes a tiger skin. Seeing them strung out so far, several thousand in number, I wondered where in the world there could be enough jungles to breed all the spotted cats—the leopards and the tigers—to furnish them their garments.

So far in the rear that I couldn't see them until they drew up for camp, passing by in ever-coming lines as I sat on Old Anak, were the African spearmen, red-hooded, goat-skinned, the dark, naked parts of them all tattooed; the Spaniards, in white woolen tunics bordered with scarlet; and a shorter section of Gauls, every one a redhead, made so with flaming dyes.

Upon the elephants was piled baggage by the ton. Old Anak was the treasury animal. "Nothing else but the moneys he must carry," declared General Samnis, "and you will give him the early teaching, will you not, to hook with his tusks if people fool around with the sacks?" Old Anak indeed had a very good load of it, together with some bushels of cheap bracelets, necklaces, rings, and other baubles to give as presents to the barbarians and Gauls. General Samnis felt he should ride Old Anak too, companionably with the army's wealth. By the time of the noon halt he had changed his mind: "Already Old Anak keeps everyone away at arm's length, so General Samnis now has peace of mind to ride a horse."

For a while he jogged along beside General Gisbo. Since he cut anything but a martial figure, I think General Gisbo was just as pleased when he considered it safe to be still farther away from the money, and pulled off to the side of the road, and waited until General Hanno came up at the head of the Numidians.

The elephants also freighted the records and equipment of Gillimas and Misdes. I tried to persuade this pair to travel aboard Old Yenbo, the Roman Crusher, who wasn't carrying anybody except the driver, but the two rhetoricians said maybe it was better, after all, just to know elephants out of books.

Once, as they were riding on horseback beside my elephant, the men all along the column as far as the ears could hear, burst out into that song we had listened to on the night of the debate:

> Across the Alps and Apennines,
>   In battles far from home,
> His elephants lunge at trembling lines—
>   When Hannibal conquers Rome.
>   His elephants large,
>   With tusks they charge,
>   They gore to death
>   And tramp out breath—
>   When Hannibal conquers Rome.

"Hear that, Gillimas?" inquired Misdes, grinning from ear to ear. "Not bad, what?"

"Very good, in fact," agreed Gillimas, as expansively smiling, "especially the tune."

"Misdes," I demanded, "did you write that? And you put in all those things in favor of the elephants when you were getting ready to argue against them as hard as you could in the debate?"

"A debate's a debate, Agenor, the same as a song's a song."

The singing broke out again. The two rhetoricians joined in, as they turned their horses about and galloped back along the ranks. They were in a gay mood at being relieved for a little while from their army paper work, riding free in the fair Spanish weather.

We traveled without incident until after we crossed the Ebro the middle of July. Then trouble began.

The savage natives of the Catalonian wilds barred our way to the Pyrenees.

These tribes, friendly to Rome, could not be left to rise up against Carthage in Hannibal's absence. In spite of his haste to get across the Alps before the dead of winter, he had to subdue them. He chose the fastest way, not taking their towns by slow siege but at once by assault. In this quick work he lost thousands of soldiers. But time was worth more to him than blood— since it was mostly the blood of Spaniards and Africans and other allies, and very little of it Carthaginian.

In this great army of his, the twenty-five hundred of the Purple Band accounted for a good third of the pure Carthaginians.

Carthage has been much condemned for so largely fighting her wars with mercenaries and hirelings. Yud and Dor, the Balearic twins, so sure of cracking enemy skulls, and thousands of others almost as good, were trained to be the best slingers in the world—for Carthage. Tattooed African lads in the desert and in the dunes practiced at throwing the spear far and certain—for Carthage. Spanish boys learned the skill of cut-and-thrust sword and the defense of the bull's-hide buckler—

for Carthage. Numidian youths perfected themselves and their runty mounts into the earth's best cavalry—for Carthage.

While far and near these valiant striplings were preparing to die for Carthage, the young Carthaginians were themselves getting ready to live until their beards were long and to yield up the ghost at last in a soft bed. They sent ships to Sidon for glass, to Tyre for purple dyes, to Egypt for linen, to Cypress for copper, to Spain for gold and silver, to Elba for iron—and the coins of Carthage, nearly always with a horse on the tail's side, came countlessly from the mint. By these means the grand city, there on her high peninsula in the bright African sunshine, grew ever fairer and stronger and greater and richer.

Even the sublime Hannibal was a true Carthaginian in prodigally drenching the Catalonian wilds with his mercenaries' blood, so he could get to the Alps before the deep snows did—and before the Romans could head him off in Spain.

In the latter he succeeded. His spies brought word that Cornelius Publius Scipio had landed at the mouth of the Rhone with more than twenty thousand troops and sixty large ships. Scipio's soldiers were seasick from their Mediterranean voyage, and were resting up. They rested too long. Hannibal crossed the Pyrenees and traveled fast to the Rhone. He arrived at a crossing twenty leagues from the mouth of the river to by-pass Scipio.

The Rhone was a mile wide in places, running full and muddy and swift from the melting snows in the mountains that fed it far away. There were islands in many sections of it, but we camped at a place where the river flowed in a single stream, and waited to cross. It was now the twenty-second of September.

The country bordering that great river seemed far off from

everywhere and lonely, with autumn beginning to color the leaves and ripen the wild fruit, and with bird nests frayed and their sticks awry from being long forsaken. I found it pleasant enough when we arrived on that September afternoon—except for one thing. The place was infested with mosquitoes. The elephants, though thick-skinned, were vulnerable and sensitive to their attacks.

Called "Rhone-Scipios" by the waggish soldiers, they afflicted us during the five days it took to get the army over this rapid, brimming watercourse. As we looked at it from the banks, the vast mass of its waters rolled along, with dead logs bobbing upon it, and green, uprooted trees wallowing deep, and with heavy gurglings and lappings at the edge that made a mournful sound.

All the forces came up and camped in as compact an area as possible. Yet a large acreage had to be cleared to make room for so many men and animals and tents.

The hostile barbarians lined the bank on the other side menacingly, sang their war songs, and made signs of what they would do to us. Hannibal sent General Hanno up the river several miles with a detachment of Numidians to cross and come back and surprise them from the rear. This cleared the opposite shore for our landings.

Then General Hanno, with five hundred Numidians, went far down the Rhone to scout out the position of Scipio's army. They ran into several hundred Roman horsemen traveling the trail upstream on a similar mission to learn about Hannibal. After a clash, in which a number were killed on both sides, the Numidians fled back up the river with the Romans in yelling pursuit at their heels, following them all the way to within sight of Hannibal's camp. Then they wheeled and galloped off.

We realized that from now on there would be Roman outposts scattered along everywhere between us and Scipio. But they would be down the river and we would be going up it. Hannibal was anxious to get away and be far gone from this spot by the time Scipio's main army could arrive.

"You run," commented General Samnis to General Hanno. "The tellings of the spies say the Romans have much seasickness."

"Not these," said General Hanno. "They're good fighters. As for the running, that was upon Hannibal's orders to make them think we're poor fighters."

The horses swam across, a soldier in a boat holding the reins of half a dozen of them. The men and baggage were carried in the numerous boats that endlessly went filled to one bank and came back only with two oarsmen from the other.

The elephants were left until the last. So difficult was the problem of getting such unwieldy creatures over the broad and swollen stream, with them ready to stampede in panic, that poor Scarbas was much worried lest the disgusted army consider this a sample of what to expect right along. Most of the army was on the other side by the evening of the fourth day. With us were the Purple Band, which had been given the duty of getting the elephants across the following day. A few other forces still remained to be put over ahead of us early the next morning. Hannibal and his headquarters staff were also still on our side of the river.

After dark, Scarbas sent me with a message to Hannibal's tent. I rode Little Enoch.

In returning to the elephant pickets, I took a route at the backs of the farthest line of tents. I passed the outer guards, and was about half way along, guiding Little Enoch to the left to avoid the farther-out stakes of Gisbo's big tent, when I heard talk and the mention of elephants, twice of Old Anak. Stopping Little Enoch was innocent enough on my part, and the talk maybe innocent enough on theirs, since they had the duty of getting the elephants over. But then, as I started to ride on past, a statement came to me that sounded evil and sinister there in the September night:

"You understand, then, that in spite of all we can do, Old Anak will probably not get across."

The voice that said this was the voice of Gisbo.

I did not ride on. I stopped Little Enoch again, and, deliberately this time, prepared to listen.

FIVE

THIS TENT, BESIDES BEING MUCH LARGER THAN THE OTHERS, HAD longer guy ropes. This caused me to be far enough away to miss some of the conversation that went on in low tones. So I slipped off the elephant. I tapped his trunk three times with my elephant staff and his right ear three times, as a sign that he was to stay where he was until I returned. I couldn't tell him, in addition, for fear my voice might be heard.

I crept up between two slanting ropes to the edge of the tent. The bottom hugged the ground closely all around. But there was one small tear through which I could peer as through the knothole of a fence.

One torch was burning. Gisbo was seated at a camp table, with him were two of his officers. Standing in front of them was a Purple Band sergeant.

"First," said Gisbo, "all the remaining forces and baggage will be taken over. By that time the rafts can be made ready and covered with earth. Then we will begin the transportation of the beasts. It will be slow work and will take several hours. The river is wide and turbulent. The animals will be nervous and frightened. The raft can take no more than two or three at a time, probably only one in case of the biggest. We can count on at least twenty trips for the thirty-seven elephants.

45

The supreme commander might have assigned someone else to
the dirty business, but since he picked on us we must go forward with it and follow the arrangements he has worked out.
In a way it is a compliment to the superiority of the Purple
Band, since the elephants are the biggest problem of the
crossing."

"But this Old Anak you mentioned, sir," said the sergeant,
"this head elephant that is old and dangerous and might become crazed on the way across—what about him, sir? Will
you cover the particulars again, sir, to make everything absolutely clear in my mind?"

"He is to be left until the very last. Then, if anything happens, all the others will be over. So much good work to our
credit. Our main duty will have been performed."

"But you think it is doubtful, sir, whether this dangerous
old leader will ever get across?"

"You have the idea, Sergeant Dokobal. In my opinion, the
elephants had better been left behind in the first place. We are
pressed to reach the Alps in advance of the winter snows. Yet
we must spend the better part of an additional day putting the
beasts over. None can be drowned through obvious carelessness.
If any are lost, it must appear to all observers that it couldn't
be helped. Indeed, unless there is actually an unavoidable accident, all will land safe and sound on the opposite shore except
this savage Old Anak."

"Do I understand correctly, sir, that the ropes attaching the
raft to the three boats upstream to keep it from drifting down
and getting out of control in the swift river, and that the big
rope in front to tow with, will all be tied by me?"

"Yes, Sergeant, that will be your responsibility. Ropes accidentally come untied."

"But there will be four, sir—three attached to the boats upstream and the big tow cable pulled at by many men on the far bank. If four ropes come loose, will I not be blamed for a careless job of tieing them?"

"Only one will come untied, Sergeant—the big tow cable. This is not unnatural, with so heavy a load and with so many men pulling. The other three will draw the boats downstream in wake of the wild raft. To save themselves and the boats in a losing game, I expect that the oarsmen in their own excitement and fear will cut the ropes."

"Then, sir, the raft will be loose in the raging current with the elephant on it. Won't a driver be on the raft with this Old Anak?"

"Yes, but he won't be Scarbas. I imagine he will throw himself in the river to save himself and be picked up by a boat, especially if the scared and excited oarsmen encourage him and yell at him to jump for his life."

"And what do you think, sir, will happen to the elephant?"

"Poor animal." Gisbo smiled. "He might lose all control of himself and jump into the broad, wild river and drown right before the eyes of the men on both banks. He might stick with the raft. In that case, he might come ashore somewhere much farther down, and barbarians will happen upon him, and return tremblingly to their camps to report to their chiefs that they saw a great demon out in the wilderness. Or he might come ashore among the Romans and what a grand scattering there will be. Or the raft might carry him clear out to sea and I think the sea can take care of him—and again imagine the Romans, down there with their navy, when they see this strange craft and this strange cargo, drifting out on an ebb tide to be dashed back by the surges of a flood tide to destruction upon the beach. They will find him lying on his side, very big and black against the yellow sea sand, and they will whisper in awed tones to each other, 'Hannibal's elephant.' And it will seem like a terribly bad omen. So you see, Sergeant, if some of these things happen, Old Anak, even in his demise, will not be without his good effects upon the enemy, and we are well rid of him."

"I understand, sir, that I will be alongside the raft on a swimming horse. I don't fancy the position, but be it so."

"The boats and ropes will be at the upper side. I advise that you be at the back end, not on the lower side where the raft can drift against you and bear you down."

"And if these things should happen, sir, I am to do everything I can to save the elephant?"

"Everything, in sight of everybody. Work frantically. But I am afraid fate will be against you—fate and the panic-stricken elephant and the swift current. This Old Anak and the raft will get away from you, in spite of everything you can do."

"I understand. Is that all, sir?"

"That is all, Sergeant Dokobal."

He saluted and left.

I slipped back to the elephant in the dark. He curled his trunk around and held it and I stepped upon it. He lifted it until I could swing my legs astride his neck. The moment I was mounted, I looked to the left into the face of a Purple Band guardsman. He had come up behind Little Enoch so I didn't see him at first.

"What are you doing?" he demanded.

He took out a whistle and blew on it. This brought another guardsman, whom he tersely directed:

"Hold the boy and the elephant while I report."

He returned very soon and ordered: "Get off. Come with me." To the second guardsman he said: "Keep the elephant."

"He can't keep him," I put in, "not if Little Enoch makes up his mind to go. He's much stouter than the soldier. He'd just go anyhow."

"He wouldn't go far with a spear through his neck," observed the second guardsman.

"We wish to avoid anything like that," cautioned the first guardsman. Then he spoke to me: "Give him the sign to stay still."

With my elephant staff I tapped his trunk three times and his right ear three times. "Stay," I commanded. "Stay till I come back."

Then I left Little Enoch and the second guardsman, and walked in front of the first guardsman, with his spear point at my back, into the tent and into the presence of Gisbo. My knees were knocking against each other because of the angry words he would begin hurling at me.

But he was not like that at all. I could hardly believe it.

"Good evening, Agenor," he greeted me pleasantly in a voice that had no anger in it, only softness. "Little pitchers have big ears. The guardsman tells me you were listening to a conference of the officers of Hannibal's army. That is a very serious offense. But you were not eavesdropping, were you, Agenor?"

"Yes, sir," I replied, "I was."

"And what did you hear, Agenor?"

"You said all the elephants will probably get across except Old Anak, but you intend to let his raft loose in the river—and that will be the last of him."

Still Gisbo didn't lose his temper. I couldn't understand it.

He laughed. His two officers laughed. "Hear that," he said to them. "Hear the boy." He turned to me: "Agenor, that is the way false and harmful reports can start. Guardsman," he ordered, "recall the Sergeant Dokobal."

"How long have I been here?" I asked irrelevantly. Gisbo seemed surprised at the question and I saw him cast quick looks at his officers. But he examined the small water-clock on his camp table.

"About five minutes," he answered.

"That makes me feel relieved," I said.

The sergeant entered and Gisbo addressed him: "Sergeant Dokobal, this boy here who helps take care of the elephants, heard a part of our conversation in reference to the animals and got some quaint ideas about Old Anak's not safely crossing the river tomorrow. You will be in charge out in the current in the most dangerous part of the arrangement. Tell him what your instructions were."

"Sir, in order to insure the safety as far as possible of the very large elephant, the one called Old Anak, he is to be taken over last. I am to see that the four ropes attached to his raft are most securely tied. You pointed out to me very strongly, sir, what might happen if a single arrangement went wrong. You made me aware, sir, of all the risks in this difficult undertaking. You cautioned me to be careful in every detail."

"Now, Agenor," inquired Gisbo, "do you see how you misunderstood? Do you not believe that you owe us an apology?"

"I am sorry, sir, but I still don't understand the mean things you said about Old Anak."

"Mere opinions, Agenor, mere personal opinions, probably wrong and not ill-meant. I indeed feel, though, that Scarbas and you, accustomed as you are to having the elephants obey

your every word and nod—I feel, Agenor, that you haven't
fully noticed Old Anak's bad disposition growing constantly
worse. Now and then, in my quick impatience, I have so much
forgotten myself as to strike him and he has struck back,
which is a sign, a bad sign, of this increasing ill-temper I mention. Someday, all of a sudden, he might easily become savage
and unmanageable. In the past, he has mowed down plenty
of Romans and barbarians. What if he decided to do a lot of it
on his own account? Among the Carthaginians? Among ourselves? You can see, Agenor, how terrible it would be. And it
might happen. You have another elephant almost as big, who
is in his prime."

"You mean Old Zain, the Ear Flapper? He's a little bigger
but not so good as Old Yenbo, the Roman Crusher. He's lazy
and wants to take things easy. Old Yenbo's a better fighter."

"How old are these two?"

"Old Zain's seventy-one, sir; Old Yenbo sixty-five."

"I had suggested to these gentlemen and to the sergeant,
and perhaps you heard me speaking somewhat of it, that this
Old Zain, or Old Yenbo, as you prefer, could act as leader in
case Old Anak were retired on account of his age and his great
services to the Carthaginian army. Merely my own opinion,
Agenor, nowise important and nowise affecting our duty to
get the elephants over the Rhone tomorrow. The supreme
commander appointed the Purple Band to do this with as little
risk as possible, and an order of the great Hannibal is never
disobeyed nor overlooked. There may be accidents we cannot
avoid, caused by the elephants themselves. But we shall do our
utmost, and with the caution I have given the sergeant about
every detail, we shall expect thirty-seven elephants to go safe
and unharmed from this side to the other side. Sergeant, you

have passed on the caution to all your men, have you not?"

"Yes, sir."

"How long have I been here now?" I asked.

I thought I saw annoyance appear this time upon the face of Gisbo, and concern as well, but he quickly routed this to be as amiable as ever.

"About ten or eleven minutes."

"I feel relieved," I said again.

"And, Agenor," said Gisbo, "I hope you feel entirely relieved about the elephants. I am sorry you misunderstood our discussion. It is best that you do not mention anything of what happened here to a single soul."

"Not even to Scarbas? Nobody is more loyal than he is."

"But, just the same, Agenor, not even to him. Then I have your promise, your sacred promise, that you will say nothing to him about it?"

"I promise, sir."

"That is well."

"How long have I been here now?"

"About thirteen minutes."

"Then I must hurry."

"Agenor," he asked, his own curiosity becoming too much for him at last, "this is the third time you have asked how long you have been here. Have you been expecting somebody? Have you been expecting Scarbas?"

"No, sir. He might wonder about my delay and come, but I am not really expecting him. I was worried about the time because of Little Enoch."

"I don't understand."

"He might leave. I can't count on his staying longer than fifteen minutes."

"Isn't a guardsman with him?"

"Yes, sir, but a guardsman couldn't hold him. He would pull away and start out fast. And he'd go back to the other elephants in a beeline and maybe run into the guy ropes and break through fences, and Scarbas would blame me for injuring the reputation of the elephants."

"In that case, Agenor, you had better leave at once."

"Yes, sir."

He rose and walked with me himself instead of letting the guardsman take me to Little Enoch, saying to me on the way:

"You will not even report to Scarbas that I have discussed the elephant plans with you. I could be censured for telling you. They are very confidential. You promise that your stopping in my tent, our talk, our plans, the fact that you have seen me, will all be silent upon your tongue, regardless of the questions of Scarbas?"

"I promise, sir."

SIX

Overnight, Hannibal decided to start at once to keep ahead of Scipio. By daybreak he was on the move north along the Rhone with his main forces that had already crossed, doubling up and trebling up his columns on the road. On our side, the tents were taken down and the men and baggage were carried over immediately to join the march.

All that remained on both sides were about four hundred and fifty men to manage the crossing of the elephants—two hundred Purple Bandsmen under Gisbo, two hundred Africans and Spaniards under General Mago, together with the drivers and Scarbas and me. It was nearly noon before the arrangements were completed for the first elephant load to start.

A big raft two hundred feet long was securely anchored to the bank by means of strong ropes. This was covered with dirt until it was level with the bank, which meant not a great thickness of earth because the water was so high. It was made to look like a peninsula running out into the river. It stayed anchored and was never moved.

At the farther end of this was a smaller raft, likewise covered with earth and with a stout fence running around it. This, with wide gates at each end, was tied to the big raft, but tied with slip knots so it could be released as soon as a load of ele-

54

phants was upon it. It was the actual ferry, the other being merely the ferry slip.

Elephants are good swimmers in water that they trust. But they were terribly afraid of the swift, wide current of the Rhone. It would have been impossible to get them to step into the muddy, lapping edges of its flood.

Two and three at a time were led along the length of the big stationary raft. They did not object or hold back, since this seemed to be merely an extension of the land. Once on it, they became somewhat frightened when it sank deeper into the water and wobbled from the level and had a more uncertain feel than the solid earth.

When they came to the smaller, inclosed raft, which had a thinner covering of earth and to which they had to descend slightly, they hesitated and wanted to turn back. The drivers had all they could do to urge and coax them forward upon it. A she-elephant, having less timidity somehow than a male, was often led out first, and a male or a pair of them followed her.

When the ferry was let loose, and they saw themselves moving and surrounded by water, they became agitated and walked around the rectangular fence, making the raft shake under them, and causing it to teeter as they crowded to one side or the other. They leaned their heavy shoulders against the fence until its posts and planks cracked. They stopped at intervals to look out upon the angry current, and the drivers were not able to calm them.

In a few instances, their fear increased to such a degree that, before the farther bank was reached, they broke through the fence and threw themselves into the water. Then the drivers all but drowned; yet the elephants themselves, in this shallower part of the river, managed to stand on the bottom. Though the water flowed over their backs and over their heads, they were able to lift their trunks high enough above the surface so they could breathe. These few swimmers or, rather, deep waders, all landed safely and little damaged by their ducking.

At each trip this elephant-laden raft was held from drifting too far downstream by three boats with strong oarsmen. One of these moved diagonally behind, one at the center, one diagonally in front, and all about eight yards upstream from the raft. A still larger boat pulled it in front. A big rope went from the forward end of the raft to the stern of this towing boat. Another rope, which had to be exceedingly long, went from the boat's prow to the farther shore where about fifty men hauled at it, with their bodies sloping backward, as in a tug of war.

Sergeant Dokobal, swimming his horse, had a place at the upper rear corner of the raft, alongside the first diagonal guy rope, but sometimes riding directly and closely at the back. For every trip in this repeated convoying he swam a fresh horse. At the start, at the leaving side, there were twenty lined up and in charge of two men, one to look after them, the other to deliver them as needed to Dokobal. Two men were on the other side to receive the used horses and to rub them down after their work in the cold water. Thus Dokobal was sometimes mounted on a black animal, or a bay, or a white, which in every case was chosen for its strength and size from the Purple Band cavalry. The sergeant himself was not spelled by others but remained all the time in the cold flood of the Rhone, except when he would be rowed back in a boat after each delivery.

At last, thirty-six elephants were safely across.

Such big fellows as Old Zain and Old Yenbo had voyaged one to a load. Little Enoch had been allowed to travel with his mother, making the passage for him relatively tranquil. Well that it was so, for, if he had been one of those to pitch himself off into the river, his trunk wouldn't have reached high enough and the muddy water would have poured in and strangled him.

Scarbas and I were both on the arriving shore. Even here, where the Rhone was narrowest, it was still over a half-mile wide.

As I looked across, I saw three objects at the end of the stationary raft. One was the red-cloaked Gisbo on his white horse. The second was the last fresh mount for Sergeant Dokobal when he should come, for he was still with us—a black horse, bigger and more powerful than any of the others. The third was Old Anak, with his driver.

Separated from all the others, the last when he was accustomed to be the first, the great leader appeared to be eager rather than reluctant to make the journey. He trumpeted loudly across the swollen waterway to the herd he wanted to join. The herd trumpeted in response. These calls went back and forth, the shriller noises of Little Enoch, out of key, joining the chorus on our side that answered the lonely, repeated and prolonged bellowings on the other side.

Sergeant Dokobal was stepping into the boat to go for this final load. Scarbas started to get in with him, saying, "I will go and bring him over."

"It will be much better," explained the sergeant, "if you remain on this side as you did for the others and call out encouragement to him if he should get nervous when the raft is cut loose from the slip or should become excited on the voyage."

The driver, mounted on Old Anak's neck, guided him forward from the end of the man-made peninsula where he stood, onto the repaired and re-earthed raft that was to carry him.

Then this ferry started across as it had on the previous trips. The elephant was a great bulk of blackness in contrast to the muddy expanse of the Rhone. The protruding head and neck of Dokobal's horse occasionally showed around the corner of the raft. This animal swam mostly at the back end, as if towed, to be seen between the treelike legs of Old Anak. A third of the distance was made, a half. Everything promised success, although the elephant went round and round inside the inclosure, and tipped the raft by his single, mighty weight, and looked out upon the turbulent current, swung his trunk, and trumpeted loudly.

"Anak!" called Scarbas in a loud voice across half the wide water now. "Anak, it is I! I am waiting for you, Anak. Do not be afraid. Come, Anak, I am waiting!"

Then the rope between the pulling boat and the raft gave way. The fifty men on shore who sloped rearward in their tugging, backed away rapidly, and some lost their footing and fell, as the heavy load was suddenly released. The towing boat was pulled swiftly forward, in considerable separation from the raft, before the hauling men saw what was the matter and stopped.

The loose raft with Old Anak on it began to speed downstream. The three ropes reaching to the three boats upstream, tautly held. But the raft drifted relentlessly, dragging the boats after it, in spite of the frantic work of the three crews of oarsmen. Sergeant Dokobal, on his black horse, kept close to the rear of the raft, shouting directions.

The elephant became crazed with fear. Swifter than ever he went the rounds of the fence, crushing against it with such force as to shatter it, but seeing the same tumultuous, muddy current wherever he looked here in the center of the river. His driver was powerless to quiet him. One side of the raft lowered in the water, then another in his milling. The driver talked to him, commanded him, cut his ear with the elephant staff. But he only became wilder as the drifting boat gained momentum.

"Do not jump!" screamed Scarbas. "Do not jump, Anak! Quiet! Anak, it is I calling. It is Scarbas."

"Hold with all your might, men," Sergeant Dokobal called out to the rowers. "Dip your oars to the middle. Hold! Work! Hold!"

The towing boat had been moving rapidly back to reattach the tow line. An oarsman stood up in the stern of the boat. With a coil of the rope in his hands he tossed the end to the driver on Old Anak's neck. "You'll have to get down and tie it!" he yelled.

While the driver was working to fasten this to the front cross-beam, the frantic elephant for a moment stopped his milling round, with his throat and tusks and trunk above the squatting man busy with the rope. Then his trunk went round the leaning-over body of the driver. He may have meant only to lift the man back to his neck. The effect was to cause the driver to lose his balance at the edge of the raft and to tumble, head-down, into the river. He came up several yards below, pawing at the water and beseeching the oarsmen, "Help! Help! I cannot swim." The boat hastened to pick him up before he sank.

Scarbas waded out into the water waist-deep. "Come back, Scarbas!" shouted the men on shore. "You will drown in that river. Come back!"

"If I can reach him, I can calm him," Scarbas insisted. "Let me go. Let me go, I say!"

A half-circle of horses were soon athwart him, crowding him back, returning him to shore. A boat was got for him, with oarsmen, and in this he started out toward the drifting raft, calling over and over: "Cease, Anak! Quiet! Anak! Anak!"

Just then, before the towing boat could regain its position to refasten the rope and replace the driver on the raft, Old Anak paused at the end, where Sergeant Dokobal and the black horse's head were under his extended throat and tusks and trunk. With a swift, angry movement, he picked the sergeant off the horse's back and held him aloft as he ran around the inclosure for all the horrified watchers to see. The rear end of the raft swung round, pushing the riderless horse with it, and the boat at that corner cut its rope to keep from being also thrown in front and smashed. Old Anak hurled the sergeant away from him out into the river beyond the struggling horse. But the sergeant himself did not struggle or clutch at the horse. He sank, with his red cloak floating above him on the surface as he went down.

The center boat was now drawn close alongside what had been the upper end. And it was pointed straight downstream. The mad elephant could grab up the oarsmen one by one as he had the sergeant. Fearing they would be next, they cut loose. The third boat, though out of reach of the elephant, was now helplessly and dangerously dragged along. A man at the stern leaned over with his Spanish sword and severed the rope.

All this was happening quicker than I can tell it. The loose raft, its back end now the front end, raced downstream. It went for its whole length over the struggling horse and Dokobal. A corner of the red cloak reappeared in the wake of the swift, runaway raft.

With a swift angry movement he picked the sergeant off the
horse's back

"He's a killer!" came the shouts from the shore. "The elephant's a killer. Let him drown!"

The great animal rushed to the upper end of the raft and stood there trembling.

"Don't jump, Anak!" called Scarbas. "No, Anak, no!"

But Old Anak threw himself into the torrent. The raft sped on ahead of him.

"He's a killer!" came the repeated shouts. "Let him drown!"

All his body went under, and his lifted head, but, as his feet struck bottom, about six inches of Anak's upheld trunk remained above the surface. This rose until about a foot showed. Then suddenly it sank lower as he stepped into a deeper place. Only two more inches and water would pour into it as into a drain, and I thought this was the end. But as he was borne downstream he made some gains toward the shore. His head reappeared, the ends of his tusks, the black edge of his back.

"A killer, a killer!" came from the throats of the mob. "Don't let him get out."

At this continuing mob call, the rowers made for shore with the boat in which Scarbas had been riding toward the elephant.

"Turn back!" he shouted. "Row to him, I say. I can jump from the boat to his head and guide him to safety."

"Let the killer drown," said the rowers.

I ran along the shore, keeping even with him and calling out: "Come, Anak, come! It is I, Agenor. Come, Anak! Swim for your life."

The boat with Scarbas in it had not yet landed but was remaining near the shore to put off again. "Give us spears," they asked. "Hurry with spears so we can approach and kill him."

"No!" cried Scarbas, and he threw himself upon them. They

finally overcame him and two men held him. With a dozen spears they set out upon their work of execution, but the elephant was now far downstream.

Old Anak at last reached shallower water and made straight and fast headway toward the bank. I was even with him, a good distance in advance of the others now hastening along the shore. Two spearmen and two bowman ran ahead of the crowd. They were still in far shooting range behind me as the elephant waded the last few yards, with the water dripping from his black surface.

"Stop the killer! Stop him!" shouted the mob to the spearmen and archers. "Strike him down! Don't let him escape!"

The spearmen, though having to make long throws, put one lance in his shoulder and one in his flank. One arrow fell with a sharp plop into the water. The other hung and shook at his side, and the ends of the long spears dragged, as Old Anak emerged from the river upon the dry shore, trumpeting in pain and I knew not how much in anger. And though I did not know, I put myself directly in his path.

"Agenor!" shouted one of the spearmen. "Not there! Out of his way! He's mad. He'll gore you. He'll trample you."

Even Scarbas yelled a sharp warning from the boat arriving too late to join in the attack. But I stood without moving as the elephant came straight toward me. I stood there and held up my hands in a kind of supplication.

"Lift me up, Anak!" I called. "Take me, Anak! Fast, take Agenor, and flee!"

As I remained steadfast in my tracks, facing the river and the oncoming immensity of the elephant, two objects showed instantaneously in the swift, wide sweep that the eyes have. One was diagonally to the left, so far downstream as soon to disappear—the empty, outlaw raft, looking very small now, speeding toward the sea. One was diagonally to the right, a good distance upstream and across it at the end of the ferry slip—scarlet-cloaked Gisbo on his white horse, a solitary figure now, a passive, guiltless observer of all that had taken place.

Two more arrows came. One went into Old Anak's front leg. One hit and stuck just below the ridge of my right shoulder.

"Cease! Stop!" commanded General Mago in a loud voice. "You'll murder the boy. Stop!"

"Take me, Anak!" I stood pleading with uplifted arms.

Old Anak reached down his wet trunk, encircled me with it, lifted me up, and I jumped to his head and astride his neck.

"Killer, killer!" shouted the crowd in pell-mell haste along the shore.

"Fast, Anak!" I cried. "Hurry for your life!"

His pain from the spears and arrows, and the shouting and all the hostile tumult, added urgency to the command.

He started with the swiftness of a running horse. On the right was the mighty Rhone from which he had just emerged. On the left was a wilderness and beyond it were the rising slopes of mountains. Somewhere ahead were the Romans. But immediately behind us were those who so briefly before had been our best friends—our worst enemies now, our own men in mob savagery, the Carthaginians.

The only way, in the grim choice of ways, was down the Rhone toward the approaching Scipio.

In that way we went as fast as a horse can run.

All the time I was saying: "Faster, Anak! It is to save your life. Faster, Anak, faster!"

SEVEN

THE BARBARIANS AND THE ANIMALS THEY HUNTED HAD MADE A trail. This ran crookedly through the trees and brush and heavy vegetation, the thickness of which soon hid us from sight. Vines trailed along the elephant's side, the overhanging volume of greenness was thrown back by his passage, thorny branches scraped him like the claws of cats. These obstructions added to the pain of the missiles he still carried. One, the spear in his flank, was not deeply imbedded and had shaken loose. When he trumpeted in pain from the lances and arrows, or in protest at leaving the herd, I bade him be silent. In our own concealment I could not look back and tell whether we were being pursued by the Purple Band horsemen.

Then came the voice of General Mago, shouting loud enough for me still to hear: "Halt! Do not follow. If he is not mad, the boy will calm him and bring him back."

General Mago probably thought that the elephant was the one in headlong flight and that I was the willy-nilly one. He did not know that the elephant, innocent of his guilt and his danger, would gladly go back to the rest of the herd, and that I, Agenor, had to urge him on—hammering the heels of my sandals against his thick hide, tapping him with my elephant staff, even touching his ears with the blade of that staff, and

calling out, repeatedly calling out to him: "Faster, Anak!
Faster, to save your life!"

Reassured by General Mago's command that we would not
at once be pursued, I looked for a side trail where we could
stop to get rid of the two arrows and the lance which he still
carried, and the arrow in my shoulder.

We came to a little stream, three or four yards wide and
about a foot deep, that flowed across the trail to empty into the
river at our right. The elephant splashed through this. Then
I turned him in a short curve to the right into the small creek,
to look by our tracks as though we had entered it and gone
down its bed toward the Rhone. Instead, I headed him up it,
wading its shallow channel all the way.

We ascended the creek a few hundred yards until its wind-
ings and the trees and underbrush entirely concealed us from
the trail. Here I found an open area and stopped the elephant.
The arrow in my shoulder stuck out straight behind. I could
not reach it with either hand to pull it directly back and out.
Here the flesh was thin, and some of the point was lodged in
the bone, but I could feel that it was not in past the barbs. I
made Old Anak take hold of the shaft with his trunk and pull
it out.

Three times I did similar service for him. The spear, and
the arrow in his side were removed by quick, hard pulls. The
arrow in his leg required some cutting with the blade of the
elephant staff.

I took off my tunic, cleansed it thoroughly in the stream,
and washed out his wounds and my own. I wrung out the
garment and hung it on a limb to dry before we started forth
again.

No sounds came from the trail. The caw of crows, the whir

of birds, the humming of insects, and the gurglings of the little stream over its uneven bed, were all the noises I heard on that late, sunny afternoon. It was a calm respite from all that had gone before; from what, beyond my knowing, might come after.

We seemed safe in an immediate way. But for this outlaw elephant and for the boy with him, there was no permanent safety. To the east was a wilderness inhabited by savage tribes and beyond them were the mountains. To the west was the mighty river whose turbulent width we knew so well. Behind were the Carthaginians, waiting, upon General Mago's orders, for me to bring the elephant back so they could kill him. In front, I knew not how far, were the Romans of Scipio.

But the main Roman army had been at the very mouth of the river, sixty miles away. The cavalry troop that had come within sight of the Carthaginian camp after their successful skirmish with the Numidians, had probably gone back to report. In that case, the upper part of the trail would be free of Roman presence for a while. Of all the possibilities, ahead seemed at the moment to be the best.

In the end, what could I do? What could I expect to happen? A boy and an elephant could not live forever in a wilderness cut off from friends. Disaster was sure to overtake us at last. But I had not the heart to go back now and deliver up Old Anak to a mob calling for vengeance upon him for the murder of Sergeant Dokobal.

Maybe their anger would cool, maybe General Mago would get them under control, maybe the matter would be reported to Hannibal and he would use his great power to save Old Anak. Whatever might eventually happen, it was clearly an advantage to keep the elephant in seclusion for the immediate time, for a day, two days, three. For that long, unless we met up with the Romans or the barbarians, Old Anak and I could live off the country. He could live very well on all the rich pasturage the wild region afforded. And I could subsist upon wild fruits and nuts. If the Carthaginians marched on without us, thinking us lost or destroyed or captured—and a big army racing to beat the snows to the Alps could scarcely be expected to waste much time on our account—well, in that event, Old Anak, carrying nothing but the hundred-odd pounds of a boy, could travel twice as fast as the army and be once more in its midst before the mountains were reached.

Of course, I didn't want them to think maybe we were captured by Scipio, and expect to see Old Anak looming up some day on Scipio's side in a battle in Italy after the Alps were crossed.

I put on my dry tunic, mounted to Old Anak's neck, and we started forth again. When we came out upon the trail, Old Anak turned his head toward the north, whence we had come, toward the Carthaginians.

"Not that way," I called softly. "Not back that way, Anak. There now are our worst enemies. There now for you will only be execution."

But, with determination, he started forward. I kicked him, I gave him direction with my staff for him to turn around. He refused, and I changed my voice into stern command. He trumpeted loudly, and I was afraid this trumpeting would reveal us. But soon that consideration lost its importance as he threw his trunk around in an effort to pull me off. Still trumpeting, now with short, hoarse blasts of anger, he shook his head and neck to dislodge me and swung around his trunk again and again.

A cold fear came upon me. Had Old Anak indeed got beyond control? Had he become a killer? In the end he responded and obeyed, and, oh, the relief it was to me that this last fear was not to be added to all the others.

We went on for perhaps five miles. The sun was now low and the trees cast long shadows over open, grassy places. Here, off the trail a safe distance, we could spend the night, by another little brookside and at the edge of another small meadow.

We ate and drank and waited for darkness, and as we waited my eyelids became heavy. The night before I had slept but little. How much better if I had not allowed the experience in the tent of Gisbo to keep me awake. I needed now to be wide-eyed, and I saw that I had to be or else find myself back in the dangerous Carthaginian camp. Old Anak was increasingly impatient to return and join the other elephants. There was no rope, no chain, with which to tie him up.

In his homesickness, he was ready to take advantage of any short absence of mine to escape. If I drowsed off ever so briefly, I would be awakened by the noise of his going. There was nothing I wanted so much as a long, full sleep. Yet I was condemned by the elephant to watchfulness all through the night.

I began my long vigil, hardly daring to turn my back to pick wild fruit as the dusk fell. Then I bethought me of at least some assistance.

With my Spanish sword I cut resilient willow stalks which I could twist into a kind of rope. I put this makeshift rope around his leg and tied it to a tree. I knew he could break it at one heavy pull, but his feeling of being bound would to a considerable degree keep him from testing its strength. I still dared not go to sleep, but I was not held quite so close to him. I could

walk about. If the heaviness of my eyelids became overpower-
ing and I drowsed off for a minute or two, I could count on
the willow rope's restraining him or his breaking it to wake
me up.

I pulled grass in the darkness and brought it to him to eat.
I caressed him and talked to him soothingly. I walked back
and forth over a beat of a few yards. I bathed my eyes with
cold water. If I slept it would mean, it would almost surely
mean the death of Old Anak. A sleepy boy, sleepier than he
had ever been before, had the responsibility of staying awake
to save a great and useful life.

I came to in a panic. I had drowsed off in spite of everything,
had lost complete consciousness for I knew not how long. It
seemed far in the night. And I was cold. But the elephant was
still at hand. I could hear the noise of his eating of the abundant
grass I had supplied him.

As I jumped to my feet, I was aware of a light to the south.
At first I thought it was the rising moon. Then I knew it was
a campfire. Was it the fire of a troop of Carthaginians come
to find me? Or was it a detachment of Romans from Scipio's
army?

It would be fairly safe in any case for us to remain where
we were, unless Old Anak got to trumpeting. I was tempted
to go out to the trail and along it to see whose camp it was.
All this thinking brought me wide awake. I wondered if I
could leave the elephant that long. But I was pretty sure that,
if he saw me leave, he would take it into his head to make a
heavy pull with his great leg, and would at once be trailing
a part of the willow rope, and trailing it fast, back toward the
Carthaginians. No, I didn't dare leave him.

I untied him, very carefully retaining the willow rope. First, we went straight west to the trail. Here we turned south. This time Old Anak obeyed me without protest. The light that showed through the interstices and across the low places of the thicket, may have meant to him a Carthaginian camp and other elephants.

We rode along the trail slowly, stopping often. "Quiet, Anak!" I cautioned whisperingly. "Soft with your tread! Slip through the overhanging bushes. Quiet!"

We came within a hundred yards of the light. Two men placed wood on the fire and then sat down. There could be no mistaking who they were. They were Roman cavalrymen. All the rest of the camp, how big it was I could not tell, seemed to be asleep.

I gave the sign for Old Anak to let me down. I crept ahead of him. We made no noise. I halted. Then I went forward a few feet, Old Anak treading softly at my heels. Some bushes arched above the trail. These would surely shake and make a noise as they ripped apart and swung back from the elephant's progress.

I stopped and considered. I caressed the elephant's trunk as I stood and thought. This was as far as we dared to go. We must retreat. I backed up Old Anak to where there was a wider place in the trail. I signed to him to lift me up. I turned him around but in doing so he brushed heavily against the bushes. I looked back and saw the two Romans jump to their feet with their spears ready.

"What was that?" one of them asked.

"The horses," said the other.

"They are staked out in the other direction."

"That is so. Then it is a panther or a bear. These woods are wild."

They threw some more wood on the fire and sat down again. One of them slapped his jaw. I knew it was a mosquito—the enemy alike of Romans and Carthaginians.

When safely out of hearing, but before we had regained the place even with our camping spot, I stopped Old Anak. The camp was asleep and carelessly sentineled. If the elephant and I charged among them, the awakening soldiers would believe we were the vanguard of many others and would certainly flee without waiting to find out. Was it not the kind of thing that had occurred again and again in wars where elephants were used? There were ninety-nine chances in a hundred that a vast, black apparition like Old Anak, appearing suddenly in their firelight, would stampede them completely. Yet I hesitated. Then I was ashamed of what I had to admit was my timidity, my fear.

If we did this and on the morrow returned, might it not bring forgiveness for Old Anak? And these same Romans, when they were wide awake and the sun was bright, would they not see his huge tracks upon the trail, which I thought of now as a threat to our concealment, would they not find us and capture us—unless we hastened at once to the Carthaginians with no worthy act to save us from condemnation?

I was unarmed. I had only the elephant staff with its blade. I had only the Spanish sword dulled by the willow withes it had cut. The spear I had pulled out of Old Anak at our first resting place, was now too far away to get. But the camp was asleep. We had proved that we could slip upon it so close that one sudden dash would put us in the midst of it.

I turned the elephant around. "Anak," I announced, "we are charging the Romans. Do you hear, Anak, the Romans? They are asleep, all but two, and we are charging them. Just one elephant and one Carthaginian, just Agenor and you, but making them think that many elephants and many Carthaginians are right behind us."

We slipped quietly back over the ground we had covered. I gave the elephant the sign to rush. His great legs went into rapid, sweeping motion. The foliage tore and parted and whipped my body and face. The two Roman sentinels were on their feet as we dashed into the clearing and into the full glare of the fire, along the trail between soldiers who lifted to a sitting posture as the elephant swept between them.

"*Elephantes Annibalis!*" came a dozen exclamations. "Hannibal's elephants!"

They saw only one but they said elephants.

I knew little Latin. There had been a few renegade Romans in Hannibal's army in Spain and there had been a good many of them at Saguntum during our eight months' siege of that city. I now cried out: "*Multi elephantes! Multi elephantes! Dedite manus!* Many elephants! Many elephants! Surrender!"

Their officer, a centurion, was on his feet. The two sentinels brandished their spears, which the elephant snatched from their hands and lifted up for me to take. Then he circled the centurion with his trunk and held him.

Meanwhile, all around the edges of the camp, soldiers had jumped up and fled, leaving their weapons. "Halt! Halt!" I shouted, but the first fugitives never stopped, and still others slid out of reach of the elephant and took to their heels. Fifteen I managed to hold, besides the centurion who was encircled by the elephant's trunk as by a boa constrictor. These fifteen, now hopeless of escape, stood as if petrified.

With signs more than with my limited and outlandish Latin, I ordered them to throw their weapons under Old Anak, one man at a time. I made the centurion understand if he did not instruct these men to obey me to the letter and without treachery, he would be trampled to death by the elephant.

There came back to us the noises of the main group escaping through the thickets. If they went to their horses, I could not help it.

I now had the fifteen, unarmed, and sufficiently cowed and expectant of other elephants to behave like prisoners. Besides, they had some consideration for the centurion, not to bring on his horrible death by attempting to flee.

I had them but I was now greatly perplexed what to do with them. I backed up Old Anak so the pile of weapons would be under his trunk. Then I ordered the prisoners, the whole fifteen, under his belly, like a brood of big fowls under a giant hen. A terrible dread was upon them at doing this, for they thought I surely meant to have the beast drop his immense weight upon them and squeeze their lives out. All the time the centurion was held by the elephant's trunk and I could see the sweat upon his face in the firelight. "Easy, easy," I called to Old Anak.

I was now free to look the place over. In my examination of the Roman gear and equipment, I found plenty of leather straps and several lengths of rope. I summoned from under the elephant one of the two who had been acting as sentinels. He seemed happy that he was to be spared. I gave him a long piece of rope. I called another man out, backed him up to the sentinel with his wrists crossed behind him, and ordered him manacled. I called out a third. The sentinel tied all of them he could with that rope, like men in a chain gang. He knotted on another length of rope and proceeded with the business of tieing up until all but the centurion and himself were thus securely fastened. Then I commanded Old Anak to release the centurion, who was ordered to add the sentinel to the handcuffed line. The centurion then accommodatingly placed himself in front of me with his wrists crossed behind him, for me to do the same with him. Bad as this was, he rather fancied it, I gathered, in preference to the embrace of the elephant's trunk.

"*Non id,*" I said. "Not that. There is still work to do."

I went along the line of men and had Old Anak cinch all the knots tighter. Then, with the centurion's help, I connected all the men by another rope that went round the waist of each. I tied an end of this rope to a tree.

I made a sign to the centurion that he was to be lifted up to the elephant's neck. I myself mounted to show him how it was done. He sat there, wondering and afraid.

"Where are the horses?" I asked him.

He pointed to the south. I started out that way afoot, leaving the centurion atop the elephant quite unbound. In my best Latin, putting the words together slowly, awkwardly, I said: "If you try to get down, the elephant will kill you."

I went out among the horses. Apparently none had been taken by the terror-stricken men, who also had not yet found courage to come back for them. I must have smelled of elephant or they were naturally afraid of strangers or the fleeing men had excited them, for when I tried to approach them they pulled back at the ends of their lariats and went around in a circle. At last I calmed one and led him to camp, but when he saw the elephant he snorted, lunged and broke away, so that the rope burned my hands before I could release it. I saw there was no use trying to capture any of the horses. I went out again and began cutting each lariat with my Spanish

sword, because I did not want to leave the animals for the
fugitives to get later. Finding this slow work, I returned to the
fire for the elephant, and, with the centurion sitting behind
me, rode him out among the herd. Soon in the darkness there
was the sound of rearing and snorting and the whole herd in
headlong flight, trailing ropes and uprooted pegs. I saw that
the meadow was entirely clear. All the horses were loose and
gone. Back at the fire, the centurion and I were let down to
the ground.

"*Cena*," I said, "supper. I'm hungry. Fast! We cannot linger
here."

He supplied me and I gave a quantity of the Romans' ground
corn to Old Anak.

With additional ropes and straps, I fashioned a kind of
harness for the elephant, one rope across the front of his
shoulders, and two going from this as traces, held in place
by a backband and bellyband, with a long stick of wood for a
whiffletree behind. To the center of this whiffletree, I tied both
ropes along which the prisoners were strung. The one connecting their wrists was left looser than the other, so they
would be pulled along by their waists.

We were now ready to start, except for some work of
destruction. I motioned to the centurion that he was to help
me. We threw wood on the fire. We tossed in weapons, shields,
garments, helmets, even some armor which a few soldiers had
apparently not found comfortable to sleep in, saddles, bridles,
food. I saved one good spear to carry.

Then, the centurion with me on the elephant, and with the
fifteen prisoners dragged along behind, I set out north, up the
Rhone, toward the Carthaginians. In the triumph of the capture we had made, I felt that Old Anak would be pardoned

The fifteen prisoners dragged along behind

and restored to favor. I realized the need of traveling fast. Sooner or later, the escaped Romans would reach another Scipio detachment and tell the news of my presence. Already I had spent a good deal of time here.

"Non multi elephantes sed unus elephantus et unus puer Punicus," remarked the officer sitting behind me in a tone of self-censure. "Not many elephants—only one elephant and a Punic boy."

"That is right," I admitted. *"Quid nomen est, Centurio?* What is your name, Centurion?"

"Cornelius Draccus."

"Well, Draccus, if you will give me your word of honor not to try to escape, I will not bind you, and I imagine it will be easier riding for you up here with your arms free. But you could grab my spear and run me through. Of course, the elephant would immediately kill you and all those tied up behind us, but sometimes men in your mood do suicidal things. Your word of honor or I tie your hands behind your back."

"I pledge my word as a Roman knight."

"Do you pledge also that the men won't try to get loose?"

"No, I cannot pledge them. Only myself. I do not now command. It is you. You are responsible for them. I no longer. I pledge only myself."

"Do you promise not to help them? If you don't, I'll have to tie you up."

"I promise not to help. To hinder them, I do not promise."

The man seemed to have very fine distinctions as to what he would do and what he wouldn't.

Old Anak, pleased at last that he was headed toward the Carthaginians and the other elephants, moved forward at a stride that would have been hard for the men to keep up with

—except that they put the burden of their keeping up mostly on him. They merely stood up and leaned back and let the elephant pull them. The fifteen of them averaged at least one hundred and fifty pounds apiece, which made over a ton. It was a heavy drag upon the elephant. I called to them to stop it, but they paid no attention. I halted Old Anak and went back to them. I told them if there was any more of it, I would untie the rope around their waists and let them be pulled by their wrists. I said I didn't think then that their holding back would be so comfortable for them. They didn't think so either. They were much better for a while but kept yelling protests that the elephant was going too fast, and then lapsed into being dragged in the old way.

I stopped the elephant and addressed the centurion. "I told them," I said, "and I meant it. It's wrists for them. I was trying to spare them. They're a mean lot."

"I will speak to them," consented Draccus, "but only to explain, not to command."

This he did and matters improved.

At daybreak we reached the crossing. Nobody was there. Nobody had waited for us. Every Carthaginian had gone off and left us.

I stopped to let the elephant rest. He stood contentedly at this place where he had last seen the herd, as if expecting them to come back. A great fatigue fell upon me. My drowsiness, long interrupted by exciting events, returned still more heavily, more insistently. I had now gone two days and most of two nights without closing my eyes. I fought against it but nodded in spite of myself. Finally I did not care what happened. I fell asleep there on Old Anak.

I awoke with a start, and then I did care. Why, the centurion might have killed me and slid off the back of the elephant without being killed himself as I had told him. He might have released the other prisoners. But he hadn't. There he was behind me, and I wasn't hurt, except my shoulder wound was beginning to get sore.

"You slept long," he said, "two hours. It was tiresome sitting here."

I looked at the prisoners. It had probably been much more tiresome for them. Then I came to life. Some of the prisoners were gone. In the handcuffed line there were now only ten.

I had Old Anak put me down to inspect the situation. The rope between the first ten and last five had been worn in two. There was a protruding boulder with a sharp edge like a fish's back. They had probably put the rope over this while I was asleep and rubbed it back and forth until it was severed.

The released five were still manacled. They were still as helpless as ever in all ways but one—they could go, the five of them together, back toward the Romans. The other ten made no response when I questioned them. I looked up at Draccus. I took a piece of rope and rubbed it across the sharp edge of the rock in the way I thought the escape had been made.

Draccus nodded his head yes, then bared his teeth and pretended to be gnawing. So between rubbing, and gnawing like mice, they had managed it. The others couldn't reach the boulder to do the same and gnawing wasn't enough by itself.

"Why didn't you wake me?" I demanded. "Why didn't you prevent them?"

"I only pledged you not to help. Not to prevent."

"In not waking me you helped."

"By waking you I would have prevented."

All this was the sort of thing Misdes and Gillimas would need to clear up with their rhetoric.

"Anyway," I acknowledged, "you kept your word the way you see it. I must give you credit for that—I suppose a good deal of credit. They must have urged you to go with them. They must have begged you with your free hands to release them."

"Yes," he explained, "they urged, they threatened. They came close and threatened until the elephant reached forth with an angry trunk."

"You kept your word very well this time," I said, "but I am not going to let you be tempted to break it while I bring back the five runaways."

I motioned him to get down and began tieing his hands behind his back. He made no protest, though he looked surprised at this treatment after the way he had kept his pledges.

I tied him to a tree by himself. I tied the others to a second tree out of reach of any sharp-edged boulders and where they couldn't get at the centurion, in case they resented his lack of assistance to their companions.

I removed the harness from Old Anak. The five men had a start of me. How long, the centurion would not tell me. Certainly not two hours, if I had slept for that period. A good part of that time would have been used in rubbing the rope in two. They might be an hour ahead. They might be only started. Draccus refused to enlighten me. And the others only grinned at me derisively and triumphantly. They also yelled at me to take their helmets off. In this early daylight, the mosquitoes were bad. The prisoners shook their heads to brush the insects off, having no other way to do so, and the headgear made this shaking heavy business. They also found their helmets very itchy, when these stayed on so long in the same position.

"I'll take them off for you," I proposed, "if you'll tell me how long the five have been gone."

All ten of them spat in my direction.

As it turned out, the fugitives had been gone only a short time. When I caught sight of them, they were running as fast as their legs would carry them. But Old Anak could go faster than they could. They looked back and let out a cry. They darted off the trail to the left where there were steep slopes and bluffs. They went up one of these steep places, like mountain climbers tied together.

The elephant could not follow them over such rough and tilted ground. I now had a spear. They had no weapons and were bound. Yet if I charged them, climbing up the slope below them, they could roll together down upon me, and kick the life out of me. And all the while the elephant could render me no assistance.

They scrambled up to a kind of ledge and stood there. With their feet they rolled down sizable rocks that fell forward of the elephant, for we were not closely under them. I held up the spear as a sign that I could spear them to death one by one. I asked them to come down and give themselves up.

"*Canis Carthaginiensis!*" they spat out. "Dog of a Carthaginian!"

I aimed the spear and they ducked flat on the ledge. I did not make the throw. I had little chance of hitting them now. Besides, I had no heart to drive the weapon into a tied-up man.

"Come down," I called. "You will starve. You can only

drink. You cannot eat. You cannot untie yourselves. Sooner or later you will perish."

"The Romans will find us—find us soon," said the one who had been a sentinel and was so quick to do my bidding back there at the camp. "Maybe too soon for the elephant, maybe too soon for the dog of a Carthaginian boy."

Whereupon, they yelled with all the force of their five throats. This could be heard a considerable distance. The menace of it to me was clear. The Romans would indeed come within range of their shouting and find them and release them. The tables would turn, and I would be the one captured.

I turned the elephant around. He carried me away in sweeping, rapid strides. The men's loud, insulting voices rang in my ears, now yelling for the Romans to come, now calling me a dog of a Carthaginian.

When I returned to the crossing, my eleven prisoners were still there safe enough at their two trees. But twenty horsemen were there also, wearing leopard skins. They were twenty Numidians come back to find me.

EIGHT

THE NUMIDIANS, IN CHARGE OF A SERGEANT, HAD DISMOUNTED. Their ponies, far from being afraid of Old Anak, were gathered companionably in front of him, where his waving trunk above them helped to keep off the mosquitoes.

"You have done well, Agenor," said the sergeant.

"There were five others that got away. I have just been after them."

"So the centurion told us by signs. We could make naught of the gibberish of his speech."

"If you will go along with a few men, we can fetch them back easily enough. They were too much for me alone on the elephant. They climbed up on a shelf of rock and kicked down stones. They screamed at the top of their voices. I was afraid they would be heard by Roman detachments riding about. They were very insulting. They called me a dog of a Carthaginian. Let's go after them."

"The army is already far ahead," explained the sergeant. "Also, it isn't safe for us to loiter here, on account of the Romans. We have the eleven prisoners, one of them a centurion, a very good haul without the others. It's as many as we can carry anyhow. We'll have to travel too fast to make them walk. You can take the centurion and maybe four others—the

84

biggest ones—on the elephant. We'll carry the rest double, spelling the horses every four or five miles. Then we can make fast time. We not only have orders to reach the army as soon as possible, but Scipio's advance patrols may arrive here any minute. Did you find out anything about Scipio from the centurion?"

"Not a thing. He has strict ideas about what's right for him to say and not to say, to do and not to do. He wouldn't open his mouth about Scipio. Otherwise, he behaves all right. But the others are a mean lot. All they ever had on their ill-mannered tongues were complaints—I caused them to walk too fast, their helmets made their heads itch, they couldn't keep the mosquitoes off, I tied their wrists so tight that they swelled and hurt."

When we were about ready to start, hardly any of the Romans had their helmets on. These had been shaken off in vigorous agitation to loosen the biting mosquitoes. I went along the line helmeting them up again.

Four of them were placed on the elephant, not on his neck, but widely spraddled on his broad back, where, handcuffed as they were, the riding would be a little slippery and insecure. And they didn't like that either. The centurion was put on his neck behind me, unbound as before.

"Draccus, do you promise upon your honor as a Roman knight not to try to escape?"

"I promise," he said.

"Don't tie him," I told the Numidians.

Six horsemen took the other six prisoners in front of them bareback on their ponies.

When I asked the sergeant what he thought the army would do with Old Anak, he said he didn't know. He merely told me that Hannibal had asked General Hanno to send out a small detachment to find me if possible. He and his nineteen men were the ones detailed to make the search.

"When you didn't return," he said, "Hannibal, and General Hanno too, thought you had fallen into the hands of the Romans. Instead, we find they fell into your hands."

"Will that speak for us, do you think?" I asked.

"I don't know," said the sergeant.

Every five miles or so, according to the plan, six other Numidians took the six prisoners in front of them on their ponies, which seemed small to carry two men but which moved along at a rapid gait with the double load. We traveled twice as fast as the army did. Even so, it was dark when we came in sight of their campfires.

"I'll go and report," said the sergeant.

When he returned, he said we were to camp by ourselves where we were. Some men from the commissariat came with him, fetching blankets and food for me, for the Numidian escort, for the prisoners, and for Old Anak. This remembrance of his needs, as well as our own, made me hope that some relenting had gone on toward him. A doctor also came out a little later to look after my wound and the four wounds of the elephant. I construed this additional attention as a good omen for Old Anak.

When I awoke in the morning, the sergeant had already reported and had received orders regarding our action for the day. We were to march at our present distance in the rear, having no contact with anybody except the men of our escort. When the army camped for the night, there would be a trial of Old Anak for the murder of Dokobal, the Purple Band sergeant, at the crossing of the Rhone.

"Gillimas and Misdes drew lots," said the sergeant. "Gillimas is to prosecute. Misdes is to defend. They will conduct interviews during the day's march and will have witnesses on hand."

"Will I be a witness?" I inquired.

"I heard Gillimas and Misdes agree not. You would be a prejudiced witness."

"Scarbas?"

"No, for the same reason."

"Gisbo?"

"Both sides will interview him."

"That isn't fair," I protested. "When you report again, will you ask Gillimas and Misdes if the Roman centurion can testify whether during this capture of himself and his men the elephant has been under complete control?"

"I'll ask them," promised the sergeant. "Meanwhile you will talk to nobody. In fact, we have orders not to let anybody come near enough to you to talk."

"Not even Scarbas?"

"No, not even him, not anybody."

The ten prisoners had to walk now, of course, and a complaining lot they were.

At nightfall, as we topped a high stretch of ground, we could look ahead and see the army preparing to camp. We were given our own supper. Old Anak was given his. The sergeant returned with orders for us.

"Agenor," he explained, "you are to arrange your rope harness on the elephant and drag the prisoners along, just as you did from where you captured them to the crossing where we found you. The centurion can ride unbound with you on the elephant just as he did then."

The army was gathered in a great natural amphitheatre,

lighted with many torches. In the center, General Hanno sat at a camp table. On the ground on either side of him sat Gillimas and Misdes, very sober and formal now. The elephant was placed in front of them, a few yards away, with the line of prisoners behind, wanting to sit down but not being allowed to. On the neck of the elephant with me was the centurion. This man now sat very haughtily, suiting me all the better so. It let the army see I had captured an arrogant Roman.

As soon as we came into the amphitheatre, a group of Purple Bandsmen began to shout: "Execute the elephant! He murdered Dokobal, the sergeant. He's a killer. Execute him!"

This time there was no beating with an iron club upon an iron sheet. A soldier blew a bugle for the trial to come to order. Even after his loud blast, the mob was not quiet: "Stand the elephant up before a squad of spearmen at ten paces. He's a killer. No trial for the beast. Execute him! We don't want to see him tried. We want to see him die."

At a sign from General Hanno, the bugler blew again for order. There was a sufficient interval of quiet for him to be heard. "By the fires of Moloch, this mischief must stop," were his first words. "The supreme commander has ordered a trial, and, by the scorched sands of the desert, a trial it will be. If the elephant is found innocent, he will be fully reinstated in the army. If he is found guilty, he will be shot with spears until he is dead. We will now proceed."

"Kill the elephant! Kill him now! No trial! Execute him!" came from a single voice in the crowd.

The bugler blew a loud blast.

"Who said that?" demanded General Hanno. "Let the culprit make himself known." He looked in the direction whence the voice had come. "You men in the back there, who said that?" They did not answer. No man admitted saying it. "By the fires of Moloch," declared General Hanno, "if a man is caught interrupting again, he will be court-martialed."

Draccus, the centurion, looked scornfully out upon the scene, and the more scornful he looked the more pleased I was. There was greater honor to me in sight of the army for bringing here a haughty Roman than in having captured a scared and timid one.

"Officers and Men of Carthage," announced General Hanno, "we are met here for the trial of Old Anak, aged eighty-seven, the chief war elephant of thirty-seven in this army on its way to Rome. Old Anak is accused of killing Sergeant Dokobal of the Purple Band while crossing the Rhone, and is further accused of having been unmanageable and viciously out of control. This is the accusation. If it is substantiated, the elephant stands condemned and will instantly be removed from the army, notwithstanding his previous long and great services to Carthage. If the charges are not substantiated, he will be reinstated as though nothing has happened, an honored elephant in the Carthaginian herd. The prosecution will be conducted by Gillimas, the defense by Misdes. These lawyers have held interviews during the day with various persons of the four hundred and fifty who assisted in getting the elephants over the Rhone."

While General Hanno was talking, a messenger had gone from General Gisbo to Misdes. Misdes nodded yes to the messenger, who then returned to General Gisbo.

"Gillimas," said General Hanno, "you may begin for the prosecution."

"Honorable Judge," interrupted Misdes, jumping to his feet, "will the court allow a short recess? General Gisbo originally

asked for execution of the elephant. This was changed into a
trial by the supreme commander. General Gisbo, who brought
the accusation, since he was in whole charge of the elephant
crossing, now petitions for an interview with the boy, Agenor."

"Does the prosecution approve?" asked General Hanno.

"The prosecution does not object," said Gillimas.

"There will be a short recess," announced General Hanno.

The messenger came to me. I got down from the elephant,
leaving the centurion up there to be gazed upon by the enemy
army, and to gaze back upon it with haughtiness and pride.

Gisbo said: "My purpose in petitioning the court for this
interview is to ask you if Old Anak has been under your complete control during your absence and at no moment unmanageable. This, told upon your honor, would be sufficient and
satisfactory evidence to me that the elephant is entirely
responsible."

I told him how Old Anak had obeyed me in every particular. This was indeed true, though I did not describe what
had nearly been my failure upon the trail in keeping him
from heading back to the other elephants.

"Through Misdes, then, I shall ask that the charges be dismissed. I shall also ask permission to make a statement, and
you may be sure this will absolutely exonerate Old Anak.
First, however, I should like to have your solemn promise that
you will never speak of the interview held in my tent or discuss
any misunderstandings you may have had about the elephant-
crossing."

I promised and it was an unfortunate moment when I did so.

As soon as we returned, the same messenger went to Misdes.
When the trial was called to order, Misdes said to General
Hanno: "Sir, General Gisbo wishes permission to address to

the court a request that the charges be dismissed and that the elephant be fully restored to favor."

"If Gillimas does not object," said General Hanno.

"I do not object," said Gillimas.

General Gisbo stepped out in the center of the amphitheatre, his helmet shining in the torchlight, his left hand raised graciously, with all the rings upon it, the folds of his red cloak hanging becomingly, his neck and body straight with generations of Carthaginian pride.

"Honorable Judge," spoke General Gisbo, "I superintended the Rhone crossing. I preferred charges against Old Anak, since I was responsible and since a man had been killed in such a way as to show the elephant had become ungovernable and a murderer. It now appears that the animal was in the stress of excitement and fear and that the killing of Sergeant Dokobal was innocent and unavoidable. I therefore petition the court that the charges be dropped."

While this speech was going on, I had motioned to Misdes. He came over to me.

As soon as Gisbo ceased, I said: "This centurion here saw how the elephant behaved. He is willing to testify. Will he be permitted, adding to what General Gisbo has said?"

"I will see," said Misdes.

"He will have to talk in Latin. Can it be interpreted?"

"We can take care of that."

Misdes addressed General Hanno: "Worthy Chairman, the boy, Agenor, while riding the accused elephant, took eleven prisoners who are here for you to see. One is a centurion, a Roman knight. He is willing to add his testimony as a character witness for the elephant."

"If there are no objections," replied General Hanno. "General Gisbo?"

"No objections, sir."

"Gillimas?"

"None, sir."

"He may speak."

Then the centurion, addressing me, made an unexpected request: "May I speak from here?"

I asked Misdes. Misdes asked General Hanno. It was allowed. The centurion stood on the elephant's neck, and, from that high witness stand, he answered the questions of Misdes.

"Your name?"

"Cornelius Draccus."

"Nationality?"

"Roman."

"Position?"

"Formerly centurion in the Roman army; now captive in the Carthaginian army."

"Did this boy, Agenor, on the elephant known as Old Anak, capture you and fifteen of your men?"

"Yes. We supposed there were many of the great animals attacking us. Not one only."

"Was the elephant at all times under complete control of the boy? Did he obey every command?"

"He did so. He even waited through the two hours the boy fell asleep, during which time five prisoners escaped."

I felt embarrassed. I would rather he had not spoken of my going to sleep and letting captives get away. It did not sound well without considerable explanation.

"In no instance, then, was the elephant out of hand?"

"In no instance."

Misdes himself had interpreted this. He now turned to Gillimas: "Do you agree that the interpretation has been correct?"

"Entirely correct," said Gillimas.

General Hanno stood up and announced: "The trial is dismissed. The elephant known as Old Anak is restored to the
Carthaginian army, with all the privileges and all the respect
hitherto enjoyed by him."

"Hurrah! Hurrah for Old Anak!" shouted the soldiers by
hundreds, by thousands, it seemed to me, so loudly did their
shouting fill the amphitheatre. Those who had previously asked
for his death were silent now or their voices too had become a
part of this deafening acclamation.

Scarbas joined me. "Old Anak is free," he cried. "We have
done General Gisbo wrong in our thoughts. We owe Anak's
freedom to General Gisbo."

I stood and listened to these things. A boy ever looks forward
to the time when he will be a man. As a man he ever looks
back upon the time when he was a boy and upon the un-
troubled mind he had then, filled with thoughts that were like
a fresh wind blowing. Here was I now at this turning point,
I, Agenor of the Elephants, burdened with the first dark
secret that had ever weighed upon me, not really the second,
only the first questionable one continued. But Old Anak was
saved and for that at least I was glad.

NINE

THE ARMY, STRETCHING OUT FOR MANY LEAGUES, MARCHED northward over a wilderness route. It was old to the feet of barbarians, but, since the world began, this was the first time the trail had given passage to a civilized army or received the heavy tread of elephants. On the fourth day, or the fifth, I do not remember exactly which, we came to another river athwart our way, the Isere, pouring into the Rhone a current almost as deep and broad as the mighty Rhone itself.

Here we halted for a few days.

Two brothers, both claiming to be kings of a Gaulish tribe, came to Hannibal for him to decide which of them was the rightful monarch. Hannibal's judgment of the case was perchance shrewder for benefits to the Carthaginian army than it was for justice. With the tribe itself the younger brother was in somewhat better favor. So Hannibal could get more food and shoes by deciding for the elder brother, which he did. This grateful king, called Brancus, liberally furnished Hannibal with provisions and supplies, particularly with new shoes which the troops badly needed for the Alps ahead.

With Brancus were left the ten Roman prisoners, who only encumbered the army. Hannibal kept their Roman uniforms for his spies when we should reach Italy. The last I saw of them, they spat out a good-by to me: *"Canis Carthaginiensis!* Dog of a Carthaginian!"

"Will the Gauls make them grow their hair long and dye it red?" I asked Draccus.

"Poor fellows," he lamented, "I caused their misfortune, but they are spirited men. They will escape sometime and perhaps get back to Rome."

Draccus himself had been assigned to us and the tusker herd. He called Scarbas "sir" which was all right, but he even insisted on so addressing me. We had already found him an unusually good hand with the elephants. He worked long hours feeding them, watering them, washing them, waiting upon them not only in the few ways they require but in the many ways they will accept. I expressed surprise that he, a Roman knight, should put so much zeal into these lowly tasks.

"Agenor, sir," he replied, "what you do counts less than how well you do it. When I was a centurion, I tried to be a good one, though you who captured me so easily may not think so. Now that I am an elephant servant, I want to be the best one possible."

And on that very account we nearly lost him.

"Agenor," said Scarbas to me, "the elephants are getting too fond of Draccus. It is dangerous. They might lose their zest for killing Romans. They'll come in time to think each one is a good friend like Draccus. Old Zain, who likes nothing better than being waited on, may be spoiled already. It can't continue."

"Do you think, Scarbas, that he's making them fond of Romans on purpose?"

"If so, he'd be more useful in taking the fight out of thirty-seven elephants than if he were free again and leading a hundred cavalrymen for Scipio. He may be doing it with guile. He may not. The effect is the same, and we can't have it."

"Would it take care of the trouble if he wore Carthaginian clothes?"

"Yes, that—and if he never spoke Latin around the elephants. And if you, Agenor, never had him teach you Latin words where the elephants can hear."

"What of his Roman smell, Scarbas? We can't do anything about that."

"Nonsense, Agenor. He smells the same as you or me, and I suppose that General Gisbo would say that all three of us smell like elephants. No, get rid of his Roman clothes and his Roman speech, and he can stay."

Draccus at first stoutly refused. I told him he would be detailed, then, to another part of the army, or, what was more likely, would be traded to Brancus for more shoes. So he consented. His centurion's uniform was carefully saved to be worn later by a Carthaginian spy.

We crossed the Isere, with much help from Brancus, who also furnished us with guides. We continued up the Rhone for some distance, then quitted its familiar shores, and turned east, across the final margin of the plain, into the limestone mountains that are the beginning of the Alps. Ridges uplifted tier beyond tier. There were wooded slopes of misty blue. There were bleak surfaces of tilted stone. These formed the lonely, inhospitable threshold of great peaks running up to the clouds, and given by their snowy covering the whiteness of clouds.

"Look," exclaimed Draccus, "they mingle with the sky!"

From the neck of Old Yenbo we gazed out upon these ramparts greater than ten thousand times ten thousand walls of Carthage or of Rome.

It was past the middle of October as we began to penetrate and to scale those lofty barriers. Brancus' guides left us. We secured new ones.

We had scarcely started to climb this far-reaching steepness before the neighboring heights along our crooked and ascending trail were held by defiant mountaineers.

Men, horses, and elephants made a winding, climbing column over twenty miles long. Sometimes at switchbacks, Old Anak at the head of the elephant section would be directly above Little Enoch at the end. At that moment the whole herd would make a sharp-pointed lazy letter "<" upon the canyon wall. Half their heads would be turned in one direction, half in the opposite direction.

Deeper in the mountains, the barbarians attacked in many places at once, killing men by hundreds.

The wild disorder created an equally wild tumult of sound that echoed and re-echoed in the gorges. The yelling barbarians, the neighing horses, the cries of soldiers forced from the crowded ledges, the crashing of men and animals far below —these made a noise and clamor that were repeated and prolonged in reverberations from the cliffs.

Nothing ever happened to the part of the line occupied by the elephants, which the barbarians regarded with superstitious terror.

Hannibal himself led a force of men up the heights above the attackers. He went on to capture the barbarian strongholds. For three days after this, the higher and ever higher paths were nearly free of enemies.

Then the army passed into a defile, with precipices overhanging it on either side and a river at the bottom. Multitudes of barbarians, in ambush on the heights, rolled down rocks

and boulders. A big stone, loosened from its shallow anchorage
in the sloping earth, would tumble and drop, gaining speed as
it came. There was no room on the narrow, crowded trail to
get out of the way. Everywhere, the relentless and inescapable
stones were descending. This caused an immense loss of men
and horses.

Again the elephants were not attacked. Behind them and
before them, the deadly avalanches took heavy toll of soldiers
and animals, but the whole line of thirty-seven elephants, from
Old Anak back to Little Enoch, was clear as they moved along.
As soon as we passed a spot, its immunity ceased. As soon as
Old Anak arrived at one, sanctity lay upon it until Little Enoch
had gone safely by. Then the bombardment started again.

The trail through the beleaguered defiles and canyons sometimes hugged the margin of the river, with an abrupt cliff at
our shoulders on one side and a mountain torrent close at our
feet on the other. At periods of low water, travelers probably
found passage, dryshod or by shallow wading, around the projections. But at this flood season, we often came to where an
outthrust of cliff filled and choked the narrow roadway. The
natives usually had an upper trail along the declivity to by-pass
such obstructed spots.

One afternoon, in a lull of the boulder rolling, we came to
such a hillside path which led up from the water-level trail we
had been upon for a while. This looked long and steep and
difficult, and another fierce company of stone-pushing savages
might be in ambush above it. Hannibal wished to avoid it, if
the route at the bottom could still be followed. Yet he did not
want to lead his army along the river only to find the way
shut off, and have to come back and take the upper route after
all.

We could see but imperfectly ahead on account of a bend in the river. We could tell, however, that in at least two places the cliff wall bulged out in capes or peninsulas, of the sort that had stopped us several times before. One was a kind of hogback looking more than twice as high as an elephant. The other was a sharp-edged buttress appearing still higher. Both seemed to extend right into the water.

"Scarbas," directed Hannibal, "will you take Old Anak and go forward to see if the path is open to the army around those two points? If there are stone-rolling barbarians above, they will not harm you because you are on an elephant—at least this has been the case so far."

"Yes, sir," said Scarbas.

"Can I go too?" I asked. Scarbas nodded approval and I took my place behind him on Old Anak.

"Meanwhile," suggested Gisbo, "the guides can be scouting out the upper trail, in case we have to take it. I will send two of them to do this, sir, if you approve."

"Send them," agreed Hannibal. "It will save time."

Scarbas and I each carried a spear. We took along a piece of white cloth and a piece of red cloth. If we found the road open for the passage of the army, we were to tie the two spears together and signal with the white banner over the top of the first projection. The army could then move on toward us at once and we would not have to come back to report.

If the road were impassable and completely blocked, we were similarly to hoist the red banner. In that case, the army would immediately proceed along the upper route if the guides reported it clear of barbarians. We would fall into line when we returned to the junction of the two trails.

We found that Old Anak, carrying Scarbas and me, could

squeeze around the first outthrust, though on the left his big side rubbed the granite and on the right the swift stream rushed by almost under us. But Old Anak was the biggest thing we had in the army. If he could get by, all the rest could.

The other projection reached clear out into the rapid current and lifted sheer from its angry wash. The river, as it hurried past, was too deep and tumultuous to be waded at all, much less upstream.

I tied the two spears together, fastened the red piece of cloth to one end. I stood up on Old Anak and lifted the scarlet banner as high as I could.

Just then a boulder came rolling down. It hit Old Anak's right tusk with a jar that threw his head to one side, and made him shake it several times afterward, as if he would get rid of some lingering pain and dislocation. A smaller stone hit his back. One as big as a horse's head landed in the trail right behind us. One as big as an elephant's head went right over me as I stood, knocking the upheld spears out of my hands. It fell into the water with such a mighty force as momentarily to splash a spot in the river dry.

We looked for a place of refuge. There was a concave area in the wall at the junction of the cliff and buttress, with the solid rock curving inward at its back and outward above it.

"Down, Anak!" cried Scarbas. The elephant lay down close against the wall, with us two on top of him, while stone after stone, some of them as big as barrels, came tumbling down with loud cuchugs into the river or falling with great thuds and making indentations on the trail.

Were the barbarians getting bolder? Had they now become fearless and reckless enough to attack the elephants themselves?

Just then a boulder came rolling down

The stones stopped coming for a while. At last Scarbas said to me: "I think all is clear."

Hardly had he spoken than another projectile came over and fell in the trail at the very margin of the river. Only this projectile was not a stone. It was a man. A spear was deep in his breast. The handle had broken off in the fall.

I crawled out away from Old Anak. I took hold of the man's arm to drag him toward us. But as I gripped his lifeless wrist, another human form hurtled over.

Now I dragged in the first man. He was one of the two guides sent on the upper trail at the same time we were sent along the river. We saw enough of the one landing in the water to make out that he was the other guide.

As we examined the first one, I cried out: "Look here, Scarbas! Look at this!"

On the third finger of his left hand he wore a ring, a very expensive ring, a Carthaginian ring. We took it off. I put it in my pocket.

A Numidian horseman appeared. "Hannibal was worried about you," he said. "He was afraid you may have been killed, both of you and the elephant. Are you all right?"

"Not hurt at all," replied Scarbas. "But see this man here."

"I know. Our men killed him, and the other one. When these two guides didn't come back, and we heard the stones rolling down, a cavalry detachment hurried up there to see what had gone wrong. They found that it was the treacherous guides themselves, at work in a concealed place, who were hurling down the stones. So our men killed them on the spot without further ado."

"Up, Anak!" said Scarbas.

Old Anak still shook his head occasionally. I felt his right tusk. He did not want me to pull on it. It seemed to be very tender. I called out to Scarbas: "I think it's loose. I think the rock jarred it loose."

"Hardly so," answered Scarbas. "But if it's loose, it will soon grow tight again."

When we returned to the junction of the trails to take our place in the climbing line, I changed from Old Anak to Old Yenbo. Draccus rode with me on this elephant.

"Draccus," I asked, "was General Gisbo on the upper trail? Did he go up there at all?"

I fingered the ring in my pocket as I talked, but I did not wish to show it to him.

"No, Agenor, sir, he was with us at the river, with us all the time. I remember it clearly."

"Are you sure he never left the junction of the trails, never rode off somewhere else for a little while?"

"Never for a moment. When the stones began to roll down, he was the one who sent the Numidians up as fast as their horses could run, with orders to kill whoever was doing it. He said loud enough for us to hear that if the guides had turned traitor and were the guilty ones, to put spears through their hearts. He was within a few yards of me all the time. He stood leaning on his big, white horse, with his left hand on the animal's withers and his right tapping the ground with that stick he carries."

"Did you notice anything about his left hand?"

"You mean a scar or something? Nothing, Agenor, sir."

"Are you certain, Draccus, that you saw nothing at all special about his left hand?"

"Except his rings. I thought maybe he liked to hold his hand up there on the horse's withers so his four costly rings could be seen by everybody. Why does he wear so many? A Roman knight wears just one. See mine, Agenor, sir. Why does he wear four?"

"Each ring is for a military campaign he's been through. You say he had four. Are you sure?"

"Oh, yes, Agenor, sir. I was fascinated by them. I was close enough to see that he had a different kind of gem in each one."

Gisbo and the cavalry of the Purple Band had gone on. I did not myself see his left hand until the next day. On the fingers of it were six rings as usual. Had he replaced the two from an extra supply? Or had Draccus been inexact in his observation, unreliable in his recollection? Or had Gisbo's fingers been mixed with the horse's mane so that two of the rings were concealed?

I hesitated to call to his attention the one that I had. Then, in desperate need of setting my mind at rest one way or the other, I took it out of my pocket.

"I have here a ring like yours, General Gisbo. I took it off one of the dead guides that rolled down the mountainside."

"It is mine," he acknowledged, quite without hesitation and quite without embarrassment. "The two Gauls coveted my rings. I gave one to each, promising them yet another apiece if their services were well and faithfully performed. Do you also have the other, Agenor?"

"No, sir, only this one," I said, giving it to him. "The second man landed in the river."

"I regret the loss of the other ring," he said. "Such bodies are fit rubbish for the river, but it is wasteful to feed the stream good jewelry."

TEN

As we toiled upward toward the summit of the alps, the barbarians continued to roll stones down upon us in the gorges. Bodies of our men and horses fell far below into the river, or lodged against obstructions, or piled up on rocky shelves. One moment a Carthaginian was alive. The next he was a part of that dead multitude in the abyss.

Hannibal decided to put a stop to it, not only where we were but all along ahead of us.

He took a force above their ambush, and captured a hundred of them. He brought them down to the trail and sent for Gillimas and Misdes.

"You are rhetoricians," he said. "You ought to be full of ingenuity. Give these hundred murderers a taste of mental torture. Shock their senses with a subtle and cunning torment. Kill ten of them, ten only, in a way to fill the other ninety with such terror that the dread of Carthaginian cruelty will spread like a contagion from here to the summit."

"We shall devise something, sir," promised Misdes.

"At once," declared Hannibal. "We have no time to lose."

In a few minutes, tall, stooped Gillimas stood beside the trail with ninety straws four inches long and ten straws two and a half inches long. As you can imagine, he had a big fistful.

All protruded evenly about an inch above the top of his hand.

Misdes was several yards ahead, attended by a sergeant. Soldiers herded the prisoners.

The barbarians passed along. Each took a straw, as chance willed, from the grasped collection that Gillimas held out. All then passed by Misdes, surrendering their straws to him. When a prisoner held a short one, the sergeant pulled him out of line. These ten were kept by themselves until the sergeant was sure he could identify them. Then they were thrown back into the general group.

The spot selected for this diabolical ordeal was a rocky point that had room at its edge for Old Anak and Old Yenbo. These two elephants stood with their forefeet at the brink, their heads and tusks and trunks sticking out over it. The precipice went straight down for three hundred feet.

Fifty of the barbarians were lined up to the left of Old Yenbo, fifty to the right of Old Anak. They were prodded with spears to stand close to the edge so each could witness what was happening.

Regular drivers were on the two elephants. I wanted to direct Old Yenbo but Misdes said to me shortly: "You're too young, Agenor, for this stern business. You oughtn't to be here even to watch it."

Two burly Carthaginian soldiers, assisting the sergeant, brought forward two short-straw barbarians. Old Anak held out one over the abyss. Old Yenbo held out the other. Their faces were down so they could look at their landing place two hundred cubits below. They squirmed and wriggled and turned their eyes imploringly toward us. Their wails and screams came back to us in echoes. I could see the ninety-eight others trembling.

"Hold!" said Old Anak's driver.

"Hold!" said Old Yenbo's driver.

"Drop!" said both simultaneously.

Their cries were smothered in their throats. In fascination, I saw that one fell more rapidly than the other, though both were released at the same instant. They made that awful plunge and hit bottom, with the ninety-eight others viewing it all. Two of the prisoners became so wobbly-kneed that they squatted to keep from going over the edge in their agonized dizziness. Soldiers prodded them to their feet.

At once, two long-straw prisoners were brought up. The two elephants held them out over the abyss, while they screamed as the others had done. Then they were set back on the bank. By twos this happened as fast as they could be given to the elephants. As soon as there was any noticeable lessening of suspense and dread, two short-straw men were dropped.

Then all those that had been set back began to tremble with fresh terror. Gillimas went along the two lines and held out another fistful of straws. Each man drew a short one. That was the only kind Gillimas had now. This second lottery in truth meant nothing. It was just an added Carthaginian refinement to destroy all feeling of reprieve, all sense of security, among the barbarians.

At last the ninety were released. Hannibal had not been on hand to watch. He came up now, as Gillimas and Misdes wiped their sweating faces. "Sir," said Misdes, "I feel as if I had been held out over the cliff a hundred times."

"In my dreams," observed Gillimas, "I will be drawing short straws."

"You have done well," said Hannibal, as the barbarians hastened away. "Give them an hour's start so they can tell their tribesmen ahead of us. Then I think we can travel in peace."

This indeed ended the rock-rolling attacks the rest of the way.

Upon the summit of the Alps, on an icy level of ground, the army rested for two days. Much new snow had fallen upon the old. The soldiers were exhausted with toil and fighting. They were hungry, shivering, weary, hopeless, and the death of thousands of their comrades lay heavy upon their spirits.

No forage of any kind was to be found for the elephants in that wilderness of white. There were no trees whose leaves could be given to the famished herd in place of other herbage. For two days on that snowy summit they went without food and without a fire to give them any relief from the cold. The drivers, Scarbas, Draccus, and I stayed up most of the two nights, spelling each other with brief snatches of rest, covering the elephants with our own blankets and leading them back and forth to put some warmth into their frozen bodies.

"They will die," declared Scarbas. "They will surely die. Do' you remember, Agenor, that Gisbo said they would? Their lungs will be sick, their breathing will be clogged, they will grow weak and fall down in their tracks. If they do not perish here, the seeds of death will be planted in them. They cannot fight again, they will be useless, they will be distempered and diseased."

The way down the Alps was even steeper than the way up. The fresh snow that had fallen on the summit continued its covering everywhere over the landscape as we descended. Underneath it lay the old ice, a buried pavement, smooth and treacherous. It was both steep and slippery, and so was doubly upsetting to the weary marchers. Those who made the least stumble could not prevent themselves from falling. And when they fell they could not remain in the same place, but men and animals rolled together upon one another.

The narrow trail itself did not afford a slender, level terrace. Its bottom was not deeply enough worn to keep it from lying at a slant. Thirty feet uphill to the left was a rocky wall. Thirty feet downhill to the right was the edge of the precipice. The elephants, even with their big feet, would slip and go halfway toward the brink before they could stop themselves.

As we marched through the center of this tilted lane, we had in front of us only about a hundred of the Purple Band cavalry scouting out the trail. There was a commotion ahead of us. The horsemen in the lead came to a standstill "No trail," they shouted back. "It's caved in."

The horsemen behind them kept on crowding up. Gisbo and a Purple Band officer, who had been riding immediately at our rear, started around us to reach the difficulty ahead. They rode close to the wall above us at our left, not attempting to pass us on the lower side because an elephant might slip down upon them.

Gisbo's big, white horse, and his companion's black one, that looked all the blacker against the snow, could hardly keep their footing without any trail at all. Their downhill legs would slip from under them sideways. They would scramble some distance toward us before they could get straightened out. When they neared the head of the elephant line, they diagonaled down to regain the trail in front of us. Both horses began to slide, stirring up the loose snow in dust about them. They could not dig in their forefeet enough to stop themselves.

I saw the Purple Band officer do everything possible to get the hoofs of his horse anchored in the ice. I cannot be sure of one momentary act of Gisbo. His horse's forelegs were braced forward in a noticeable halt of the descent. I saw, or thought I saw, Gisbo's heels dig into the animal's flanks.

First the big, white horse, then the big, black one, hit against Old Anak. The jar threw him off his balance. He began to skid helplessly toward the precipice. On him was Scarbas. On him was most of the Carthaginian treasure. I was with Draccus right behind him on Old Yenbo.

"Jump, Scarbas!" I yelled. "He's going over the cliff!"

The two horses were sliding with him, without grip upon the slippery ice swept clean by his four huge feet. The white horse was at his side. The black horse was behind him. He was turned so that Gisbo's horse, at his middle, was still lodged against him. Gisbo was doing everything he could to stop him now. His face looked as white as the snow.

Scarbas did not want to jump. Gisbo did not dare to, amidst those four great legs and eight smaller ones in helpless motion on the ice.

Old Anak managed to get his head turned forward. He buried his tusks through the loose snow into the ice. They plowed for about a yard and then held him. But he was within half his own length of the precipice. The officer's horse was halted behind him. But when the elephant turned to a straight-ahead position, the white horse, no longer having his support, skidded swiftly past to the rim of the cliff and on down into space. The horse had his forefeet ahead of him and he went over in the manner of a leap. The folds of Gisbo's scarlet cloak were whipped back from him.

We thought it was the end of them.

A soldier, digging places for his feet, went down to look over the rim where horse and rider had disappeared. There was a ledge as big as a tent floor before the precipice continued at a sheer drop of seven or eight hundred feet. The deep, fresh snow, with drifts heaped upon it, had deadened the fall of the horse. He was not injured but stood buried halfway up his sides. The soldier saw him thus with Gisbo still mounted on him.

It was about twenty feet down to the ledge. Gisbo himself could be drawn up with ropes. But we considered that the animal was doomed.

"No," said Gisbo, "we must get the horse out."

The trouble ahead was serious for that exhausted army. An avalanche had taken away a section of the trail between a bluff and the precipice. It ended in a chasm a thousand feet deep. There was no way around. The army set to work to bridge the gap and dig a new path along the stony wall of the overhanging bluff.

There were some trees at this elevation. When these were cut down, we shook the snow and ice from the withered leaves and fed them to the famished elephants. In one day's time a trail was made for the men and horses, but it took three more days to build a passage wide enough and strong enough for Old Anak, Old Yenbo, and the others. So, counting this stop and the one at the summit, they had to go six days without any food except the winter leaves.

"They can't stand it," said Scarbas. "They can't go through this and ever be the same again. They'll be too weak to recover."

But here we could build fires with which to thaw out their blood. Occasionally Old Anak shook his head as if his right tusk had been given another wrench at the roots.

During the first day of the halt, while hundreds repaired the trail over the chasm, a considerable number were employed in rescuing Gisbo's horse. The men felled twenty trees about the size of Little Enoch's legs and cut them into lengths of twenty-five feet. Back from the edge of the cliff the snow and ice were cleared away. The logs were laid down in two sets of ten each, fastened together, with poles laid crosswise over them, so no single log would trip up.

The two raftlike contrivances were the length of the horse apart. About six feet of both projected out over the precipice. Here on one stood Old Anak. Here on the other stood Old Yenbo. Each was balanced by five or six elephants standing on the nineteen feet of the platform that stretched back upon the upward-sloping ground. Across the necks of the two big elephants a large pole was laid like a long yoke. Ropes were put around the horse, with padding, and were then brought over the pole. Men and elephants pulled the cables up the slope, the horse rising like a bucket from a well. By this arrangement the animal was saved from collision with the jagged cliffside. When he was lifted up to where his back nearly touched the pole, other ropes pulled him forward onto the bank.

All this work by weary men and beasts for a horse, the best one in the army, to be sure, better than Hannibal's, but still only a horse, made me realize how powerful were the words and wishes of Gisbo.

He was very grateful to the elephants. He thanked Scarbas over and over. To me he said never a word, but I thought he eyed me questioningly. They were the lingering and repeated glances of one who wonders if another knows something not meant to be known.

It was the first of November when we reached the foot of the Alps and rested in the broad plain of Northern Italy.

We had started out from New Carthage just five months and two days before. We had started then with one hundred and two thousand men. We had left the Pyrenees with fifty-nine thousand. We had left the Rhone with forty-six thousand. We rested here now in Northern Italy with only twenty-six thousand—as worn-out and feeble-looking an army as ever stood upon the threshold of a country it meant to conquer.

Of course, Hannibal expected the Gauls and Celts on this side of the mountains to join him. And they began to do so in large numbers.

We rested through November. Then, in the early part of December, Scipio led out his troops to meet Hannibal. The consul had come from the Rhone to head off the Carthaginians in Northern Italy.

Hannibal's spies reported that Scipio had given an oration to his soldiers. They repeated such parts of the arrogant Roman's speech as they could remember:

Soldiers of Rome: As I, Scipio the Roman Consul, lead you into battle, you have reason to be strong of courage.

Back at the Rhone, did not a few of our cavalry rout many of Hannibal's horsemen? Did not Hannibal himself take to his heels with his whole army, in terror of Scipio?

How much less cause is there now to fear these enfeebled Carthaginians. From crossing the Alps, they are but the resemblances of human beings, the shadows of men, the wraiths of soldiers. They are worn out with hunger, bruised by rocks. Their joints are frostbitten, their sinews stiffened with snow, their limbs withered up by frost.

Their elephants are but great skeletons, their wrinkled hides hang upon them as loosely as the folds of a toga, distemper is planted in their lungs, their energies are gone. Our spies have seen these emaciated wrecks and so report.

The Alps have conquered these Carthaginians for you. Go forth, soldiers of Rome, go forth under Scipio against their last remains.

"It is all as we wished it," said Hannibal. "We have them overconfident." To his own soldiers he gave a speech, every word of which I drank in, and all the others no less:

Fellow Soldiers: On the right and left two seas inclose you. The Alps behind hem you in. Before you is the only way out. Before you is Rome. Soldiers, you must conquer or die.

Here Fortune will end your labors, load you down with spoils, cover you with glory.

You will fight with a raw army and a six-months' general.

To this untried, upstart Scipio shall I compare myself, bred in the tent of my father Hamilcar, myself the conqueror of Spain and Gaul, of the Alpine nations, of the Alps themselves? Soldiers, there is not a man among you before whose eyes I have not achieved some military exploit. Soldiers, there is not a man among you who before my eyes has not performed glorious deeds. I was your pupil before I became your commander.

There is a necessity for you to be brave. All between victory and death is broken off. You must conquer or die.

After these two speeches, was fought the Battle of Ticinus, wherein the Romans met shameful defeat, wherein the wounded Scipio would have met death but for his son.

In this engagement the elephants were not used. They were still so completely unfit for fighting that Scarbas was sure the excitement and activity and getting heated in battle would have been the end of them. We continued to win over Gauls and Celts, to gather booty about the country, and to give the men, horses, and elephants as much rest and recovery as possible from the terrible experience of the Alps.

Near the end of the month, on the twenty-sixth of December, we fought the great Battle of Trebia, in which all the sick elephants took part—and of that battle I have much to say.

ELEVEN

O<small>N DECEMBER 25, THE DAY BEFORE THE BATTLE OF TREBIA,</small> Hannibal said to his younger brother: "Mago, come with me."

"Yes, sir."

They rode out along a waterless creek that made with high banks a deep ravine across the plain. There were no trees but it was heavily bordered with thorns and brambles.

Hannibal led the way through this thicket. Descending to the dry bottom of the creek, they went up it toward the north.

"Two thousand men and a thousand horses could be concealed here. Is it not so, Mago?"

"Without difficulty, sir."

"When the Romans see places with trees, they think something's wrong. They are used to finding the Celts and Gauls in ambush in wooded areas. But they will not be suspicious of this dry stream that has only brush growing along it. Mago you will spend the night here. You will be hidden here to fall upon the Roman rear at the proper time in the battle tomorrow. Go find ten of the best horsemen and ten of the best foot soldiers you know. Bring them to me after supper."

"But, sir, you know what our spies say. The enemy has forty-five thousand troops. What can I do against their rear with twenty men?"

"Find the twenty, Mago. Let them be strong and fearless."

Hannibal had scarcely finished his evening meal than Mago appeared with ten fine specimens each of cavalry and of infantry. "Here they are, sir," announced Mago.

"They look capable," said Hannibal.

"They are, sir. They can do anything that twenty men can do, but they are not magicians."

"True enough. Each of you go and find nine men as good as yourself and come to me."

When the two hundred stood before him, half on horses, half afoot, Mago said: "This is better, sir, but hardly enough for an ambush against forty-five thousand men."

"No, it is not enough. Each of you go and find nine men as good as yourself and come to me."

This force of a thousand cavalry and a thousand infantry was led by Mago in the darkness some distance up the dry stream bed. Snow fell in the night, and the cold wind rustled the thickets, but they themselves remained without noise, without motion, in no way disturbing the solitude of the dried-up watercourse. Mago cautioned them to lie low in the reeds and brambles, to keep their helmets off, to carry their spears and all their long weapons close to the ground and not let them stick upright, and for the horses to stay in the creek bottom. Men's teeth chattered as the snow fell; there was the whir of an occasional bird; the cold wind continued to rattle the thick shrubbery. There was no other sound.

The Trebia River is about fifty miles long. It rises in the Apennines and flows into the River Po. Scipio, still wounded and still in bed, had stationed his army on the western bank, with breastworks and trenches. He was joined by Sempronius, the other consul, and his big army that had made forced marches after being landed from Sicily.

These two consuls—sick-a-bed Scipio, and Sempronius—had forty-five thousand men there on the Trebia. Enough Celts and Gauls had joined Hannibal to give him thirty-eight thousand. On account of Scipio's illness, Sempronius commanded both Roman armies and was eager to fight. He had to work fast for the glory of defeating Hannibal before his successor was elected.

Hannibal had found out all about Sempronius. It was his habit to size up an enemy general inside and out, and act accordingly. He used stratagem to draw this vainglorious consul into battle and destroy him.

That twenty-sixth of December was a cold, snowy day. Before the enemy had time to eat breakfast, Hannibal sent a troop of Numidians across the Trebia to throw darts and shoot arrows into them, just as they were getting out of bed. The Numidians called them dogs of Romans and shouted other insults. To have such a thing done by these leopard-skinned desert savages was too much for proud Sempronius.

The Roman cavalry chased them away. And they allowed themselves to be chased without making any sort of bold stand. They seemed like a cowardly troop when real horsemen took after them.

The Roman cavalry returned. The Numidians approached again. This was kept up until Sempronius ordered out his whole cavalry, then his whole army, to finish the Carthaginians and be done with it.

The snow and sleet continued, with intervals of cold rain. It was in the midst of winter between two great mountain ranges—the Alps and Apennines.

Sempronius ordered his men out before they had breakfast. The wide, icy current of the Trebia they waded up to their breasts. They emerged thus drenched into the chill of that snowy day.

Hannibal's men had had a good breakfast. They oiled themselves all over to get the stiffness out of their joints, Hannibal having sent around barrels of oil for this purpose. They put on their armor in front of warm fires. Then they waited for the whole Roman army to get across and be drawn up in order of battle, shivering as they stood in the ranks in their wet, stiffening clothes. This took several hours. Finally, with the snow falling between them, the Roman legions opposed the Carthaginian phalanx.

Sempronius, the confident consul, arrayed his legions in three lines. His Gauls were on the left. His four thousand horsemen were on the wings.

Hannibal drew up his infantry in a deep formation. His nine thousand cavalry—besides the one thousand hidden in the ravine—he placed equally on both flanks. On one wing he placed eighteen elephants, on the other nineteen, including Little Enoch.

"I dread what will happen to them," confided Scarbas to me. "Did the rhetoricians, this Gillimas and this Misdes, did they tell of elephants ever before fighting in the snow? They are not recovered from their sickness. But we must put them into the fight. The supreme commander is expecting them and he must not be disappointed. Breathe no word to him of our fears of their bad condition, and of this intolerable cold and the snow."

Old Anak, Old Zain, Old Yenbo, Old Sapor, and Old Bolobo had two-bladed, sharp-pointed scimitars fastened on as ex-

tensions of their tusks, carrying on the upward curve of them.
This made the elephants much more terrible in one way, while
actually rendering them less so in another. It limited the free
use of their trunks, which would be cut or pierced by any
collision with the sharp blades. Old Harab, among the first-
sized animals, was not armed in this way, on account of one
stumpy tusk. The rest of the herd also fought with tusks bare.

As we led them out, Draccus was sad. "When you bring them
back, Agenor, sir, with tusks all red—from piercing Romans—
I will have to wash them off."

"Red they will be, Draccus," I answered. "Buckets of water
will be dyed in cleansing them. But I will do it, and the drivers,
not you."

Scarbas did not ride Old Anak but lazy Old Zain so as to
get the best service out of him. Yud and Dor and one other
slinger were on Old Anak, each with a long sling for distance
and a short one for close up. I wanted one of them with me on
Little Enoch, but my request was ignored. For one thing, the
twin slingers would not fight separately. For another, their skill
was too valuable to be frittered away on the back of a half-
grown elephant. So I had a spearman with me. Since I was not
high up like the rest, Little Enoch was placed between two
big elephants, whose drivers had orders to keep their eyes on
me, and to pull Little Enoch and me out of any difficulties we
might get into.

The Romans, as usual, took the offensive. Their archers,
slingers, and light-armed infantry advanced. Sempronius rode
at the head of his men. The Romans cheered but their cheers
were hollow and faint. Their throats were soon silent; they
soon ceased to blow the snow away with shouts as it fell in
their faces. They were hungry and numbed with cold. Their

The elephants had two-bladed scimitars fastened on their tusks

garments, drenched in the Trebia, had frozen on them rather than dried. With nerveless hands they threw their javelins; with stiff arms they pulled back the strings of their bows; with wild aims they slung their stones.

While Sempronius was leading these men up, Hannibal's Numidians and the dread, oncoming elephants put the Roman cavalry to rout. The gray sky, the whitened ground, the snow-flakes descending slantingly through the air—out of this blurry paleness appeared the black monsters. The enemy horses became at once unmanageable, rearing, snorting, and darting away, like wild ponies on the plains.

This left the flank of the legion exposed, and our eighteen tuskers and Little Enoch fell upon it. I was with the half of the herd that now moved against the enemy left. Much the same thing was happening on the Roman right where the other eighteen big elephants attacked.

The legion's ranks turned to face us, the ones here at least not made timid by the cold nor shocked into helplessness by the apparition of the black beasts bearing down upon them. At once they presented a front with six extended spear points to every man of them. They were six deep and each row held out lances to make this thick barrier of barbs between us and the first line of men. We headed the elephants into them. They stood firm, they did not waver, not a man in the front line moved his feet backward; if they trembled we noted it not. In as even and unbending a line as theirs, the elephants rushed upon them.

Now was shown how wise Hannibal had been in putting Balearic slingers in the howdahs. With a swiftness and precision greater than I had seen in practice at New Carthage, the three combatants on each elephant, using their short slings, threw and ducked and rose and threw again. Those protruding spear points began to thin. The Romans in the front line, felled by the slingers, toppled to the ground toward us, their upturned heels in the way of others stepping unhesitantly forward to take their places.

They did not hurl at us their own spears. They continued unflinchingly to hold these out as spikes for the elephants to be impaled upon. That line of brave men, though wavering not in the face of those charging mountains of flesh, could not be as instantly filled from behind as they were dropped by the Balearics in the howdahs. There were gaps for elephant trunks when the elephants arrived.

In the first clash, the animals received many wounds. That avalanche of great bodies did not move on through this puny wall of men with overwhelming momentum. Those six rows of Romans stood steadfast, with spear handles jolting their arms as thick hides struck the points.

The Romans stopped a general trampling-down onslaught, to become victims, one by one, of those same great crushing feet, and angry trunks, and piercing tusks and scimitars. And all the while the Balearics would carry on a second warfare from the howdahs. For some time the crowded Romans could not get out of the way. The elephants mowed them down and mowed ever a new swath, as a harvester cuts a field of wheat with a sickle.

When at last the legionaries had more room, they did not at once use it as a means of flight but for energetic retaliation against their monstrous attackers. Fresh spearmen arrived with extra weapons, who dodged and side-stepped, and followed the animals as they turned. The enemies, emboldened by this success, came up in larger numbers. They assaulted the elephants at their sides, at their rear, and all around. No longer were the tuskers in an orderly line with victims only in front. Circling and facing in all directions, they mixed with the enveloping legion in a fierce melee. Every elephant was wounded; every one was bleeding; but they all remained on their feet and all went on fighting savagely.

During this period, a Roman slinger, some distance back, hurled a stone and hit Scarbas on the temple. It did not kill him but it stunned him so that he fell from Old Zain. One of the three Balearic slingers, though unfamiliar with elephants, showed great presence of mind and took Old Zain under control. Old Anak was the one that got out of hand. Seeing Scarbas lying there, he rushed toward his fallen master, and his driver could not stop him.

When old Anak reached Scarbas still insensible and motionless upon the ground, he acted at once, not to lift him to remount in the ordinary way, but to carry him out of danger. He meant to pick up the limp and unresponding Scarbas on his tusks, hold him and carry him, as a father would hold and carry an infant child in his outstretched arms. He forgot about the scimitars with which his tusks were pointed and extended.

"No, Anak, no!" shouted his driver, cutting at his ear.

But he went madly, irresistibly on to carry out his intention. Some men stooping over Scarbas were knocked aside. Anak leaned and shoved forward his head in a way which normally would let his tusks go under the body and hips, and so furnish a safe support for an unconscious man. But the longer, upcurving scimitars pierced the body of Scarbas. With all of us looking on in horror, the elephant, still not realizing what he had done, lifted up his beloved master, turned, and, holding his head high, trampled down all before him that could not get out of his way, and hastened with his precious burden from the field. For some distance we could see the elephant, in swift, terrifying progress through the ranks, his head high above all, and holding aloft the body of dead Scarbas.

Yud and Dor, the twins, and the other Balearic slinger with them in the howdah, had seen they were being taken willy-nilly out of the fight. So they had swung down along the sides of the swift-moving elephant, while holding onto the howdah with their hands, and then jumped to the ground, sprawling as they fell. Yud and Dor said afterward that they had never left a battle before it was finished, and did not mean to this time. But the battle was hastening to an end.

All over the field, as here against the elephants, the army of Sempronius had been meeting defeat and ruin. The first to turn and run were the horsemen. Next the Gauls took to their heels. Then the Numidians and the Balearic foot soldiers moved around the Roman flanks. Finally, Mago with his two thousand men came out of the ravine all along their rear. Everywhere over the plain, the Romans broke and fled.

The day had grown colder. The snow was falling heavily and relentlessly.

The fleeing Romans bunched up at the Trebia, where the swift, frigid current was choked with waders desperately trying to get across. The cavalry killed many; the infantry killed many; and the elephants, on grim duty along the bank, crushed them and pierced them and slung them into the river, so the live ones fording the river intermingled with the dead bodies floating down stream.

Of the Roman army of forty-five thousand, one-third escaped. A total of thirty thousand were made prisoners or wounded or slain. The fugitives were not chased beyond the Trebia. Ten thousand made off toward the River Po to find safety in a fortified city there. The pursuit ended because the winter darkness came on, with the bleak day ending in a thawless, bitter night, and a thickening of the snow, and a mountain wind driving the flakes at a long slant into our faces and against the shivering bodies of the elephants.

The Carthaginians returned to camp so benumbed that they could scarcely feel joy for their victory. Even when the Romans, who had waded the Trebia, recrossed on rafts during the night to escape to the Po, the Carthaginians were frozen into such inactivity that they pretended not to hear. This remnant was led by the wounded Scipio.

After that hard day of battle, the drivers and Draccus and I worked all through the night to save the elephants. As soon as they cooled off after the action and excitement of the day, they began to keel over dead. Even there along the Trebia, some would cease from killing Romans and throwing them into the river, themselves to sink to the ground and never rise. More than anything else, it was the severe, intolerable weather that killed them, just as Scarbas had feared it would. In their already weakened condition from the Alps, this battle in the snow, the prolonged fury of the conflict, their getting overheated and then freezing, the absence of any shelter—all these things, made worse by their wounds, were the influences that took them off. One after another they died through the night.

By morning all were dead except Old Anak.

After the battle he had been found in the Carthaginian camp, still standing over the man his love had slain, where he had laid him carefully upon the ground. At last the elephant allowed himself to be led away. Scarbas was taken to his tent, never to breathe or speak again.

The next morning I went with Hannibal over the battlefield and along the Trebia. Under the snow, lifting up its white sheet, were three sizes of mounds. The smallest were men, the middle-sized were horses, the biggest were elephants. Hannibal as a general looked upon death as it affected his army, and what he regretted most were the thirty-six white knolls of the elephants.

"It will be much work to bury them," I remarked.

"There is no energy for that," said Hannibal.

"You will take the ivory, won't you, sir? It is valuable. Sixty-nine big tusks. Little Enoch's don't count and one of Old Harab's isn't much good, that's why we called him Old Broken Tusk. All of them together, sir, will make about five thousand pounds of ivory."

"You are right, Agenor. We must not leave it for the Romans. But we cannot take it with us. It is too heavy. We will bury it. Then we will return and dig it up after we have conquered Rome."

In the end, only three graves were made—a very large one for Little Enoch, a very large one for the tusks, and in between a small but deep one for Scarbas. We left no markers of any kind. We fixed the location of the graves in our minds in relation to a bend in the Trebia River.

The Africans who used elephant hide for their shields and bucklers, skinned the animals. Then vultures came in high, slow flight from the Adriatic, from the Mediterranean, from all along the Valley of the Po, for their greatest feast since the beginning of the world.

Old Anak was kept in a tent. Draccus and I spent the whole of every day with him. Through the night we took turn about sitting up with him, in watches of two hours. For some time, while the extremely cold weather lasted, we often despaired of his recovery. Finally, he began to improve and each day we could see he was getting a little stronger. The elephant drivers were transferred to other duties in the army. The elephant brigade had been reduced to Old Anak, to me, and to Draccus.

Before we buried Scarbas, we took a little piece of paper out of his pocket. It had this written on it:

> Gisbo
> Old Anak
> H——

"What does it mean?" asked Hannibal. "The H could stand for Hamilcar or Hannibal."

"Or Hasdrubal," I suggested.

"What makes you say that, Agenor?"

"Wasn't Old Anak in Hasdrubal's army, sir, when he was supreme commander before you were? Scarbas sometimes talked of those days. The H could stand for his name too. Once—only once—Scarbas spoke of Gisbo's beginning to be against Old Anak after the death of Hasdrubal. And Gisbo still doesn't like Old Anak and wants to get rid of him."

"Be careful of your speech, Agenor. Hold your tongue."

"Yes, sir."

Nevertheless, Hannibal directed that the slip of paper be kept with Scarbas' things and not be destroyed.

One night while Old Anak was so sick, Draccus said that during his watch Gisbo had passed by the tent and had stopped to ask if the elephant would pull through. As Gisbo had walked away, he had made a remark to the Purple Band officer with him: "Thirty-six elephants died and this Old Anak lives." Draccus thought he was speaking in admiration of Old Anak's remarkable hardihood.

Soon after the death of Scarbas, I was summoned by General Samnis to his tent.

"Agenor, my good friend," he announced. "I have here a good-sized sack of silver moneys with some mixtures of gold pieces. It belonged to Scarbas. Now it belongs to you because of his much love for Agenor."

He took out a sheet of paper which was in the leather sack with the money. It said:

The Will of Scarbas
Head Elephant Keeper to Hannibal

If Scarbas dies or is killed in battle, he leaves this money to Agenor. Only a common man's son is Agenor, but his mind is bright. It is not suitable for him to spend all his days with the elephants. Scarbas requests that Hannibal use his great influence to have him admitted to the best rhetoric school in Carthage— when Agenor is fifteen or when Hannibal thinks best. This money, saved by Scarbas for twenty years, will pay his expenses. Perchance he will grow into a wise and great man. This will please Scarbas, who has loved Agenor as a son.

Scarbas
Witnesses:
Hannibal
Samnis
Gillimas
Misdes

"Why did Scarbas do that?" I demanded sadly. "I do not

want to leave the elephants. I do not want to leave Hannibal."

"It is much better for you already," said General Samnis.

"Anyway, I don't have to go until after we conquer Rome. Do you think, sir, that Hannibal will get more elephants as soon as he can from Carthage?"

"General Samnis cannot know of an exactness, but General Samnis thinks he will ask Morbal for fifty, maybe a hundred. An army without elephants has a lonesomeness for Hannibal."

"Sir, will you go on keeping the money for me as you did for Scarbas?"

"General Samnis will keep it, and safe it will be just like the treasure of the army."

Before this new world, this tame, tame world, reached out and took me in, I would have another year, possibly two years, with Hannibal, and Old Anak, and the new elephants. And now I was head elephant keeper, though I had only one man to work for me, the centurion Draccus, and only one elephant, the sick Old Anak. So reduced we were from a herd of thirty-seven, and all the drivers, and somber, unforgettable Scarbas.

Before I left the tent of General Samnis, he showed me a sack of rings taken from the fingers of dead Roman knights. "We would have more already," he observed, "if only they wore many rings like General Gisbo. But each wears only one. In all battles General Samnis will take them and save them and send them to Carthage for the Senate and Suffetes to see, and their eyes will pop out at so many."

TWELVE

We spent the winter in the valley of the po. so many Celts and Gauls had come over to our side that the army now numbered sixty thousand.

Two great mountain ranges were behind us. A third was still before us—the Apennines. Dark memories of the other two climbs should have made us downcast and unhappy at the prospect of this final one. But the soldiers began the march with the familiar song:

> Across the Alps and Apennines,
>   In battles far from home,
> His elephants lunge at trembling lines—
>   When Hannibal conquers Rome.

They sang as if we still had the thirty-seven elephants and not just Old Anak. He had fully recovered his health. He was well and strong again in body, though lonesome in spirit —he seemed always to be expecting other members of the herd to come; little noises caused him to listen; in the solitary night Draccus and I would hear him murmuring as if talking to the ghosts of Old Yenbo, lazy Old Zain, Old Sapor, Old Harab, Old Bolobo, Little Enoch back there in his Trebian grave, and all the rest.

131

As we began crossing the Apennines, nearly a year after leaving New Carthage, I, Agenor of the Elephants, was fourteen years old; Hannibal was thirty; Old Anak eighty-eight. My age and Hannibal's added together amounted to just half of Old Anak's.

We ascended the mountains along the Serchio River. On the summit we ran into a violent storm. When the infantry tried to advance against the gale, it was as though flat hands were pushing back upon their breasts and stomachs, and they made no headway. The horses lowered their heads between their forelegs. Old Anak, with so much surface exposed to the hurricane, braced himself to meet it, and rocked as he yielded to it or shoved back against it. All the men sat down for a while with their backs to the wind. I put Old Anak on his side upon the ground, while Draccus and I found shelter to the lee of him, between his legs. Then the sky resounded with thunder. The lightning flashed between its terrific peals. It was followed by a long rumbling that rolled and gathered sound as a snowball gathers snow until it ended in such a deafening crash that all the heavens seemed torn asunder. A torrent of sleet and hail poured down.

When we came off the Apennines into Etruria, a still worse experience was in store for us in the marshes. It took us four miserable days, and three still more miserable nights, to get through these never-ending fens. We marched up to our knees in ooze and water. When darkness came, there was not a place where we might stretch our weary bodies. All along the route, beasts of burden slipped in the mud, fell, and perished. These dreadful moors were bad enough for everybody, but while they were still fresh and untrodden they afforded somewhat easier passage for the Africans and Libyans. By the time the Celts and Gauls waded into them they had become a deep morass. The barbarians dragged their tired legs through the clutching slime; they bore the fatigue with anger and impatience. They wanted to turn back, but General Mago and the Numidians prevented them.

Old Anak would put his huge feet into the mire with a squashing sound, and would draw them out with a smacking noise.

Hannibal rode with me on the elephant. Draccus was made to walk, for Old Anak still carried the army treasure for General Samnis, including now a large quantity of Roman coins, and the sack of rings taken at the Battle of Trebia. Sometimes Hannibal was low-spirited.

"Agenor," he said in such a mood, "we have an army of sixty thousand. We ought to have one of a hundred and sixty thousand. I thought all under the Roman yoke would come over to us. But those who are slaves for a time seem to lose the courage, even the desire, to be free men again. I expected all the peoples to see in Hannibal their one great hope of deliverance, so that we would approach the gates of Rome as an overwhelming multitude."

"Won't Carthage send you many more men, sir? Won't Carthage send you thousands more of good Libyans and Africans and Numidians?"

"Carthage, Agenor, though able to do much, may do little. Many men in Carthage are sorry they did not give me up when the Romans asked for me. But this ring, Agenor—you see I wear just one—you have no doubt heard what it contains?"

"Poison, sir."

"I can drink it quickly. The ring never leaves my finger. So of one thing be sure—Rome will never have Hannibal alive."

At another time I asked him if he meant to go on with just Old Anak in the army or to get a second large herd. "Will you send for others, sir?"

"For a hundred."

"Won't Morbal object to sending so many? Won't all the empty stalls make him unhappy?"

"Morbal will come with them. Too long he has indulged his ease. A little activity will do him good."

"Will he be in charge as Scarbas was, and will I be under him?"

"Yes."

"I do not wish to be under Morbal, sir."

"What's the matter with Morbal? Doesn't he understand elephants?"

"Yes, sir. Scarbas said that next to himself he was the best elephant man in the world."

"Scarbas is now dead, and how much I miss him, Agenor. From him I took rich values. Every great man owes his worth more to some common man than to another great one . . . With Scarbas gone, Morbal is the best elephant keeper I could possibly get. But Agenor does not wish to work under him. I suppose you consider that a good and sufficient reason why he shouldn't take charge of my new elephant herd? Get the habit of letting your tongue be one step behind your thoughts, Agenor, instead of always ten steps in front of them."

"Yes, sir, I will try."

The Romans had elected two new consuls, Servilius, an aristocrat, and Flaminius, a plebeian, a mob-rouser, rash, conceited. Two new armies were raised. Scipio had gone to Spain to join his original army and fight against Hannibal's older brother, while Sempronius went to Rome and tried to explain away his Trebia disaster.

Flaminius, with forty thousand men, was camped on the Etruscan plains. Hannibal by-passed him after issuing from the marshes, and the vain, benighted consul took this as a sure sign that Hannibal was afraid of him. To egg Flaminius on, Hannibal began to plunder the rich country far and wide. The ruse worked. He followed Hannibal.

Some of Flaminius' officers tried to restrain him, wanted him to wait for the other consul, but he said: "Shall we remain inactive and let Hannibal waste Italy through and through, ravage and burn everything, let him arrive at the walls of Rome?"

The Etruscan citizens, listening to his grand speeches, thought the Carthaginian finish was right around the corner. Thousands followed along behind his army, carrying chains, fetters, rope, and all such gear, with which to truss up Carthaginian prisoners and lead them home like dancing bears.

Hannibal lured Flaminius into a defile between Lake Trasymene and the lofty hills that bordered it.

It was early morning. There was a heavy fog. Flaminius marched along with his army, eager to catch up with Hannibal. The thick vapors covering the lake and the lowlands kept them from seeing the trap they had entered—thousands of Carthaginians in ambush on the hillsides.

It was not an ordered battle, but fierce, individual fighting. It was each Roman for himself. His only hope was in his right hand and his sword. There in the opaque mist it was man against man in scores and hundreds of duels.

I was astride the neck of Old Anak halfway up one of the high slopes, above the fog. About me were some hundreds of

Carthaginian soldiers. We looked down upon the dense clouds.
To the left were the loud and never-ceasing noises of conflict
and carnage. Immediately below was only the sound of marching feet—Roman columns still coming up, like oxen to
slaughter, but with whom our forces were not yet mixed.
Upon these we rolled down rocks—a grim lesson we had
learned in the Alps. I directed the elephant here and there to
loosen big boulders that were deeply imbedded.

The battle lasted three hours. Thousands of Romans were
driven out into the lake. Some in desperation tried to swim
with their armor on.

During the main part of the conflict I was not allowed to
descend into the fog with Old Anak. "In the confusion," said
General Hanno, "you and the elephant will be killed. Stay
right where you are until the battle is over."

Draccus was not with me. He was always left behind in these
battles with his own people.

As men and horses dashed away down the hillside into the
fight, I remained alone. Then I began to notice big boulders
rolling down, bigger than the ones we had loosened a little
while before. I looked to see who was doing it. There was no
one. Of its own accord a great rock would start moving. It
was as though unseen soldiers, ghosts of Carthaginians, were
helping us. But there was equal menace to us now in these
bombardments. Our men also were down there, mixed with
the Romans in combat and as likely to be hit as they.

At the mystery of it, dread and awe fell upon me, all alone
there with the elephant on the slope. Boulders would rise out
of their depressions as if pushed by invisible hands. I had a
terrified sense of the phantom presence of a third enemy, de-
structive alike to Romans and Carthaginians. Then I became

aware that the whole earth was shaking and trembling. It was an earthquake.

When the battle was practically over, and the fog had cleared away, I came down with the elephant to the edge of the lake. General Samnis wanted another sack of rings from the fingers of the dead Roman knights. Many centurions and other officers had drowned or been killed in the lake. They had been weighted to the bottom by their armor. Here was work that Old Anak could do.

"Agenor," ordered one of the men, "get into the water with your elephant, if you mean to help us, and begin lifting up the bodies."

Still out there were perhaps a hundred Romans who hadn't been killed. They were up to their chins in the waves of the lake. They cried out time after time in a kind of refrain: *"Misericordia, misericordia, amici!* Mercy, mercy, comrades!" We left them for the time being, muttering their supplications, while we took off the rings of the sunken knights. I rode out little by little, first in the shallows, later in the deeper water, with a horseman at my right.

While we were thus engaged, I again heard big boulders rolling down the slope back of us. Some of the stones came close to the water's edge.

At the same time a thing happened that made us look at each other in fear and amazement. The elephant and horses at once stood in shallows. The live Romans out in deep water, which had been lapping at their chins, suddenly were only waist deep. Astonished, they started wading out, away from us across an arm of the lake. They were allowed to escape because the Carthaginians thought this an intervention of the Roman gods.

"It's an earthquake again," I shouted to them. "Don't be scared. The earthquake has pushed up the bottom of the lake. That was what caused the stones to roll down just now. Anak and I will catch the Romans if you want them."

"Let them go," ordered the officer in charge. "An earthquake or whatever it is—let it save them, let them go. And all of you come out. If General Samnis wants any more rings, let him get them himself."

In this battle, carried on in the fog and during an earthquake, fifteen thousand Romans were killed or wounded, with Flaminius himself among the dead. Another fifteen thousand were made prisoners.

Four consuls had come out against Hannibal. One had been killed. One had been wounded. One had fled to Rome with excuses for his defeat. During his few months in Italy, Hannibal had killed, wounded, or captured nearly seventy thousand Romans.

What wonder that he now seemed an invincible demon let loose upon the world. What wonder that all citizens of the Eternal City trembled at his name. What wonder that Roman looked into Roman's face for courage and found it not.

THIRTEEN

After the battle of lake trasymene, all of hannibal's generals wanted him to march upon Rome. No use, they said, to take time for the army to rest—they could do that in thousands of soft couches on the Seven Hills. A short distance off were the upper reaches of the Tiber. Not far beyond it was the Flaminian Way, paved for their eager feet to the very gates of the hated city.

In four days, they promised, Old Anak could be standing like a living statue in the Forum. Hannibal could be sitting down to a dinner of fish livers, flamingo tongues, and peacock brains in that rich man's house on Palatine Hill that had cost four million silver *dinarii*.

"Your talk," replied Hannibal, "your talk, gentlemen, reminds me that I am hungry. I have been too busy to eat. But a thick steak from a white Etruscan ox is what I want. Tell the cook."

"Sir," urged General Hanno, "now is the time. Underneath every toga is a heart quivering with fear. The proud nation is prostrate. Let us fall upon it, sir, and finish it. Remember your oath, O Hannibal, your oath and your hate."

General Mago, Hannibal's brother, agreed.

"Everywhere, sir," said General Gisbo, "the men of the

139

Purple Band are crying out: 'To Rome! On to Rome! When do we go to Rome?' "

To the same tune spoke his other high officers. Even General Samnis, treasurer of the army, chimed in with his urging. He wanted to clean out the pockets, the tills, the vaults of Rome to add to the many sacks he already had of captured money. I had good reason, of course, to know about these sacks, because Old Anak carried them upon the march. In the treasurer's tent I sometimes untied the strings and buried my arms up to the elbows in the coins. I scooped up double handfuls and let them pour out tinkling. By torchlight I looked at their designs, heads and tails. They were mostly minted by Rome, but there were many from other lands—Egypt, Syria, Greece, Syracuse, Utica, even from Carthage. I found two stamped with the elephant of Pyrrhus. They were not round but rectangular. I was allowed to keep them. To show how elephants are honored, I held them up before the small, bright eyes of Old Anak, but when he saw they were not good to eat he lost interest in them.

As soon as General Samnis was through speaking, Hannibal answered them all:

"Consider what you are proposing. Consider well, gentlemen. We have been everywhere victorious, but many victories can be forgotten in one defeat. The name of Hannibal has become a name of terror wherever the toga is worn. But consider well, I say. Rome has walls high and thick. And what is the condition of our artillery, our siege machinery? How many towers do we have, scaling ladders, crossbow engines, movable sheds, catapults, battering rams? Our cavalry is strong, but cavalry would be of little help in an assault upon the impregnable ramparts of Rome—a horse, gentlemen, is not a ghost to pass through a wall thirty feet thick, he is not a winged Pegasus to jump over one fifty feet high. Of elephants we are reduced to Anak—and think you that the mightiest push of his head could loosen a single stone in the solid masonry that incloses the Seven Hills? No, gentlemen, let us win over the allies of Rome. Let us make a treaty with the King of Macedon. Let us add still other thousands of Gauls to the army. Let us get help from home, artillery and siege equipment, men, horses, elephants, aye, a hundred elephants. Then the walls of Rome will be no more than cobwebs that a spider has spun in front of a cave."

There was another round of argument and insistence by the generals. To them Hannibal again made reply:

"We shall march southward, gentlemen, south and east, but we shall by-pass Rome. We shall pillage the country as we go. We shall proceed to Cannae on the Adriatic. From there we will send out ships to summon aid. General Hanno, have no fear that my oath and my hate have been forgotten. Doubt not that in due season we shall go to Rome, perchance I will sup on the Palatine Hill in that rich man's house you spoke of, but we shall go when there is no chance of failing, for I cannot fail, by all the gods of Carthage, I cannot fail."

He stopped as a thought held him. "Perchance we can send a man inside Rome to find out things for us—if we can find a man."

"Or a boy?" suggested Gisbo.

"By the fires of Moloch, yes, a boy!" cried Hannibal.

"Is it Agenor of the elephants you have in mind?" asked Gisbo. "Of him I was thinking. He understands the language and speaks it. For hours he has listened to the captive centurion telling the tales of Rome, the geography of Rome, the customs

of Rome. He knows more about the place than many a Roman.
A little disguise can alter Agenor into a Roman boy."

"A spy dies when he is caught," said Hannibal. "Agenor
must volunteer. We cannot order him. And a way must be
found not only of getting him into Rome but of getting him
out again, else what advantage would it be to us?"

I stepped forward and saluted. "Sir," I said, "I volunteer."

"Could he not go as the son of Draccus?" proposed Gisbo.

"Draccus," explained Hannibal, "has refused many rewards
to act on the side of Carthage. He is a good prisoner but he
will do nothing against Rome. Also he would run the chance
of being recognized. No, we cannot use Draccus. We shall
study the matter."

So were the plans left at the end of the first discussion. I
was commanded to secrecy. No one outside of the highest
officers and myself must know what was afoot, except I was
to study the diagrams, maps, and charts in the tents of Gillimas
and Misdes.

As we took up the march again, Old Anak carried Draccus
and me, his customary burden of money sacks, together with
a bushel of gold rings. The Tiber was a narrow, unimpres-
sive stream where we crossed it over a makeshift bridge built
by the army engineers.

The army despoiled wide countrysides belonging to the
Etruscans, the Umbrians, and the Sabines. All the baggage
animals were loaded to the limit. Cavalry horses carried much
in addition to their riders. Foot-soldiers doubled the ordinary
weights of their packs. Confiscated carts and wagons were
filled: fruit, vegetables, wheat, barrels of wine, all the yield of
the rich farmlands, passed from the wailing owners to the
Carthaginians. Chickens, ducks, and eggs were gathered up in

large quantities. Herds of cattle, droves of hogs, flocks of goats, were driven along by the soldiers. Meager hoards of money, a little at one place, a little at another, nevertheless all mounted up to an additional good-sized sackful to be borne by Old Anak.

During several days, Hannibal had his headquarters on a high, isolated hill within twenty miles of Rome. He said this was as close as he would be to the city until he came back. So my journey was to be one of twenty miles; it could well be the last one which I, Agenor, the Carthaginian boy, would ever take.

At this camp I had my first chance to visit Gillimas and Misdes. I asked to see them in a tent by themselves. I then requested all the information they had on Rome.

"We have a good deal," said Misdes, "and we'll get it all out here on the table."

"I wish I could go with you," announced Gillimas out of a clear sky.

"Go with me where?" I asked in pretended innocence.

He became serious as he addressed me: "It is easier to get just the right information when one is told what it's for. In any case, it will be hard to foresee every need. To know a thing out of a book, off a map, by report, any second-hand way, isn't the same as knowing it like a native—and that's how you ought to know it but can't. So we'll have to come the closest thing to it. I suppose you have pumped Draccus dry?"

"Ever since we captured him, in all the months of his homesickness, he's filled my ears with Rome. I taught him Carthaginian and he taught me Latin. Once or twice lately, I thought he looked a little surprised at my questions and I had to leave off before he covered all the ground I needed."

"A little slip can mean death to a spy," declared Misdes

soberly. At the words my insides felt all empty. "Your head works fast, Agenor. It is possible you are sometimes too eager to speak up. A good rule in what you are about to undertake is to let any Roman start the conversation and carry most of it along."

We began studying the sketches, the charts, the maps. The town did not seem to have any particular shape. It wasn't a square, nor a circle, nor yet a rectangle. As much as anything its outline resembled that of a roughly-fashioned arrowhead with the shaft off to the left instead of properly in the center. And those walls seemed as much built to let Romans in as to keep enemies out. For there were eighteen gates.

I memorized the names of the Seven Hills and tried to fix in my head the location of each. I gave my attention to the public buildings, the principal streets, the roads, the market, the Camp of Mars, the Roman Circus where the elephants were killed, and the Tiber in a double bend in front of the town. Then I must needs become wholly familiar with that assortment of gates.

"As though you have been going in and out of them all your life," said Misdes.

"Will you trace out for me a map of the city like this one?" I asked.

"No, Agenor, no," objected Gillimas. "One on a mission like yours has no papers."

I remained three long hours with the relentless rhetoricians. It wasn't as easy as working with elephants.

"Is Rome really a great city, as Draccus says?" I asked just before I left. "Is it the greatest city in the world?"

"In one way, yes—in their water supply," answered Misdes.

"You'll see their two big aqueducts. Otherwise I am afraid the toga-wearers have some rather enlarged and fanciful ideas when they call it the Mistress of the World. Carthage is richer, bigger, and decidedly more healthful, in spite of the two rivers of good water which the aqueducts bring into Rome. Just the same, it is the city all of us would most like to see. You are the luckiest person in the Carthaginian army to be going there."

"Even as a spy?"

"Just remember what I said—think fast and let the Romans do most of the talking."

A trusted squad of Numidian horsemen had been ordered as they pillaged to watch for a father with a son about the size of the boy Agenor of the Elephants. The corporal of these cavalrymen came to Hannibal to report. He wore, as always, a leopard skin over his shoulders and nothing else, but he saluted and observed all the military courtesies.

"Sir," he said, "we have found a boy, a Sabine farmer's son, yet a citizen of Rome, both man and boy being privileged to wear the toga. He is sixteen years old, but is only the bigness of Agenor of the Elephants and with looks not hard to make correspond. Nearly always he accompanies his father who hauls vegetables and other things of the farm once a week to the market in Rome."

"You have taken this man's cattle and wheat?"

"We have stripped him, sir, of nearly all he has."

When the man was brought in, he was so much afraid that words would scarcely come out of his mouth.

"Your name?" asked Hannibal.

"Titus Sabinus."

"Your son's name?"

"Pulvius."

"Do not be alarmed," said Hannibal. "We mean no harm. We merely wish your services and the identity of your son—and his clothes."

"I do not understand."

"When you next go to market, which will be tomorrow—, starting at twelve tonight—you will take as your son this Carthaginian boy you see here. He will spend a day with you in Rome, a long day. Then you will return, and you and your real son may leave for your home. We have taken your wheat, your fruit, your vegetables, your wagon, and your oxen, two white ones, I believe. We shall resupply you in everything so you will have more than your usual load for the market. On this trip you can even take beef to Rome, where no doubt it will sell."

"It will sell quickly and at good prices. To a few noble citizens, old customers, I could give a sign that I had it, though the rule is to sell all things through the market."

"Of a truth, noble citizens! We have not a few of the like in Carthage." And Hannibal winked at his generals who were present. "But for the business in hand—if everything is done well, you will get your cattle back, your wheat, your wagon, all your goods. You will be paid for what we cannot restore and be given much money besides."

"If I go, no harm will come to my family, my boy? My property will be restored?"

"This is promised, with a thousand silver *dinarii* besides. At present you will leave your son Pulvius with us as a guarantee that you will return with our boy by midnight tomorrow

—or let us say by two o'clock in the morning, in consideration of the distance and of possible delays on the road. Your son will be well cared for. The real Pulvius can amuse himself all day with the elephant."

I took Titus Sabinus with me to pick out everything needed for our trip. We went among the captured herds in search of his own two white oxen. At last we found them and, of a truth, they were fine specimens—big and fat, with their white coats glossy in the sun.

We likewise found his wagon, a vehicle of two wheels, with high, bent slats supporting a hood that covered the whole bed. The back end was closed with a curtain that hung down from the top.

The butcher supplied us with several two-pound and three-pound packages of beef and pork. He also let us have a number of chickens and ducks, as well as two dressed peacocks, which Sabinus said would bring a hundred *dinarii* apiece, these fowls being highly esteemed by the Romans.

Hannibal summoned me. "Agenor, I overlooked possible damage to our plans in promising the boy Pulvius amusement with the elephant tomorrow. He and Draccus must not be allowed to spend the day together. During your absence, therefore, Draccus will be assigned to duties in a different part of the camp. One of the former elephant drivers will take charge of Old Anak."

The next item of my preparation was to see General Samnis, treasurer of the army. He was alone in his tent with the money sacks.

From his supplies he took out a big leather pouch. Then he picked up a measure and scooped it brimming full of coins out of one of the large sacks of silver *dinarii*. He stood with the empty pouch in one hand and the filled measure in the other.

"General Samnis," I protested, "I won't need that much."

The container of coins was heavy and he set it down on a camp table. Then he answered my protest: "I tell you the example of three guards at Roman gate—one shakes the head against a hundred *dinarii;* not honest but cowardly on account of others finding out; a hundred *dinarii* to each one is better maybe; three hundred no difference from a hundred, if Agenor has plenty; with three hundred, he walks through gate; with only a hundred, in prison maybe or something worse, which we better not describe on account of making you nervous; ten guards same way, a thousand *dinarii,* and something extra maybe to corporal or sergeant, but no difference to Agenor with big sackful which army takes from Romans in first place. Moneys is a spy's best friend. Remember such fine wisdom from General Samnis."

I held the pouch while he poured the coins into it. You may be sure I now made no objection when he said, "A few more it will hold yet," and added a handful of gold pieces to the bag already bulging with silver. Then he tied it securely with its buckskin thong, and handed it to me. I took it, thanked him and left.

It was not until close to eleven at night that I changed my clothes for the complete Roman outfit of the boy Pulvius. Sabinus was on hand to instruct me. I felt a surge of pity for the innocent Roman lad awaiting a deadline only twenty-six hours away, and then I realized that I was equally involved in that grim appointment, for nothing would happen to him unless it happened to me first.

The sandals and tunic offered me no difficulty, except Sabinus had to show me how to make the tunic skirt short or long by the way it was tucked in at the girdle.

The toga was the real problem in my new accoutrement. The one I was to wear was between four and five yards long and between three and four yards wide. Since it belonged to a boy, it was white with a purple border. That of Sabinus was entirely white. When, after much practice, I had learned to put on this cumbrous robe properly, I observed a grave omission.

"It has no pocket," I cried, "and I must have a pocket."

Sabinus put his hand into the fold that crossed the breast diagonally, affording a receptacle like a little hammock. Here was indeed what appeared to be a good pocket and certainly a capacious one.

There was no headgear to help with the disguise. With scissors, Sabinus changed my Carthaginian haircut to a Roman one. My complexion was judged of a proper hue for a Roman boy accustomed to work in the fields. But Sabinus looked at my bulging forehead and shook his head with misgivings. Of this I was very proud, for it was somewhat like Hannibal's, but in the present enterprise it was a heavy liability. This and some of my other unsatisfactory features had been given me by the gods, said Sabinus resignedly. They could not be altered and we had to chance them.

Our preparations were now complete. I put the heavy money pouch in the toga pocket, extinguished the torches, and stepped out of the tent with Sabinus.

It was a clear night with many stars but moonless. The oxen were hitched to the wagon and everything was ready, but we were scheduled with the sentries to leave exactly at midnight.

And it was still a quarter to twelve. I had enough time to go and say farewell to Old Anak. As I approached him, he snorted in anger, pulled at his stake, and swung his trunk. I had forgotten about coming to him in the dead of night in a Roman garb.

"Anak!" I called. "It is I, Agenor."

I took his trunk in my arms and lay my cheek upon its rough surface. I felt the pulsation of his breath through the long nostril.

As I turned to leave, there was Draccus looking at me as I stood before him dressed as a Roman boy.

"I heard the noise of Old Anak," he explained, "and I came from my tent to investigate."

"I thought you had been taken to another part of the camp."

"I go early tomorrow morning."

"Draccus, you have kept every promise you ever gave me. You must now swear that as long as you are a prisoner you will never speak of what you may have guessed before and now know. Otherwise I have no choice but to report you to be placed under guard in solitary confinement."

"I swear," said Draccus.

"*Vale*—good-by," I called, holding out my hand and trying to be casual.

His own hands went over my shoulders and he drew me to him. "*Vale,* Agenor! *Vale!*" he said, and released me lingeringly, and I knew he never expected to see me again.

I walked fast to where Sabinus was sitting in the wagon, waiting to start. The guards were changing watches for midnight. The first crows came from our captured roosters in a distant part of the camp.

"Paratus sum," I said. "I am ready," and climbed into the wagon.

A patrol accompanied us beyond Hannibal's lines and outposts. Then I was alone with Sabinus. Behind me was everything Carthaginian and friendly—before me only what was Roman and hostile.

FOURTEEN

D<small>AY WAS ALREADY ABROAD AS WE APPROACHED THE COLLINE</small> Gate. On the high walls the patrols paced back and forth on short beats, carrying long spears diagonally. They moved in ceaseless and measured promenade against the background of the blue sky. Two men covered each thirty yards. For fifteen yards they approached, for fifteen they separated, but while their backs were turned two men at neighboring beats could ever see the intervening space. I do not believe a butterfly could have fluttered between them unobserved.

Everywhere the movements of any two were exactly repeated and exactly timed. At the same moment, all along the walls, partners faced each other across the whole distance of their common beat. At the same moment they passed each other, their spears seeming to cross. At the same moment, as far as the eye could see, two men met at the common end of their connecting beats. Always two were walking toward each other. Always two were walking away from each other. In the fresh morning, as I looked out of the front of the wagon, it all had a wondrous grace.

We had become one of a stream of market wagons. As we halted for inspection, and awaited our turn, I saw that the example which General Samnis gave me of bribery at the gate did not fit the present situation in Rome. If I gave a hundred *dinarii* to every guard here to turn his back or wink at my departure, I would need well nigh as many of the silver pieces as one of the big sacks held.

Though numerous enough, the gatekeepers were mostly in shabby contrast to the trained legionaries rhythmically treading their lofty beats atop the walls. These were clearly not regular soldiers; rather, middle-aged and oldish ones urgently impressed into service because Hannibal had slain two armies, one was in flight, and another was now desperately being raised for Fabius the Delayer to lead. What young men remained were evidently going into these new legions and this home guard, except for the wall patrols, largely a militia of the rawest and most nondescript character.

Two of them came up to us, one on either side. They looked us over, got our names, itemized our freight, and passed us. It was all done in such casual routine that my Carthaginian lineaments did not receive a second glance.

But just as my spirits were rising over this easy entry, they dropped again. Two other guards, thirty feet on at the inside edge of the gate, held up their hands for us to stop.

"Two white oxen," called out one, and the other put it down on a writing pad. "Without blemish all over?" he asked Sabinus.

"Yes, sir."

"Were both animals born between the Ides of February and the Ides of April?"

"Yes, sir."

"Do you own the oxen?"

"Yes, sir."

"Your name?"

"Titus Sabinus."

"Drive on."

Sabinus did not explain this extraordinary ado over a pair of white oxen and their birthdays, and I did not ask, for my spirits, after this causeless lull, were rising again like a summer breeze, and I was anxious to see the city that now began to appear in majesty and glorious whiteness in the sunrise.

After a short distance, we departed from the main stream of market wagons and went down a narrow by-street where for the moment ours was the only vehicle. This street was not more than twenty-five feet wide. The sidewalks were raised to a height of a foot and a half. At regular intervals, stepping stones of the same height, like those over a brook but thicker, went across the street from one side to the other. This was fine for the pedestrians but hard on draft animals.

At the third line of stepping stones we stopped amidst them, and a very distinguished-looking Roman walked with great dignity out to us. He seemed to be an important man, but he didn't look like a happy one, with his cold, gloomy, and smileless countenance. I thought his veins must be filled with the fever Misdes had told me about. I was sure he was going to ask for our identity, for mine in particular. Instead, he said in a very low voice, "Three pounds."

"You come yourself, sir," said Sabinus. "Where are your slaves?"

"They have been freed for the army."

"Pork or beef?" inquired Sabinus in an undertone. "Or I have a peacock."

"You tempt me greatly, but I cannot carry it. Pork."

"Get it, Pulvius my son," said Sabinus. Then, in a louder

voice, he addressed his distinguished customer: "Do you think, sir, that Fabius the Delayer will save Rome?"

"Too slow, too cowardly."

Meanwhile he handed some coins to Sabinus and, concealing the meat in the folds of his toga, walked away with great dignity over the stepping stones.

In a similar way, we halted to make four other deliveries to noble citizens willing to ease their gnawing hunger in advantage of others and contrary to laws they themselves had made.

Joining the now thinner stream of farm wagons, we went first to the meat market and then to the vegetable market. While we were disposing of the rest of our produce in this regular way, I noticed a woman trying to still a fretful child. It would not cease its crying. She tried various soothings and promises. Then she appeared to be listening and said, "Hush, Hannibal at the gates!" The child became quiet. Poor woman, little did she dream that an ambassador of that terrible bogy was standing so near.

After unloading, Sabinus tied the oxen to a hitching post. "We are now free," he said. "Where do you want to go?"

"I suppose," I answered, "that the whole town is beyond the limit of our legs, but I wish to go everywhere I can, see everything I can, and to hear all kinds of people talking about the war and Hannibal. At the start, to satisfy my own curiosity, I would like to go to the Roman Circus."

On our way we passed a group of women talking in excited superstition. We lingered close enough to hear, pretending ourselves to be in earnest conversation.

"Dread times," recited one woman. "Always we receive

signs of doom. Lightning struck a tomb along the Appian Way, a swarm of bees settled in the Senate, mice gnawed the gold in the Temple of Jupiter. Bad omens of the coming scourge of Hannibal. It is the end of Rome!"

"Yes, it is the end," said another. "Hannibal will destroy us. All over the world there are portents and prodigies of it. In Sicily a watchman was walking along the walls and his spear took fire. He looked up and the point above his shoulder was blazing. In Gaul a wolf snatched the sword from the scabbard of a soldier on guard, and carried it off. In Spain it rained stones. A crow flew down into the Temple of Juno. In Sardinia a man saw a pale moon over toward the west in a daylight sky, and, when he turned around, lo, there was another pale moon in the east. Ah, woe is the world, with the dread Hannibal coming to slay us."

"My false son," declared Sabinus, "such conversation ought to be pleasing to you and your commander."

"I do not think my commander will find it disagreeable when I report it," I replied.

We walked on. The Roman Circus was as vacant and deserted as some remote hollow in the hills. Empty were the sloping walls of sixty thousand seats—and because of Hannibal, I reflected, thousands who had sat there would never do so again.

Remembering what Misdes had said of the slaughter of the hundred and twenty, I went about peering down at the sand to see if any areas of it were still rusted from that vast drenching. My reason should have told me different, but it seemed to me so much blood could never entirely disappear.

"Were you here, Sabinus," I asked, "when the elephants were slaughtered? It was thirty-three years ago."

"It was part of the triumph for L. Metellus, the consul. I was but a boy of seven then. I was not allowed to come. My father saw it and was sickened by it. He was a farmer and disliked cruelty to animals. He would never talk to me about it."

Sabinus took me outside the River Gate to see the Tiber. To the north was an island, and there were many ships at anchorage or passing back and forth.

"How wide is it?" I asked.

"Three hundred feet."

"How deep?"

"Twelve feet or perhaps a little more in the center."

This glorified river! Why, Old Anak, by lifting his trunk, could have waded across it. Its reddish waters were not suitable at all for drinking, and I imagined anybody swimming in it long would come out with a coating of its deposits.

We went to the Forum, the Citadel, the Temple of Vesta, the Temple of Jupiter, the Senate, where I saw no bee-swarm foreshadowing ruin. I inspected the Old Wall of Romulus, trudged along the Sacred Way, and looked at some mansions of the rich. These and other sight-seeings added up, as you can guess, to a considerable amount of walking.

And I became increasingly conscious of an awkward embarrassment. My money pouch pulled so heavily upon the toga folds that these slipped forward over my left shoulder. Every so often I would have to stop to make adjustments.

I was an active lad, but when one has an elephant to ride he doesn't overdo his legs. As we kept journeying about, and moved from group to group to get the flavor of their opinion about Fabius, about Hannibal, about the war, I had to confess at last to Sabinus that I was weary, and hungry likewise. Could we find aught to eat in this short-rationed city?

He explained that he had reserved something from the selling. This would furnish a fuller meal than any we could get along the streets. So we made our way back toward the wagon, but by a different route to extend still further my observations.

A policeman was standing beside the oxen. He stepped forward to meet us. My time had come. He was waiting to arrest me. The price a spy pays is death. Always it had been so. Always it would be so. And at that moment, for the first time, it struck me forcibly that it had been Gisbo who first suggested that I come to Rome as a spy.

"You are under arrest," he stated.

My knees must have shaken, my teeth must have chattered, and my skin must have gone paler than a Roman's ever is. But he was not talking to me. He was talking to Titus Sabinus.

He uttered an oral warrant: "Titus Sabinus, you are arrested for five times selling meat to citizens before reaching the market, contrary to the war laws of the Roman people. Come with me to the judge."

"Pulvius," he said, "I may be long delayed. Take the wagon and drive home."

"The wagon and oxen will remain as security," declared the policeman. "The boy can wait, or he can leave by other means, as he pleases. He is but a youth, wearing a youth's toga, and he cannot be held for his father' s offense, though aiding him in it."

"They may hold me until tomorrow," cried Sabinus frantically. "Pulvius, as you have pity for the love of a father, get home before two."

"What's the urgency of a farmer boy's getting home before two?" demanded the policeman. "Cows aren't milked then. Chickens aren't fed then. I suspect you two of other evasions

of the law, of other offenses. Titus Sabinus, to what evil tres-
passes of citizenship are you training your son?"

"The hay, officer," I explained. "The hay is cut, is down.
In case of rain it will be ruined. Neighbors are coming at two to
help."

Better if I had remembered what Misdes told me.

"Your speech," remarked the officer. "It has an accent.
Information from the Colline Gate shows you to be a resident
of the Sabine country. It is not fitting that a foreign accent
should remain upon the tongue of a citizen living so close to
Rome."

"His mother, sir," explained Sabinus, "is a Gaul, from across
the northern Apennines. She never lost her brogue. This has
affected the speech of the lad."

"Pretty dark to be half Gaul."

"As often happens with mixed races, sir, he favors me."

"I see that this is so," said the officer, "but we have talked
overlong. Come with me."

Again his command was to Sabinus, not to me.

"Go, Pulvius, go!" Sabinus entreated me once more as he
was being led away. "My son, pray heed my request. By starting now you can walk and arrive in time."

He held out to me the bag that contained all the coins
from his day's sales. Though I had forgotten the advice of
Misdes, this proffered purse now reminded me of the advice
of General Samnis. The police officer could not be too intelli-
gent, after acknowledging that I, Agenor the Carthaginian, favored Sabinus, and his scruples were probably on a level with
his wits.

"Officer," I asked, "how much will be my father's fine? We
need to get home, as we have explained, on account of the hay.

If you will pay the fine for us, we will leave with you this purse of money my father has in his hand, and a hundred *dinarii* besides. You can pay the judge what is required. If aught remains . . ."

"But, my son," interrupted Sabinus, "you do not have a hundred *dinarii*." My wealth was no secret to him, so I knew he spoke in warning, but I ignored it.

I had buried my fingers in the pulled-down toga folds to untie the strings of the pouch. I drew out a big handful of coins.

"Here is the money, sir," I said to the officer. "Count it. I will add enough for the hundred *dinarii*."

From the stuffed, untied pouch some silver pieces poured out and rang as they hit the pavement. I stooped down to pick them up. The sagged, out-of-place toga pocket let the whole bag fall out. A quantity of coins hopped about, some lay in a loose, scattered pile at the mouth of the pouch, and there was the bulging pouch itself, its contents unmistakably revealed, and still slowly spilling out *dinarii* and an occasional gold piece to join the others upon the street.

Whatever the policeman had originally thought of our offer, his resistance was stiff and certain after this outlandish accident.

"The talk is ended," he ordered. "Come along."

For the third time he was addressing Sabinus, not me. Of all things, he left me standing there in astonishment, free as ever I was, hearing the appeals of Sabinus coming back to me, "Go, Pulvius, for the pity of a father, go!" This city was quite beyond my understanding. Apparently, a Roman boy could do anything. He could get his father into all sorts of trouble without getting into any himself. I gathered up my scattered wealth, readjusted my toga, and stood for a moment pondering what was best to do. Such preposterous lengths to which a Roman boy could go without being arrested!

At a distance and unobserved, I followed along after Sabinus and the policeman and stood in the rear of the curious crowd at his hearing by the judge. This was his last case before lunch and the hour of sleep. He listened to the details indifferently and then passed sentence: "Titus Sabinus, for selling meat unlawfully to five citizens, is fined two white oxen."

Sabinus, who had been so abject before Hannibal, so anguished over the desperate situation of his son, now showed a side that surprised me. As a Roman citizen, before one of his own courts, he displayed amazing courage, coolness, and dignity in standing up for his own rights under the law.

"I am a poor man, sir," he protested. "I cannot be fined two white oxen except by the people. A rich man can be fined thirty oxen, but a poor man can be fined only the value of two sheep by a magistrate. It is in the Twelve Tablets, sir."

"But the man is not poor," spoke up the policeman. "His son had a very large pouch of money."

The judge thereupon had Sabinus searched. There was found upon him, of course, only the money for which he had sold his produce.

"This," declared the judge, "is not sufficient to disqualify him as a poor man."

"It is the son," repeated the policeman. "It is the son who has the money." I thought he would surely look around to see if I were present, and I made myself very small behind some large Romans. I even expected him to bellow out, "If Pulvius Sabinus is in the crowd, let him come forward," or some such summons. But neither of these things happened. The stupid bailiff seemed to take it as a matter of course that I had hastened home to look after the hay.

"Ownership of the boy's money would have to be determined in another trial," stated the judge. "At present this citizen stands guilty of unlawfully selling meat, and his own funds do not disprove his being a poor man. So he is within his rights in protesting the fine of two white oxen." Then the judge spoke directly and sternly to the prisoner: "But, Titus Sabinus, I cannot refrain from censuring you for your unpatriotic attitude. Fabius the Dictator has ordered the sacrifice of one hundred white oxen to Jupiter. Hannibal's pillaging has made it difficult to get the full number. As a Roman citizen, Titus Sabinus, you should gladly respond in these dark times."

"Voluntary sacrifices, sir," stoutly answered Sabinus, "are the only kind acceptable to Jupiter or the other gods. These would be forced—taken away from me, sir, under the name of a fine."

"Very well," commented the judge. "You will have your appeal to the people, according to your rights under the law. This appeal will be held tomorrow morning at eleven o'clock."

I could guess what the unhappy Sabinus was thinking. Pulvius, his son, would die nine hours before this hearing, unless in some way I returned alone—Sabinus, though, tried a way out.

"Sir," he said, "no one told me of the sacrifices ordered by the Dictator. I voluntarily and gladly give my two white oxen to the state. I will also pay from the money here a fine equivalent to the value of two sheep to cover my offense."

"No," ruled the judge, "this cannot be done. Here a man refuses to be fined two white oxen. Later he offers them of his own free will. It would appear like an indirect coercion. The magistrate himself could afterward be accused and condemned by the people for violating a law of the Twelve Tablets. Titus Sabinus has asked for an appeal to the people. The appeal will be taken up at eleven tomorrow morning."

"But I want to give the oxen!" cried Sabinus. "I want to give them to my country for the sacrifice to Jupiter."

"Hold the man for his appeal," ordered the judge. "After the sleep-hour, secure the oxen also."

This case had made the judge late to lunch. What it had done to Sabinus and to me could not be measured.

But this sleep-hour, which often amounted to two hours, offered a remedy to our predicament. During this one-hour or two-hour period, Rome was as sound asleep as other cities at regular bedtime. In fact, there was a Roman ghost story, amusingly told in Carthage, in which the ghost appeared at midday instead of midnight.

I had a good chance to get away in time, and to get away with the oxen. I hastened to where they were, unhitched them, climbed into the wagon, and started for the Colline Gate. The streets were already beginning to be deserted as I drove along.

And when I arrived at the Colline Gate, it was closed. Only six of the gatekeepers were awake before the sealed portals. All the rest were lying in the shade of the walls, sleeping, or about to go to sleep. How Hannibal would have stared and gasped at this snoring scene. Even in their present extremity, these people could not keep their heavy lids from shutting at a period of the day long used for a wholesale nap.

I drove on, clear up to the gate, and halted amidst the six that were still awake. I had figured out what I would do. There could be no harm in repeating to them the urgency of the mown hay and of asking that the gate be opened under the circumstances. There could be no harm in offering them ten *dinarii* apiece in consideration of their trouble. How gladly would I have given them a hundred apiece or two hundred, but I thought the smaller amount would appear more natural and less offensive.

I was soon to find out that of all briberies this was the most impossible. The city slept. Fabius the Delayer himself could scarcely at that hour have had opened to him the Colline Gate or one of the other seventeen. If these six men had let me pass, it would have meant lances through their hearts.

For the guards on the walls would have seen and reported it. And these legionaries were unaffected by the universal torpor: always two were marching toward each other; always two were marching away from each other. From a drugged city, I looked up at their rhythm of ceaseless, vigilant motion, and briefly forgot my thwarted need in the wondrous grace of it all.

"The gate will open at two," said the sergeant. "You can leave then. But hold! This boy has white oxen. Rufus, is there now clearance to pass the animals? Go look at the latest orders from the centurion of the gates, and at the entry record of Pulvius Sabinus."

The man examined a bulletin upon the wall and some notations on a writing pad. He returned and reported.

"Sergeant, the orders are unchanged. By the time of the sleep-hour, only sixty-seven white oxen were on hand. One hundred are required. All animals are still to be turned back and delivered at the central depot. Those objecting to the sacrifice of their cattle will have a hearing before the people tomorrow morning at eleven. The records show that Pulvius

Sabinus entered by this gate with his father, Titus Sabinus, near sun-up this morning."

"Go, then, Rufus, at once. Take this boy and the oxen to the keeper of the sacrificial animals. Report also to the centurion of the gates."

Upon the order of this Rufus, I turned the wagon around. I saw not only that I, too, would be jailed until eleven the next morning, and that it would be the end of the boy held hostage by Hannibal, but heavy within me also was realization of the danger of being questioned without the presence of Sabinus.

The soldier, Rufus, walked along, never once looking back, but able to hear the tap of the oxen's hoofs and the rattle of the wheels upon the paving stones a little distance behind him. The oxen themselves needed no urging, no guiding in their slow traveling in the wake of Rufus.

I slipped noiselessly out of the seat, crawled back through the wagon, opened the curtain at the back, and eased myself out so my feet would land upon the pavement without sound. For a few steps I followed behind the wagon, to which there could be no objection if the man heard me. But Rufus did not look back, and there was no one in the deserted street to see me.

I slipped over to a sidewalk and found concealment in the vestibule of a building. Rufus and the white oxen moved on down the street. I regained the sidewalk, proceeded in a matter-of-fact way in the other direction to a corner, and went up a side street. I soon felt more conspicuous in being the only one abroad than if I had been in a crowd. Where could I go? Where could I hide myself until the gates opened? I thought of the Roman Circus, deserted even during the busy period of the day and surely a safe haven now.

In this empty place I was safe enough from all observers,

but I soon began to be oppressed by a clearer view of my situation. This last act had made me a criminal. The police would be looking for me everywhere. My name would be posted at every exit.

I was locked up within Rome.

Every means of escape that my struggling thoughts hit upon held not the smallest promise of success. The advice of Misdes and the advice of General Sámnis was alike of no use when I actually found myself a prisoner in this hostile city. The only sound advice had been ignored—that of Sabinus, and I blamed myself enough now that it was too late.

Yet why hadn't he foreseen what was to be the cause of all our woe? Now he was to be held nine hours past all chance of saving his son on account of a pair of white oxen, and I was being sought everywhere in an enemy city on account of the same animals.

I was hungry and tired and very wretched. And, in spite of my anxieties, I fought against heavy eyelids. Time was precious. Not to stay awake would be disastrous.

Remembrances of people and odds and ends of advice mixed up in my nodding head—the way the arms of Draccus enfolded me lingeringly; the utterance of Misdes, "A little slip can mean death as a spy"; the remark of General Samnis, "In prison maybe or something worse which we better not describe on account of making you nervous"; and Gisbo who had first suggested me as a spy to Hannibal.

Scarbas was gone. Now Agenor. How soon would come the turn of Old Anak?

The red cloak of Gisbo became less bright. The place out there where the elephants bled, became indistinct. Then I did not want to struggle any more against this comfortable drowsiness. I slid down in front of the Circus seat and bunched up some of the toga folds for a pillow.

When my eyes opened, they looked up not at the blue sky of day but at a few pale stars beginning to show.

FIFTEEN

MY SLEEP HAD BEEN DEEP AND DREAMLESS. THERE HAD BEEN no nightmarish specters of the sinister Gisbo, nor of Romans coming to take me, nor even of Pulvius looking at me accusingly as he was led away by the death squad. This latter phantom, spared me in my dreams, appeared before me almost immediately as I stood awake.

The Roman Circus, so thronged on holidays, still had no tenant besides myself. Sixty thousand to see the gladiators or the murdered elephants, but none now except a Carthaginian boy. Or if another was anywhere in the big amphitheatre, there was no noise of his footfall, no blur of his white robe moving in the darkness. Because of the silence, and the loudness with which a creaking board would sound, I climbed with great stealth up the numerous seat terraces to where I could look out over a portion of the unlighted city.

There beyond me, and not so high as I was, showed the shadowy and bulky outlines of the Appian Aqueduct. I had walked under it with Sabinus. In the daylight I could not have climbed inside without being discovered. But in the darkness it might be different. I contemplated it eagerly, as something full of promise.

This was the older aqueduct. It ran about eleven miles to a

spring, partly on arches which spanned the low ground between the Aquitine and Aventine Hills. The rest of it was underground. I did not know whether, if once in, I would have to wade its stream the whole eleven miles, or whether it would have short stretches above ground to enable me to get out.

The other aqueduct I had also seen. It was newer, and forty miles long. Once committed to this, with no exit, I could easily perish before reaching its far-off intake. Would my energies sustain me without food, with no means of resting, drowning if I faltered in weakness, moving on hour after hour in pitch blackness, always against a current that would be cold and deep and no doubt swift?

Both were covered so that their channels were completely boxed in to keep out the dust and impurities, and would afford me perfect concealment. The old one had a flat top, the newer one a pointed roof. In the parts on arches, both at intervals had sizable air openings. Since the whole aqueduct structure was on a huge scale, I counted on these openings being big enough for me to climb through.

I picked out the newer and longer one to investigate first. It would be about the same distance as the other one from guards but considerably freer from observation by chance passers-by, its direction was more nearly the one I wanted to take, and its conduit was bigger and would be more comfortable to walk in, if anything called comfort could apply to such travel in any case. I minimized the risk of being shut up in it the whole way. This didn't seem reasonable. Across forty miles of uneven country, it could hardly keep from rising above ground in places.

Night had fully arrived now. The stars had become bright

and numerous but there was no moon, and for this I was thankful.

I slipped up toward the reservoir on Equiline Hill to find where the aqueduct started. As the arches went into the sloping side of the hill they became constantly less high. These disappeared altogether where the aqueduct joined the reservoir. Nothing was left here but the steep-roofed conduit. But this was large itself, about eight feet high, I would guess, from the bottom to the ridge of the roof.

About thirty feet back from the juncture with the reservoir, where the arches and wall were still at considerable elevation, was the first air opening. It was quite big enough to let me through, but how was I to reach it? It was placed at the top in the vertical conduit wall, right up to where the roof began to slope.

No great distance off were three gates with their squads of watchmen. They were wide awake now. I could hear their voices and even make out snatches of their conversation, though they were not talking loud.

In order to reach the first high opening, I needed to climb to the roof where the arches ceased, slide along it, and enter from the top. Once up, I would have to proceed for thirty feet, in full view of anybody looking, and in danger of making noises.

Having to accept the roof with its risks as the only means, I still must hit upon the trick of mounting it. If I were caught— well, I would of a truth this time never see Hannibal again, nor Old Anak. As I stood by the conduit, I could hear the stream of water pouring into the reservoir like a waterfall.

The masonry had no projections for handholds or footholds. The corner at the juncture with the reservoir was likewise smooth. I was about to give up and try the Appian Aqueduct when I thought of going through the first arch and seeing what the other side offered. Here I was less in shadow, but I saw something I hoped might do. It was a staff, a flagstaff, I judged, from the top of which some sort of banner probably waved on special occasions. I suppose each of the Seven Hills had one.

It was about fifteen feet back from the juncture of the aqueduct and reservoir. Its slender summit reached eight or ten feet above the ridge of the aqueduct roof. Here, though, on account of the pitch of the hillside, the conduit was higher above me—about thirteen feet, I estimated.

The pole rather closely hugged the wall, to which it was held by a band near the top. Its base was sunk into the ground. There was barely room for me to get my fingers in between it and the wall. This interfered with my grip, all the more so because my fingers got caught when they went in past the knuckles. Nor could I assist my hands with any clinch of my feet and knees. If the contrivance had been set back a foot from the wall, the task would have been simple for a strong and agile boy. As it was, it clung to the stone surface like a round, upright molding, and halted me or threw me back as I worked to lift myself along it.

When I was up high enough for my eyes to be level with the eaves of the roof, my fingers were so weak that I thought surely I would have to relax my hold and slide down. But the pole above me was now free of the wall. Grimly I put hand over hand, gritting my teeth, breathing hard, and the sweat pouring out. My eyes were now even with the ridge of the roof. I lodged my feet in the angle of the pole and the eaves, and paused to recover my strength and my breath.

Next I had to transfer my hands from the pole to the ridge of the roof, nearly two feet beyond me. The sloping roof and the vertical wall met in a smooth edge or rim, as if folded. The slope itself was formed of solid slabs of stone, with joints running up and down but none right and left. The surface was smooth, the pitch very steep.

The ridge of the roof was rounded, affording a poor grip for the fingers, as I found when I swung over to it. In this act the heavy money bag slid out of the bosom of my toga, hit the stone with a metallic thud, rolled down the roof before I could grab it with the one hand I could free, and struck the ground with another thud. And I had added to the noise with my maneuverings.

Lying prone on the sloping roof, my fingers over the ridge, my feet in the angle of the pole and the eaves, I pondered what to do about the money pouch. I was unarmed. What if I also were without money?

My hands and fingers were still weak from the former effort; I did not believe I could make the climb again. But I felt a terrible reluctance to leave the money.

I heard footsteps and voices. I pulled myself up by my fingers so I could look over the ridge. Two men were coming up that side of the Equiline Hill.

"I heard something," one insisted. "I tell you I heard something."

"You are jittery, Balbus. Hannibal has made everybody jittery."

"But the flagpole," cried the one called Balbus. "See it! It's shaking. And there is no wind."

I gripped the ridge of the roof with the tips of my fingers, from the first knuckles onward, so they would show as little as possible, and released the pressure of my feet against the pole.

"Your imagination, Balbus, that's all. The pole is perfectly still."

"Now I don't see it move any more either. Maybe it was my imagination. It's pretty dark, but I thought I saw it shaking a little against the stars; it was along the edge of one. Then there was space between it and the star. This happened three or four times."

"Yes, and what does that prove? You looked and the star was alongside the pole. You moved your head a little and naturally there was space between them. You're seeing things. I'm an old soldier and don't get excited over little sounds and movements in the dark. You're a new man and nervous, expecting to find Hannibal behind every stone and every bush. Balbus, you're seeing things. Let's go."

"So be it. But hadn't we better pass under the arch to the other side and look at the flagpole?"

"Balbus, why do you keep harping on the flagpole? Look at it. Does it shake? No. You have a bad case of Hannibal nerves. Come on, let's go."

The vast relief at hearing them depart was followed at once by the problem of getting the purse. After they had walked clear away down the hill, I began my descent of the pole slowly and carefully so as to make no sound, not risking a jump.

I picked up the bothersome money pouch and fastened it to the girdle of my tunic to prevent its escape again. With a little less difficulty than before, I regained my old position, lay prone again upon the sloping stones to rest, and to figure out my further progress. I would have to throw my body across the eaves, and feel for the window with my toes when I neared its approximate location.

In doing this, the accursed money at my girdle struck the stone surface with a bang of the whole mass and a clanking together of the pieces inside.

"I hear it again!" came from Balbus down below. The two men started up once more, the first soldier grumbling.

I was now on their side of the aqueduct. When they approached close enough, they could see me. Swiftly I went along the ridge of the roof, one foot on either side of it. At what seemed a proper distance, I reached down both feet to locate the window, and found it. Then I felt another alarm. I had to enter the opening in a kind of curve. With my fingers holding on to the ridge of the roof, as they must now do, the distance to the opening was greater than my body could reach in safety. When I let loose my fingers to slide, I would do this fast, and at the start I would have inside the opening only a little of my legs above the heels. With the ridge released, my fingers would have no grip upon the smooth surface. As I slid down, would the rest of my legs enter the opening, or would I be thrown backward, to hang head downward with my heels over the window sill, like an acrobat, or more likely to tumble down at once to the ground at the very feet of the approaching watchmen?

"I believe I see something," said Balbus. "I know I heard something this time."

"By Jupiter, I heard something too," admitted the one who called himself an unexcitable old soldier. And they started running.

But I had succeeded in throwing my body in its half circle

through the opening, into a stream of cold water up to my waist.

Other windows at intervals along the tunnel let in light that seemed bright in comparison with the blackness of the tunnel itself. I edged my way toward the reservoir so I would not be silhouetted between two windows. The cataract of the inpouring stream would drown out all noise. There, immersed up to my chin, I waited.

The two men arrived. Above the sound of the water dashing into the reservoir, I heard one of them shout very loudly, "Corporal of the Guard! Corporal of the Guard! At the reservoir!"

Additional men came up. "Ladders!" ordered the corporal. "Two ladders, long ones."

I could catch only part of what Balbus told the corporal he had heard. After a short delay, I saw a helmeted head lean through the first opening. He looked in both directions, but toward me he peered into blackness. And I was now immersed, with only my nose showing. Sometimes I thought I would surely be borne down by the current and poured into the reservoir. I felt myself sliding inch by inch nearer the outlet.

A head looked in at the second window.

"Do you see anything between us?" asked the man at the first window, who was the corporal, as I now knew from his voice.

"I see nothing," said the man at the second window.

"Could he have got beyond your opening?"

"I can see pretty clearly to the next opening and the next beyond that. There is nothing."

"And why should there be anything?" asked the corporal in disgust. "These civilians are always seeing things."

This time Balbus stood his ground. "I know I saw a man," he declared.

I rose to my feet, waded away from the dangerous outlet, and felt reassured. Then I heard the corporal say: "Give notice to the guards on the wall, and the aqueduct posts beyond the wall, to watch that no one leaves it."

I took off my wet and heavy toga and in my exasperation threw it into the current. Then, as it was floating away, I grabbed it. It was the badge of my citizenship. On second thought, there still might be much need of it. I wrung it out, wrapped it around my upper body under the arms, and wore it that way.

I waded along, pushing one leg forward, then the other, in long, slow sweeps. I kept wondering if I had gone far enough to get through the Roman walls yet. Even in my misery I gloated over the way I was stealing a march on these vigilant legionaries, piercing the ramparts right under their tireless feet, and they never the wiser. I went through two fairly long places without windows and supposed these to be two of the Seven Hills, though of this I cannot be sure.

When I estimated my slow wading had finally taken me out of the city and some distance beyond the walls, I put my head out cautiously through an opening to look forward and backward and get the lay of the land.

Of a truth, the thick walls were now behind me—those impregnable walls inclosing and making secure the proud city of Rome. Their vast bulk loomed up vaguely; beyond them were the stars, and moving against the stars were the legionaries on their short beats by twos, in the darkness exactly as in the daylight. Standing up to my tunic girdle in water, I nevertheless felt triumphant as I looked. I had seen horsemen on parade, armies in review, elephants in stately procession, and, once in Carthage, fine ladies dancing in a great hall. Like these things in wondrous grace was this ceaseless motion upon the ramparts, which I now viewed for the last time, vaguely in the starlight, and exultantly. These men of springy step and of ever-watching eyes had let me pass unchallenged and unheeded. I, Agenor the Carthaginian, had outwitted them. I, Agenor of the Elephants, had escaped them.

This window was on the eastern side of the conduit, for its direction here was northeast. When I came to the next opening on the other side, I put my head out. Then I pulled it back quick. Jutting out from the base of the next window ahead, and here we were thirty feet or more from the ground, was a sort of slab. On this stood a sentry. It was little bigger than a chair seat, a small platform for a man to keep his feet upon during the period of a watch.

I eased out my head a little way again to reconnoiter. Below and to the west was the Field of Mars, as nearly as I could tell. Beyond was the Tiber, the outline of which I could barely make out under the stars, though after wading so long in the black tunnel, my night eyesight was good, like a cat's.

From the knees up, the man would be above me as I passed. I could probably get by without being heard, if I dived for the distance of a dozen feet. If any sound reached his ears, he would have to squat in a difficult position to peer into the opening. The chief danger was that at regular intervals he looked into the tunnel, for I remembered the corporal's orders back at the reservoir. In that case, I would be far from safe even after I passed, since he could see me for a considerable distance, give the alarm, have me blocked up between openings, and send men in to get me.

He was not standing erect, but leaning over with his belly along the sloping roof and looking toward the east. He was probably another recruited citizen, not a trained soldier. He possessed four spears. I supposed the reserve supply was because at this altitude a spear thrown was a spear lost. One he held loosely in his right hand, leaning it with himself. The other three had their handle ends at a corner of the slab, probably resting in some pocket made for the purpose, and the barb ends resting against the eaves.

At once I asked myself the question, why not get armed here? If I could halt by the window in absolute quiet, I could take one of the three loose spears without his ever knowing. And in the uncertain adventures still ahead, this equipment might save my life.

As I stopped by the window, I was certain he had heard nothing. From the position of his feet and the fat calves of his legs, so close now in front of my face, I knew he was still belly down upon the roof. His back would be diagonally turned to the disappearing spear point that projected with the three others above the eaves.

I reached forward a hand, lifted the end out of a socket, and began drawing it toward me. When I had pulled about a foot of it inside, suddenly it was held tight—probably the upper end had made a rubbing noise as it slid across the rim of the eaves. His knees began to buckle as in a stoop. I tried to jerk away the spear and dive with it under water out of sight, but he wouldn't let go. Then we were face to face at the window. A cry started in his throat. It was never uttered, for, holding on to the spear, I gave his knees a push with all my might. The impact of his fallen body was the only sound. He made no outcry, for the fall whipped the cry out of him.

I gave his knees a push with all my might

Immediately a shout went up from the walls: "Corporal of the Guard! Corporal of the Guard! Outside post of the aqueduct. A man fallen!"

The three loose spears had dropped with him. I now drew in the one I held and hurried as fast as I could. I took a quick look out of the next opening on the other side, and saw it was the last one. The conduit ran into a hill. This offered me greater security if there was suspicion on account of the fallen watchman, but would this be the beginning of nearly forty miles without any opening at all?

I waded on and on, the current going much faster toward Rome than I was leaving it. At last I saw a little point of light. It grew bigger. It was another opening. I reached it and put my head out. All about was the open country, and, as I looked and listened, there was no sound or sign of life anywhere.

Here the aqueduct emerged to cross over a ravine between two hills. I judged the height to be about a dozen feet. The opening was right over a small creek. I threw the money pouch and spear down ahead of me, off to one side, to fall upon the bank. I hung suspended for a moment with my fingers over the window ledge. Then I dropped with a splash into the creek.

I wrung out my garments and started forward. I made the toga into a wet roll to be carried over my shoulder. Constant soaking had caused the money pouch to stretch so that it was larger than ever but not so bulging.

After walking for about an hour, I came to a house where dogs were barking. I unrolled and shook out the toga, as one would shake a blanket, with the dampness of it coming into my face like mist. I arranged it upon myself to some degree as a toga should be arranged, approached the dwelling, and walked to the front door. Two dogs barked and snapped at my heels until I gave them little jabs in the sides with the spear point. I knocked loudly. A window opened, not the door, and a man stuck his head out.

"Who is it? Who is it in the night?"

"Pulvius Sabinus, a citizen of Rome. I want a horse."

"A horse at this hour? Soon the cocks will crow for midnight."

I was gladdened by this information of the hour. I had been afraid it was later. With a fast horse I could still reach Hannibal in time to save Pulvius.

"I will pay well. Hannibal's soldiers took mine, and I had to flee on foot. I wish a horse to ride to Rome to give news that Hannibal's men are abroad."

"I have only two I use for the farm. I cannot spare either of the animals."

"For two hundred *dinarii?*"

"No, no, I cannot break up my team."

"For three hundred *dinarii?*"

"I have only the two," he said, but I saw he was weakening.

"What if Hannibal comes tomorrow? They say he is marching on Rome. His soldiers took my animal. You can hide the money. But you cannot hide a horse from Hannibal."

The man came out to receive the price and show me to the stable. He required his pay first. I counted out three hundred of the silver pieces into his palms. Great as was my haste, he had to feel and examine each coin to make sure it was a silver *dinarius.*

"Light a torch," I said. "Then you can see the money." I also wanted a light by which to select the better of the two horses for the urgent ride ahead of me.

"No, no, not a torch," he objected. "Not if Hannibal's men are about."

So I had to pick out the animal in the dark, but my night eyes were still good.

"Take this one," he said.

"That one is old—is it not so? I will take the younger one."

I paid five additional *dinarii* for a bridle and mounted the horse.

"Which is the nearest road toward Spolietum?" I asked.

"To the north. Turn to the right on the second road." Then he came to life. "But why do you ask? You say you go to Rome. The road to Rome is here."

"Isn't there a centurion with a patrol on the road to Spolietum? I wish to warn him about Hannibal's soldiers being abroad."

"Twenty horsemen, then a party of fifteen, then eight, passed early in the evening. I know not where they went. The dogs have not barked to indicate their return."

It was with no light heart that I galloped along the road where I would have to run the gantlet of those three troops of Roman cavalry. Urging on the horse, and with his rapid hoofs clattering in the still night, I traveled about five miles before I came upon the first party, the largest one of twenty men, halted in the roadway. I kept my horse running right up to them, as if I were a messenger in hot haste. I drew my heaving and sweating mount up suddenly and called out: "Who is the commander here?"

"I am the centurion of the troop," answered one.

"I come to warn you. Return to Rome. Hannibal's men are abroad. All patrols are being recalled. Hasten to Rome. Report at the Colline Gate."

"Proceed," said the centurion to his men. "We return to Rome." I started on. The centurion stopped me. "Do you not go with us?"

"I go on to warn and recall the next party."

"There is no party beyond us."

"There was a troop of fifteen. Another of eight. Where are they?"

"They went north. They are not on this road."

And there I was. On the one hand, I had this news of the road ahead of me being free of Romans right to the tent of Hannibal. On the other hand, I was thus deprived of all excuse for taking that road.

"Then," I asked, "what is the sound of hoofs upon the road beyond us?"

"I hear none," said the centurion.

I dismounted, kneeled, and lay my ear upon the ground. "Yes," I observed, "it is the sound of more than a troop. It is, then, the cavalry of the Carthaginians—the dread Numidians. And they will soon be upon us. Hasten with your troop or you will be overwhelmed."

I kept my squatting position, and at intervals returned my ears to the ground.

"Do you not accompany us?" asked the centurion.

"I will listen briefly to make sure. Then I will overtake you."

When it was safe to do so, I rode on toward the tent of Hannibal with a very light heart. In truth I had heard nothing, but now I saw cavalrymen ahead of me, in single file, at a walk. They were coming down a rise, and between them and me was a thicket of growth closely bordering the road. They meant the good fortune of a Carthaginian troop in reality, when I had only invented them to deceive the centurion. But if we met in the added darkness where the road passed through the thicket, my own men, seeing me in a white toga, might mistake me for a Roman and send a spear through me before I could identify myself.

So I halted at my edge of the small wilderness and called out: "I am Agenor the Carthaginian. I am dressed like a Roman, but I am Agenor the Carthaginian." Then I was filled with alarm, for I had said it in Latin, so steadily had I spoken it during the day, and my own men would be suspicious over the use of this language. At once I began in Carthaginian: "I am Agenor of the Elephants. I am dressed in Roman clothes, but I am Hannibal's Agenor. I am Agenor the Carthaginian."

I heard a sudden clattering of hoofs and eight horsemen galloped forward, four abreast. As they neared the end of the thicket, I saw they were Romans. I wheeled my own horse about as they yelled to me to halt. I fled back the way I had come, with all eight shouting in pursuit. I dug my still wet sandal-heels into the horse, which in the first part of that mad race proved himself worth the three hundred *dinarii* I had so recently paid for him. He was fresh and the cavalry horses upon my trail had already gone far. The wind ballooned some of the toga folds and its free hangings backward in flapping banners. This scared the horse and made him go all the faster; he was headed toward home, and behind him was the tumult of the pursuing troop.

I passed the spot where I had met the first troop and sped on halfway to the house where I had bought the horse. Here was a turn in the road. Below me was the wide slope of a ravine, covered with shrubs and small trees. I had gained slightly on my pursuers and for a moment around this bend I was out of their sight. I turned my horse off the road, down the slope among the trees and bushes. But the ground here was covered with boulders among the growth that concealed them. The right foreleg of the leaping horse struck against one of these as high as his knee, and he was lamed beyond any further usefulness of travel. The Roman troop dashed past.

For the time being I was safe again. But I had lost the greater part of the distance gained on horseback. I would have to go the rest of the way on foot; there was no hope now of reaching Pulvius in time. My sorrow for this was unchanged, but my remorse had lessened. I could now have the consolation that I had tried to save him.

Had the centurion deliberately deceived me? Or had this second troop, without his knowledge, ridden along some connecting trail from the northern road to this one?

I skulked for a while through the country adjacent to the road and then, more boldly, began to travel the road itself. I threw the toga away from me, not even taking the trouble to fold or wad it up. Where it fell, it draped a bush to scare a skittish horse. I still hung onto the money, heavy encumbrance that it was.

When I reached the first outpost of Hannibal's camp, the stars had become as pale as they had been to my opening eyes in the Roman Circus. A Numidian cavalryman set me upon a horse, and galloped with me to Hannibal's tent. I dismounted in front of the sergeant of Hannibal's guard.

"The boy Pulvius?" I asked.

"He lives, but dies shortly. He was reprieved till sun-up."

"Hasten with me to where he sleeps."

The sergeant led me there, and, without speech one to the other, we took our places before the entrance of the tent. Dawn was coming up from behind the Apennines, and the stars were entirely paled out. Soon the death squad arrived, and I stood before the corporal.

"Do not enter," I said. "I am Agenor, and Agenor has returned." The sergeant nodded.

"We go, then," said the corporal to his men.

"Yes, go," I said. "Do not disturb the boy. Let him sleep."

SIXTEEN

BY TORCHLIGHT IN THE EVENING IN HANNIBAL'S TENT, I GAVE MY report to him and the generals. I described the Hannibal-fear that gripped Rome, the things that had happened to me, my preposterous misadventures with the money—whereat the other generals looked at General Samnis and laughed.

"But the horse," he reminded them, "was it not with the moneys our young spy bought the horse?"

"Yes, the horse," said General Mago, "which greatly helped Agenor to keep right on making a mess of things."

"Just the same, gentlemen," insisted the treasurer, "on the average it is exactly as General Samnis says, money is a man's best friend when he is in a tight place."

Hannibal put a stop to these pleasantries to bring the discussion back to the business in hand—whether to march on Rome and how.

"Agenor's aqueduct adventure gives us an idea," said General Hanno, "a kind of Trojan horse idea. Back, away from the city several miles, out of sight of everybody, we can put fifty men in one of the aqueducts and fifty men in the other, and start them wading. It will be easier for them because they will be moving with the current, not against it. They can pass into the city all unbeknown the same way Agenor passed out

of it. Dressed like Romans, they can emerge from the two
aqueducts at the sleep-hour, hasten to the Colline Gate, kill
the guards, and open the gate. The advance column of our
troops, coming up at the precise moment, can rush in."

"With me on Old Anak in front?" I asked.

"No, Agenor," said General Hanno, "you will guide the fifty
soldiers through the aqueduct you were in."

"Who will guide the other fifty through the Appian aqueduct?"

"I was thinking of Misdes. He knows the town in a bookish
way, which is better, I suppose, than not knowing it at all. Let
him do something real for once."

"Gillimas would be better," I suggested. "He's taller and
the water wouldn't come up so high on him."

"What about the patrols on the walls," inquired Hannibal
practically, "those trained legionaries who so much impressed
Agenor and who are wide enough awake at the sleep-hour?"

Before there was a reply, a sergeant came into the tent and
saluted. "Sir, the Sabine farmer is here, the one who took
Agenor to Rome."

"What does he want?"

"His son, sir, his pay, two more oxen and a cart. They took
his white oxen away from him in Rome and so he had to leave
his cart behind too."

"Give them to him. Let him pick out a pair of white oxen
from the herd."

Scarcely had the discussion been resumed when the sergeant
reappeared. "Sir, he does not want white oxen, but black or
brindle or any other color. No use, he says, to drive another
yoke of white ones into Rome. They would simply be sacrificed
to the gods on the order of Fabius the Delayer."

"Attend to him as he wishes and let him go home," directed Hannibal. "Agenor," he said to me, "if you want to bid Sabinus good-by, we will excuse you for five minutes."

"And do not tell him how you got out of Rome," admonished General Mago.

"And this matter of sending him home," observed Gisbo, "isn't it dangerous on account of what he will tell?"

"His boy knows nothing and he himself will be silent," said Hannibal. "What would happen to him if he confessed that he had taken a Carthaginian spy inside the walls? His lips are sealed."

When I returned to the tent, General Maharbal was beginning to speak:

"I have an idea to dovetail with General Hanno's aqueduct plan. The legionaries are ever alert, ever awake, ever pacing their beats, as Agenor has told us. I think I know how to throw them into confusion and put them out of business while our men are taking the Colline Gate."

"How so?" asked Hannibal.

"Another hundred Carthaginians, also dressed as Romans, will go at midnight and steal up close to the walls on the outside. By hugging the masonry, they will be out of the line of sight of the patrols. The latter, walking their beats along the middle of the broad top, are too far back from the edge to look straight down. Isn't that right, Agenor?"

"Yes, sir."

"At daybreak our men will be walking beats of their own, as if assigned there in extra precaution. Each of the hundred will bring with him in the night a stone jar. This can be set down out of sight in a hole beside the foundation while he walks his post. These Carthaginians cannot scale the walls. But with arms as strong as the average, they can certainly throw rather heavy stone jars thirty feet up to the top amidst the legs of the legionaries ceaselessly pacing back and forth. The whole hundred, at the same moment of the sleep-hour, will throw."

"And pray tell us," cynically demanded Gisbo, "how this pottery tossing will put the legionaries out of business. Just what will be the demoralizing effect of pitching up a hundred jars at their feet?"

"Their perfect formation, upon the instant, will be changed to frantic disorder," answered General Maharbal.

Gisbo smiled and spoke sarcastically: "Jars, gentlemen, are a very savage kind of weapon."

"When filled with snakes they are," said General Maharbal, "when crammed from bottom to lid with the living, writhing coils of poisonous reptiles. The noise of their anger will come out of the jars perpetually like steam from a vent. But in the tight-covered containers they will be harmless to the Carthaginians. Soldiers can be sent out all over the countryside to capture them alive with forked sticks. Just as the aqueduct men reach the Colline Gate, the hundred crocks will hit the top of the wall with a simultaneous crash amidst sandaled feet, breaking in pieces to release the snakes—irritable from their long durance, vicious, hissing, striking. The patrols will be thrown into dismay and confusion. They will have no eyes for what is happening at the gate."

"By the fires of Moloch, very good!" cried Hannibal, who liked stratagems.

"And it is supposed," said Gisbo, "that a bunch of snakes will thus upset perfectly trained soldiers?"

"With those reptiles in their pathway," replied General Maharbal, "entangling their feet, fastening fangs into their legs, and not a man free to aid another, do you think the legionaries would go on walking back and forth with that precision Agenor has described?"

"I think they would," said Gisbo.

"And so do I," agreed General Mago. "A soldier can be perfected to the point of ignoring any interruption whatever that does not have the physical force actually to stop him—and in this case his feet move through venom but they still can move, and they would do so until he dropped down dead from the poison. The snakes might hiss and strike and encumber his legs, but he would proceed with his duty, the same as he does when facing death upon battlefields."

"It is unreasonable," declared General Samnis. "They would forget the business of patrolling, forget everything else and fight the snakes."

The argument continued back and forth for perhaps five minutes, whether discipline would be stronger than the serpents, until Hannibal interfered.

"Let's end all this speculation, gentlemen," he said. "At present we are not taking Rome."

"Not taking Rome?" three of them cried out together.

"It will be done in good time. By the scorched sands of the desert, yes. But not now."

Maharbal, very sober and much disappointed, made a remark in Latin: *"Vincere scis, Annibal; victoria uti nescis."*

Hannibal smiled in a way almost boyish that was part of his great magnetism. "Gentlemen, what mean thing is he saying about me and in what barbarous tongue? Speak it out, Maharbal, in plain, blunt Carthaginian."

"This is what I said, sir: *You, Hannibal, know how to conquer; but not how to make the best use of a victory.*"

Hannibal continued to smile in winning good humor, but the remark went home, as we could see, and he began to explain his decision: "I am not insensible to the glory of capturing Rome, but why let glory destroy us, why lose our sense of values? We are fighting Romans, not just a place. Assume we can take their proud capital, by means of the aqueducts and vipers or in other ways. What then? We would be inside the walls, with nothing but enemies on the outside—to beleaguer us, starve us, shut us off from the world like prisoners in a cell. We would only be making a jail for ourselves. Months would pass and men on the streets of Carthage would ask one another: 'Where is Hannibal—is he dead?' And with us so neatly dungeoned there on the Tiber, Carthage itself could be attacked. We shall capture Rome when we can hold it without being isolated—when Carthage sends reinforcements, when my brother brings an army from Spain, when Greece joins us, when the Italians and the others under the yoke of Rome desert and come over to us. For the present, we are going into the Campanian Plains, the richest in the world, to gather cattle and corn and booty for the winter ahead. Then we shall march to the shores of the Adriatic to get in touch with Greece and Carthage. All of you prepare to march upon short notice. The council is ended, gentlemen."

By this decision, the supreme commander kept the Carthaginians from being cooped up inside the walls of Rome, but he brought them within walls that held them no less inescapably —as much without glory as without hope, all on account of a little slip of speech.

The clumsiness of Hannibal's tongue with a foreign word is what did it, his Punic accent, his Carthaginian brogue. The blunder resulted from the way he spoke a Latin name. It was a small thing to have such sinister consequences for a great army.

Hannibal called in the Roman guides in his pay and told them where he wanted to go—just told them without pointing it out on a map. He meant Casinum. Because of his poor pronunciation, they led him to Casilinum—the worst possible place he could have gone.

On two sides was the unbroken barrier of steep and wooded mountains, on one side a broad and marshy river, and on one the sea. He came into it through a narrow defile, the only entrance, the only exit.

He was caught in a trap. Fabius the Delayer moved up and occupied the pass, ensnaring the Carthaginians as surely and abjectly as beetles in a bottle. The dread Hannibal would soon trouble Rome no more. He had much booty, many provisions, from the rich plains of Campania. When these gave out, the end of him would be at hand.

Hannibal was aware of his predicament, his soldiers were aware of it. He was more alarmed than he had ever been before.

He went about in deep thought. Twice I rode by him on Old Anak and spoke to him without his paying any attention to me. This man who saw all things around him when his eyes looked outward, saw naught when his eyes looked inward. For a whole hour he might gaze at the unconquerable mountains, the wide river, the shipless sea. These only revivified his discomfiture as he walked back to his tent, his great mind resourceless at last.

Then one morning his face was smiling again and he was once more eagerly alert to his surroundings.

"Agenor," he greeted me, "it is several days since I last saw you and Old Anak. We occupy here a pleasant little valley. But it is rather hemmed in and I have had thoughts of leaving it. Will you go on the elephant to the edge of the camp and tell the captain of the pioneers that Hannibal wishes him to come at once?"

When the man returned with me, Hannibal said to him:

"See those high ridges north of the pass which the Romans hold. Now, listen to what you must do. Have your men make four thousand fagots out of dead vines or light brush or very dry wood split into fine kindling. Collect two thousand oxen from the herds. At midnight tie the fagots to their horns, set the fagots on fire, and drive the animals up those steep slopes with the torches burning at their heads. Put enough of your men at the work to do it quickly. Keep the cattle in orderly formation as much as you can so they will look like an army escaping over the heights by torchlight. The camp will be silent and black, without a fire anywhere, as if deserted. The four thousand Roman guards at the pass, thinking us in foolhardy flight over the mountains, will quit their posts to run up there to head us off. I will send along the light-armed infantry to handle the fighting. While the pass is left unguarded, the army will take possession of it, and march through and off and away."

"And give Fabius the Delayer the slip," I called down from the neck of Old Anak.

"Just so!" observed Hannibal. "I'm afraid he will be in for some heavy censure at Rome. And we'll make it hotter for him yet. Since he is the only Roman having my respect, we don't want him to have theirs. He owns a big farm in Campania. There, we will load our wagons down with fresh booty, take more wagons and load them down. Only we won't touch a thing belonging to Fabius, not an ox nor a peck of corn, nothing. Because he ever tags at my heels but ever refuses to fight in open battle, the peevish Romans already call him Hannibal's lackey. What will they say when I ravage every other farm for miles around and spare his?"

"They'll think he is deceitfully playing into your hands," I answered, "and there's some kind of bargain between you."

"That is it," said Hannibal, "and what a rage honest old Fabius will be in . . . Captain, are your instructions clear?"

"Yes, sir," said the leader of the pioneers, brief and timid in speech, his tongue not loosely hinged like mine.

"Be ready at the foot of the ridge at midnight. And do you understand that these arrangements are absolutely secret?"

"Yes, sir."

"And you, Agenor?"

"I won't breathe a word of it, sir."

Just Old Anak knew besides us three. I thought of how many secrets he must have heard during his long life as a warrior. One he had kept so darkly and so well that Scarbas, who had been troubled by intimations of it, and I, who saw sinister evidences of it, could not piece it together into any understandable pattern. Only the elephant and Gisbo knew it, whatever it was that made bad blood between them, and I wondered whether it would ever be fully revealed to me, to Hannibal, to anyone outside those two.

Night came, and the dead of night, the time appointed by Hannibal. There were the numerous oxen with fagots tied to every horn, as yet unlighted. There was the whole army in readiness to move. All marching preparations had been made in complete darkness, for not a torch, not a campfire, had been permitted.

Abruptly, in this universal blackness, lights started to glisten like fireflies or stars coming out. Some distance up the hillside they began to show, hundreds of them upon the instant, faster and thicker than one could count. They made a pretty sight as they moved up the slope, an even line of brightness ascending.

Then the line grew wavy, lost its regularity, and became all the more ragged and mixed up as the radiance increased.

What had happened was this: The oxen little minded that each horn was a candlestick as long as the blaze was up there some distance removed. All this simply lighted the way, enabling them to pick out the best routes up the rough, wooded, and pathless heights. But it was different as soon as the creatures felt the heat in their faces and realized their heads were afire. A stout wind blew up the slopes to fan the fagots into vigorous burning. The cattle lost all semblance of order, and the herdsmen began to have a hard time of it.

Draccus and I were mounted on Old Anak, ready with the rest of the army to move to the pass and through it as soon as it was left clear by the deluded guards. The excitement was too much for me just to watch and not be a part of.

"Let us go and help," I said to Draccus.

"Do you have orders, Agenor, sir?" he asked.

"None to go but none not to, either."

I started the elephant off at a brisk pace. When we reached the herdsmen, we found the oxen badly demoralized by the torches they bore aloft. A pair would halt, face each other with lowered heads, mutually regard their blazing horns, then snort and spring away. They butted each other's sides. As the smell of melting horn came into their nostrils, they tore through the brush with fresh speed or tried to dart past the herdsmen back down the slope. Now and then a dry bush would be ignited and flash up quick and bright with a hissing sound.

An officer approached us in rebuke: "Agenor, what are you doing here? This is no place for the elephant."

"I am helping, sir. Old Anak and I are helping."

And of a truth we were. When the frightened cattle started back down the slope and saw this huge bulk blocking their way, they turned their lighted heads and began to climb again. Occasionally the elephant slapped their flanks with his trunk or prodded them with his tusks.

One got past us and we pursued him down the slope.

"Let him go!" a herdsman shouted. But we kept up the chase until we saw there was no longer any use.

Meanwhile, cattle and men were a considerable distance ahead of us, nearing the summit. We looked back and saw a forest fire springing into big proportions in our wake. The wind still blew strongly up the slopes. This would cause the fire to leap and travel at our heels, we knew not how rapidly. We hurried Old Anak on as fast as possible. The shrubbery was pushed back by our passage to tear at our legs. Then the advancing, torch-bearing cattle had set another fire in front of us, where we could see bushes burning in a bright, spreading contagion. We turned to the right to by-pass this new danger and still keep ahead of the one in pursuit of us.

Our adventure with the escaped ox had left us behind alone. The fire at our rear now leapt up to the tops of saplings in a twinkling and jumped into the branches of trees so that a whole acreage was solid with a red blaze that illuminated our route as we hurried.

We came to a pond, a saucerlike basin on the high ridge-side, a small mountain lake.

I put Old Anak out into this as into a sanctuary.

"Hadn't we better go on, Agenor, sir?" suggested Draccus.

"We'll be safe enough here," I answered.

"You see there is much dead and fallen material about the place," insisted Draccus. "And the trees are thick and heavy-foliaged. There will be a high wall of fire around us and the pond is small."

The little body of water was roughly in the form of a circle, perhaps a hundred yards across. It was about five feet deep in the center but only a foot or less at the edges. Half of its circumference consisted of rocky walls. The rest was flat, heavily forested and thicketed with underbrush, as Draccus had observed.

"I like not the prospect," insisted Draccus. "We'll be in the middle of a furnace, Agenor, sir, a furnace a hundredfold big and a hundredfold hot. It can cook our faces and suck our breaths out."

"Not if we wet down and drench all the edges," I said, in sudden inspiration.

I set Old Anak to doing this with all the speed he could manage.

"Immerse trunk!" I commanded time after time. "Inhale! Lift trunk! Spout!"

As fast as ever he could, while I moved him around the edge, he drew up all the water that the hollow tube of his trunk would hold, and spurted it out. He soaked the bushes and dead underbrush in a broad rim, and then, lifting his trunk, soaked the leafage of the trees. The whole half of the border not protected by the cliffs, was finally dripping like a grove after a spring downpour in the Apennines.

As we were thus occupied, rabbits and other small animals came, and a deer, which trembled at sight of the elephant, turned to flee. Then, driven back by the fear of the fire to conquer the lesser fear of us, it splashed in its bouncing way through the shallows to get as far off as possible. Birds flew in so numerously as to cover the cliffside. Three terrapins hastened as fast as they could into the protection of the pond. A dozen snakes arrived, put into the water, and swam across. I thought if no more than these were driven from a whole ridge to refuge from a fire, General Maharbal might have had trouble finding enough for his attacking jars.

Last of all, and brought to an astonished stop right under the elephant's splashings, three Roman horsemen raced to this place ahead of the fire. The horses, as had the deer, trembled in the presence of this vast, black apparition which threw out streams of water upon them. The illumination cast forward by the approaching blaze, made everything as bright as a lighted hall. I saw the flesh of the animals quiver as they stood between two dreads—the devouring flame and this terrible beast. They leaped into the pond, their hoofs throwing up water in the shallows, and dashed across to the farther side by the cliffs.

"Surrender!" I shouted to them. "Cast your weapons into the lake!"

Instead of obeying, they lifted their spears threateningly.

I interrupted Old Anak's second round of drenching the border and headed him toward the three.

"Best a truce now!" cautioned Draccus. "The fire is almost here."

"And have them kill me afterward?"

For a moment I thought Draccus saw a chance for his own freedom. He divined my mistrust. "I promised not to try to escape. I never break a promise, you know that, Agenor, sir."

Yet, amounting to the same thing, his innocence might not

prevent them from turning the tables to take me prisoner or from killing me. The imminent menace of the fire was on my side now. It would not be, later, if we all came through it. I kept Old Anak going toward the Romans, who on their part still brandished their weapons.

"Surrender!" I repeated.

They cast their spears, but their terrified and rearing horses caused the throws to go wild or short. The horses now dashed out to the edge and around it. I kept them herded there, exposing them to the closeness of the fire, which filled our ears with its crackling and would soon be upon us.

"We surrender!" they said at last, casting away their swords and their shields.

We gathered together in common urgency by the cliffside, the men, the elephant, the birds, the deer, the snakes, even the distrustful horses. I made Old Anak lie down with only his trunk above the surface. Draccus and I immersed ourselves up to the chin. The Romans did likewise. The deer was in over its back. The poor shaking horses were the ones most exposed, with a good part of their bodies out of the water.

"Are you a recent captive?" one of the Romans asked Draccus. The water rippled with the breath of his speech, his mouth was so close to the surface. "This young Carthaginian is an obnoxious stripling. He has a big animal and imagines he's big himself."

"He understands Latin," Draccus replied and said no more. Nor did they.

Thus this group of strangely assorted fugitives awaited the coming of the fire. We felt the intensity of its heat. The cliffs reflected it. Burning fragments lighted upon us. But as the flame reached the wetted-down borders it was briefly halted and the instantaneous violence of the conflagration was somewhat lessened. After this fuel was dried out, it burned so long and hot that we felt the temperature of the water rise.

At last the worst was over. All of us were safe and all anxious to end this enforced companionship. Old Anak showed the most reluctance to leave. The ground was still alive with coals and embers over which he was unwilling to travel. I ordered the Roman prisoners to grope about in the shallows and fish out their castaway shields, which had iron rims, and with which I set them to scraping out a clear path for the elephant. While we were in the midst of this slow work, I heard a bugle and knew that this was the signal from Hannibal for the troops to march through the defile.

When we finally got clear of the burned section, we hastened on. It was nearly daybreak and the last of the troops were moving through the pass when we joined them. I had a pleasant feeling of satisfaction over the evening's work as we rode along. Then I saw a man on a horse, who I hoped would not see me. It was Hannibal.

"Agenor, fall out!" he commanded.

I did so, ordering the three prisoners to stay with me.

"I captured these three men, sir!" I announced.

"It's a habit, Agenor, for you to go on solitary expeditions, capture a few Romans, and think that settles the matter. You and the elephant might have come to serious harm. It was unsoldierly and I want no more of it. Sergeant, add these three men to the prisoners. Agenor, fall in!"

Draccus, Old Anak and I joined the marching column. In the days that followed, we moved on eastward, plundering right and left, went through the Apennines, and wintered at Geronium. This was on the Adriatic side of the mountains, but a good many miles from the sea.

In regard to Fabius, all turned out as Hannibal wanted. "The bungling dotard has made a laughing-stock of the army," said the Romans. "And have you heard what happened in Campania? Hannibal didn't hurt a thing of his, even put Carthaginian guards around the place to protect it. There's just one way to explain a thing like that."

When our spies brought reports of such sayings and news that Fabius was not dictator anymore, Hannibal remarked: "War kills reputations as well as men. Fabius, and he alone, might have saved them. I am glad the Romans didn't know it. I do not like his delaying tactics and I rejoice that the Romans don't either. I wish open battles and I am pleased that the Romans do likewise. The Romans want what I do—suicidally for them. Only Fabius does not. Now, pleasantly once more, they have given us two rash consuls. We have already disposed of several pairs of them. We know the trick of managing it."

The consuls did not reach a proper stage of rashness until a June day of the following year. Then took place Hannibal's greatest victory, the Battle of Cannae, between the Aufidus River and the Adriatic beach. There from noon to sunset more men were killed than ever before at once in the history of the world. Sixty thousand Romans perished, and the men of General Samnis gathered up a bushel of gold rings from the fingers of dead Roman knights.

Hannibal's brain was worth forty thousand men on that June afternoon. The Romans had ninety thousand, Hannibal fifty thousand. The supreme commander used no less than seven stratagems to outwit the Roman consuls. One of these was to time the action to a breeze that blew thick dust in the Romans' eyes.

The next day, when all the tumult and dying had ceased, General Maharbal rode up to Hannibal sitting on his horse near the seaward bank of the Aufidus.

"You do not need to speak, Maharbal," said Hannibal. "You have come to chide me—to say I know how to win victories, but not how to use them."

"I am here for orders, sir, to take the cavalry ahead to open the gates of Rome to you. I will be there before they know I am on the way."

"Not yet, Maharbal. It must be as I said. And everybody will come over to our side now. Then, by the scorched sands of the desert, we will take the capital! Do you see that ship out there? On it is Admiral Bomilcar. It will carry to the Senate of Carthage the bushel of rings taken here at Cannae, and the other bushel taken at Trebia and Lake Trasymene. I will send my brother Mago, and General Gisbo on account of his influence with the Aristocratic Party, and one of the rhetoricians to make a speech for me. I will ask for Numidians, money, elephants. And, yes, I will also send Agenor with Old Anak and Draccus the Roman. These will reinforce my request for a hundred new elephants, for a hundred, Maharbal."

I walked on air at being chosen to go to Carthage.

Admiral Bomilcar brought coins which we had not seen before, minted after the Battle of Trasymene. This had a Negro's head on one side, an elephant on the other. Gillimas and Misdes flipped one of these to see which of them should go. Misdes chose tails, and twice out of three times the tossed coin fell with the elephant up.

General Samnis summoned me to his tent. "Much moneys

you take this time," he said. "About Rome maybe General Samnis was mistaken. There is no sensible dealings with such parsimonious peoples as the Romans, slow to take advantages in getting moneys; and on the other hand squeezing every little coin tight in the fist and putting it in a pot, maybe, to be buried in a garden. Nothings of the kind you will find in Carthage where the peoples know about moneys and have eager eyes when they see it in another's palms, and are willing to make trades for it. General Samnis has figured out already how much Agenor needs and the best way to take it. A belt, ten inches in width, I will have my men make out of tanned horsehide to go around the bigness of Anak's waist. Inside will be six little belts, three of them filled with gold coins, three with silver, the whole distance girthing the elephant's body. Of so much treasure in the belt nobody will know except Hannibal, General Samnis, Agenor, and Anak who hooks anybody fooling with it but Agenor."

"Draccus will know or guess," I said.

"Draccus, of a necessity, yes, but not Mago, or Gisbo, or Misdes. The wide belt of new yellow leather will seem only something to make the elephant look nice; the moneys inside will be secret. If Agenor gets in tight place, he does bribery in big way and Carthage does not disappoint him. Anak likewise carries the two bushels of rings."

It was a ship of one hundred oars. The elephant was not towed on a raft but was given a place on the deck.

Gisbo put his handkerchief to his delicate nose. "There is something stronger here than the salt sea breeze," he said. "We have fallen upon evil days. An elephant is now a gentleman and travels with gentlemen."

On the voyage, Misdes and I worked out a big sign on white

linen which Old Anak would wear wherever he went in Carthage, for the citizens to see and read.

I was now fifteen years old. Two years and a month had gone by since we left New Carthage in Spain. It was the Year of the World 3788.

SEVENTEEN

MY PULSES QUICKENED AS WE CAME IN SIGHT OF CARTHAGE jutting forth from the powdered plains into the blue sea under the blue sky. From sea-edge to heights, the splendor of its slopes uprose in front of us—great piles of masonry that were circular and semi-circular and seven-sided and horseshoe-shaped. And this was no Rome, all white stone and white togas. Some of the buildings were indeed of colorless purity, but some were gray, and brown, and spotted-yellow from Numidian quarries, and some were as black as Old Anak.

For six hundred and sixty-eight years the city had stood here on the bright African shore, one hundred and thirty-eight years longer than Rome had stood on the hills and in the marshes beside the Tiber. And during those centuries, within its boundaries twenty-three miles around, it had become the wealthiest spot upon the surface of the whole broad earth—vastly richer than Athens or Tyre or Alexandria or Antioch or famed Babylon or Rome still clinging to its rustic parsimony after half a thousand years.

Crafty, cruel, corrupt, the Romans called it, but it was fair, exceeding fair, to look upon. What wonder that we all stood gazing from the ship, Gisbo, Mago, Misdes, and I, and Draccus whose face could not conceal a great expectancy. What wonder that I, Agenor, as I held my left wrist in my right hand, should feel the faster pumpings of my heart at the glory of it.

"Look, Anak!" I cried. "Look, it is Carthage! Do you remember it? You were already old when you left it twenty-two years ago. You carried upon your back a boy of nine who had just taken an oath in one of the temples yonder. That boy was Hannibal. That oath of eternal hate now fills every Roman breast with dread. It is Carthage, Anak. Look!"

Draccus the Roman paid no attention to this outburst. Nor did Old Anak. He was seasick from his long voyage and raised his eyes not at all to the Carthaginian capital spread out in such majesty over the slope.

I, Agenor, was returning after only three years' absence. I had left it at the age of twelve to go to Spain to the great Hannibal, and to dear Scarbas now a year in a grave beside the Trebia, between the sepulchers of Little Enoch and the tusks.

Afterward I was to think how curious it was that in this vast city of seven hundred thousand the very first man I encountered should be a Spaniard saying the name of Scarbas, and saying it intimately, affectionately, to make a moisture come to my eyes.

Our approach had been heralded and we were received with suitable ceremony. There was a functionary from the Senate, brilliantly uniformed and riding a white mule. There was a horse-drawn chariot for Gisbo and one for Mago. There was a dromedary which kneeled for the hesitant Misdes to get aboard. And there were twenty-four elephants, with Morbal atop Bostar, the biggest. They were lined up twelve on a side, facing one another and making an avenue for our passage. Their trunks were gilded, their ears painted blue, their bodies hung with yards of gold-and-crimson trappings, their thick necks girdled with little bells that tinkled musically. These richly embellished beasts were in great contrast to plain, wrinkled Anak, adorned only with the wide horsehide belt, and the cloth banner hanging at either side of him and proclaiming in red and black letters:

HANNIBAL'S ELEPHANT
Old Anak
Greatest war tusker that ever lived on earth
Only survivor of 37
36 died in battles for Carthage
Give Hannibal 100 more to conquer Rome

Our retinue moved up the ascending streets toward the citadel on the heights. The functionary on the white mule rode ahead. Immediately behind him was Gisbo's chariot. Then Mago's. Then came Misdes on the camel, white around the gills in vertigo from the rocking motion of the hump. Draccus followed on foot, symbol of the coming downfall of Rome. As I at the last moved through the avenue of elephants, these fell in behind.

I had noticed the Spaniard among the people, finding perhaps some magnetism in the fixity of his gaze. He now stepped forward and walked beside me and began to speak.

"I am from New Carthage," he said in a low tone. "I knew your master, Scarbas."

"Scarbas is dead," I replied. "A year ago."

He brushed his eyes with the side of his right hand.

"I knew him well. He was my friend, but afterward I was not allowed to see him. Will you be at the elephant stables? To you there I will bring a letter for you to carry to Hannibal, now that Scarbas is dead. Do not let—"

His talk was disturbing the dignity of our procession. A policeman quickly interfered and took him by the shoulder. "What do you mean?" he demanded. "Don't you know better than to address one in a formal march? Back in line, rude Spaniard!" He pushed the man back among the bystanders, so his last remark, some injunction he was about to give me, was interrupted upon his tongue.

All along our route, few noticed the gilded tusks and blue ears of the home elephants but all read Old Anak's banners and gave him special huzzas.

From my high perch I observed the assorted means of Carthaginian travel—white mules with dignitaries astride them, painted mares, beribboned sacred horses, chariots, ox-carts, Numidian ponies, zebras, dromedaries.

We moved up to the ramparts of the citadel at the top of the town, but we did not enter. We went along the walls to another thoroughfare, and passed down it to the Forum, which was close to the sea and not far off from where we started. This going up one street and down another had been nothing more than a parade to please the people.

At the bottom of the broad steps of the Forum, the functionary dismounted from the white mule. Gisbo and Mago got out of their chariots. The camel knelt and let Misdes stand once more on the unweaving earth. They walked up the steps in single file, one behind the other in their established order, with Draccus at the rear. I, Agenor, continued on the elephant. The wide, high, bronze doors of the Forum swung back, and Old Anak marched onto the tiled floor of the great hall.

There, seated all around, were the hundred and four Senators of Carthage and there were the two Suffetes or kings, or rather presidents, for they were elected fresh every year. We halted in the center of the floor.

"Down, Anak!" I commanded.

He kneeled.

Four guards came. They lifted off one bushel sack of rings and took it to the front of the elephant. They untied the neck of the sack. They held it bottom up as a farmer empties a bag of corn. The rings poured out and rattled and clinked and tinkled, in a prolonged and delightful clangor of gold, and some resonantly bounced and rolled away from the pile. The sack was handed to Draccus. He stood holding it a full minute as haughty before these Senate graybeards as he had been back there at the elephant trial, with the yellow mound at his sandaled feet.

Mago announced: "Honored Sirs, rings from the fingers of dead Roman knights at the battles of Trebia and Trasymene."

Draccus dropped the sack upon the heap of gold. This that he had done was as much as he would consent to do. "Agenor, sir," he had said, "I will not kneel to the Senate. I will refuse in front of them and you can have me beheaded, and that would not make a favorable impression as to the compliance of Rome. And if your guards have to force me to my knees, that would not look well either."

In the same way the second sack was emptied. In the same way Draccus did his part while Mago called out:

"Suffetes and Senators of Carthage, rings from the fingers of dead Roman knights at the Battle of Cannae recently fought."

Then Misdes eloquently presented four requests in the name of Hannibal—one hundred elephants, five thousand Numidian cavalry, twenty-five thousand infantry, and what seemed to me a staggering sum of money, of which he said: "Honored Sirs, Carthage has a single golden temple shrine worth not less than forty million silver pieces. The equivalent amount is what your supreme commander needs and requests. In manifold return, he will give you Rome."

A Senator uprose. Shaggy-bearded he was and shaggy-haired, of the Aristocratic Party with a long record of being against Hamilcar, Hasdrubal, and Hannibal. His speech was insulting in its wit and brevity: "Gentlemen, if Hannibal is winning victories, he does not need aid. If he is losing them, he does not deserve it."

Other Senators strongly objected to funds and reinforcements. I remembered now and understood what Scarbas had said of the party of rich merchants and slaveholders. Any weakness of Hannibal was not in himself. It was in Carthage.

But these Senators, in sight of the double heap of rings, were in the minority. The majority voted forty elephants, four thousand Numidians, twenty thousand infantry and four thousand horses to be raised in Spain, and forty million of the new Carthaginian coins with a Negro head on one side and an elephant on the other.

We left the Forum to go our separate ways.

Gisbo walked off without saying where. Mago departed for the wealthy suburb of Megara.

Misdes was all agog to get to Hippomedon's School of Rhetoric. "Better come with me," he urged. "I'll introduce you to Hippomedon and the other teachers, Nicanor, Diocles, Heginax, Phoxidas, all Greeks. I understand it's the school you are going to. It's the best in Carthage."

It depressed me just to think of a rhetoric school that was sooner or later ahead of me. I declined the invitation. Then

Draccus and I rode Old Anak up over the heights to the inland or isthmus edge of town to the elephant stables under the triple walls.

Morbal was seated on a stool. Another boy was waiting on him, just as I had done in the old days. He was too lazy to rise. "Come here, Agenor," he said. "Let me shake your hand and greet you and welcome you back to Carthage."

Carthalo, his second in command, came up. He was not old, somewhere in his thirties, and full of energy and good spirits. Several of the drivers crowded around and made it all seem like a pleasant homecoming.

"That sign, Agenor," said Morbal, pointing to the banner on Old Anak. "It takes in a good deal of time and a good deal of country, doesn't it?"

"No more of either than is the fact," I replied.

At this point Carthalo led us away to Old Anak's stall and our own quarters.

"I will show you the city," I said to Draccus, as soon as we were settled. "You must appear as my servant in public, but it will be better than staying cooped up here under the triple walls."

"Yes, Agenor, sir, much better."

As we mounted Old Anak again and rode past long sections of the three hundred stalls, with an elephant eating away for dear life in each one of them, I made a sweeping gesture with my right arm and remarked: "A good many elephants, don't you think?"

"*Hic et ubique,*" he answered. "Here and everywhere. So many, and such enormous appetites. Don't they ever stop eating? Carthage has to be rich to feed them. And the taxes to do it. Don't the citizens complain?"

"Oh, sometimes. Then there is a big parade of the whole herd through the streets and they forget it."

In the afternoon, along the streets and in the Square of Kharmoun, we heard talk of sacrifices to Moloch in honor of Hannibal's victories. There had been none for a long time. When things went smoothly the god was neglected. If there was a disaster to cause lamentation, or some favorable event to cause joy, then the Carthaginians thought at once of giving human lives to this monstrous deity.

Toward evening we caught the remark of one street idler to another: "The Roman with the boy on the elephant. He would be a most suitable offering."

Near by, listening, was a priest of Moloch, clothed in red robes.

"I like not this talk—it is contagious, it spreads," I said to Draccus. "Let us return to the elephant stables where they will not see you."

We started away but we had gone no more than three blocks before a patrol of the soldiers of Moloch overtook us and stood athwart our way.

"Why are you here?" I demanded. "What do you want?"

"We have come to take the Roman."

"This man is Hannibal's. You cannot have him."

"Hannibal, nor any man, high or low, can evade what is due to Moloch. There is no exemption from the claims of the god. Hannibal, did you say? Was it not he—yes, he it was, the story has gone the rounds—the boy Hannibal was chosen for the sacrifice and escaped by the base deception of his father. That this man is Hannibal's makes him all the more liable. We have come to take him."

"Get out of our way or the elephant will trample you down."

"Give us the man or we will drag him off the beast."

"It is best for me to go with them," said Draccus.

"They can't take you, Draccus. There are only eight of them. Old Anak won't let them."

"It will only cause trouble," urged Draccus. "You can oppose these eight but not the whole force of Carthage. They are determined. Let them take me. It is best, Agenor, sir."

"Draccus, when you ask me to surrender you to them, do you know what a sacrifice to Moloch means?"

"Yes, Agenor, I know. In Rome we called Moloch the abomination of the Carthaginians. We were unable to understand how civilized people could do it. It means being burned alive."

"No!" I cried. "I'll never let them! Anak—"

He clapped his hand quickly over my mouth, smothering the command I was about to give the elephant to attack and trample down the patrol. We argued back and forth for perhaps five minutes while the soldiers of Moloch waited. At last, after considering the fair chance that Gisbo and Mago could successfully intercede, I let him slide down from the elephant.

As he was being led away, I realized that he had no real hope of being saved. *"Vale,* Agenor! *Vale!"* he called back, and the solemn, mournful tone of that farewell made it sound inexorably final.

Old Anak did not move nor I on his back until the death squad was out of sight. Gisbo, who would have the most weight, had vouchsafed no information of his whereabouts. Mago was at Megara, out at the isthmus, beyond the triple walls. Misdes was closer, but he would not have enough influence to be of much use. In my nervous thinking I had been

fingering the broad tanned horsehide money belt that encircled the body of Old Anak. The money!

I unlaced an opening in the big belt and an opening in one
of the smaller belts that contained gold. I unlaced another
opening and took out a buckskin bag. I counted out one hundred and ten gold pieces into the bag, and then relaced all the
openings tight and snug.

I directed Old Anak to the canyon where was located the
Temple of Moloch, a sinister building, black as night, its ebony
walls rising out of the gorge like the sides of a sepulcher.

The guard objected to letting me inside the inky, ominous
building until I gave him a gold piece. Then he bowed and let
me pass. Successively, by means of a coin each time, I went
by several attendants. I gave three to the last, a kind of orderly
or lackey. He took me to the high pontiff of Moloch where
he was seated on a throne in a great room.

Back of him was the brazen idol, huge and intimidating.
No one could remember when this metal colossus had not
stood here in the black tabernacle ready to be hauled out into
a public square for its work of death and desolation. Rather
than the semblance, it was the malignant, cruel god itself. In
the grim, true sense, this massive image over against the wall,
behind the pontiff on his throne, was Moloch the Devourer,
Moloch the Destroyer, who exacted living sacrifices and re-
joiced in human woe and human tears.

The idol rose up several cubits high. He had the legs and
body of a man. His head was the head of a bull. His wings were
outspread along the wall. His teeth were red. In his face were
three black, yellow-rimmed eyes. A big opening was in his
hollow stomach, with one low down in each of his hollow

legs, the routes of his victims to the consuming fire at his feet. His arms were overlong, like a gorilla's, so that his hands almost touched the floor as he stood.

The high priest had on a scarlet mantle and wore a tall Assyrian headdress. "Why do you come here, boy?" he asked with arrogance and irritation.

"I am Agenor of the army of Hannibal."

"Who is Hannibal's boy and who is Hannibal to send him here to intrude upon the high pontiff of Moloch, greater than generals?"

"I came, sir, to bring an offering from Hannibal, not to the temple but to the high pontiff personally, an offering of fifty pieces of gold."

"Pardon my uncivil welcome, Agenor," he said.

"If I may give the offering, sir."

"It is acceptable," he replied, and held out his hand.

Slowly, one by one, I took the heavy and yellow disks out of the pouch and counted them with deliberate slowness into his covetous palm.

At exactly fifty I stopped.

"The equal amount remaining?" he asked, with cunning, eager eyes. "Another fifty perchance, are they not offerings from Hannibal too?"

"Not now, sir. They will be so tomorrow afternoon if the Roman centurion, the one called Draccus, proves unacceptable to the great god Moloch."

"There will be five priests and twenty soldiers of Moloch to carry on the sacrifice. What of them?"

"Five gold pieces for each of the priests, two for each of the soldiers, and these remaining fifty for you, sir. The Roman is useful as an elephant man. Hannibal would be inconvenienced to lose him."

"I had thought," he said, "that a Roman would be spurned by Moloch. It is a subterfuge of the Carthaginians to offer a Roman, of plainly less value than one of themselves. The god is not so easily deceived. It is ever a Carthaginian sacrifice that Moloch wants."

I was clear out to the elephant when the orderly came running up to summon me back to the pontiff's presence.

"Agenor," he explained, "I brought you back on account of the priests and soldiers. They will require an advance, an earnest amount, for it is indeed a sober matter to interfere with the workings of incorruptible fate."

"What sums do you suggest, sir?"

"I suggest one gold piece for each of the soldiers and two for each of the priests, or thirty in all."

I spent some more time upon the streets, feeling much better. The assurances I had received were veiled and oblique, as they ever are, I suppose, in the case of bribery.

The dreadful event was to take place at high noon in the Square of Kharmoun, whither the idol was brought and made ready. The soldiers of Moloch built a big fire all around and between his feet, out of cedarwood and laurel, so that his legs became red-hot up to the knees. Doleful music was kept up by tambourines and other instruments. One of the red-robed priests chanted continuously, regardless of other sounds and distractions. The square was packed with people. They resented Old Anak's taking up so much room and shutting off so much of the view beyond him.

With so high a stake in this unholy spectacle, I ignored

their reproaches. I had slept fitfully and uneasily, fearing the pontiff's treachery and in my nightmares seeing Draccus disappear into Moloch's cavernous stomach, down to the red-hot legs, and hearing his smothered cry as he fell.

And I had spent the whole morning in an agony of apprehension. I had been simple and guileless in advancing the thirty gold pieces. The high pontiff could keep this pay, say nothing to his priests and soldiers about it, let the sacrifice take its regular course, and he would be short only twenty gold pieces of what he would receive in any case.

Yet I did not fail to see, amidst my dark forebodings, that he might as easily keep for himself the eighty pieces I had already given him, get eighty-five more for carrying out his bargain, and simply order his assistants to spare Draccus. So I found myself hoping he would turn out to be a big rascal instead of a small one.

Gisbo, tall and straight in his scarlet cloak, was standing close up front with other Aristocrats. Mago was just back of the inner circle. As I looked over the crowd, I could not see Misdes anywhere. Morbal was some distance back, on his own feet for a change, not daring to brook the displeasure of the crowd, as I had done, by bringing an elephant into the square. At the outer rim I caught occasional glimpses of the Spaniard, whose face had a strange way of magnetizing my attention.

There were fifteen victims, fifteen innocent people picked up and fed to the fires of Moloch, most of them children. Draccus was saved until the last, prolonging my suspense, and intensifying it amidst the abominable rites that sickened me beyond aught I had seen on the battlefields.

The god's hands and arms were manipulated by chains. One of these went from each of his wrists over each shoulder. Two men worked at each chain. As the two chains were pulled down, the elongated arms and forearms lifted, and the hands moved closer together. When the slope became steep enough, the victim rolled down into the stomach opening . . . and that was the end.

Four of Moloch's soldiers led out Draccus onto the loading platform at a level with the god's great arms. He was too proud to let these cruel Carthaginians see any evidence of fear upon his countenance. They brought forth a black mask for his face and a black robe for his body. He waved them aside.

"I do not need them," he said. "Just as I am in a centurion's uniform, with my eyes open and beholding all."

He asked the soldiers what position they wished him to take. Then he lay himself down across the two outstretched arms of Moloch, with his face upturned to the blue African sky.

He lifted his head enough to be able to look down at me, unaware of what I had done or tried to do. *"Vale, Agenor! Vale!"* he called.

I hardly dared to call back, there was such a choking in my voice and a wetness in my eyes. I was now sure the high pontiff had played fast and loose with me. He was standing close to Gisbo. On his face I saw nothing but the unrelenting, inevitable processes of Moloch.

"Good-by, Draccus," I answered in a broken voice, and I gave Old Anak the sign to utter a mournful trumpet.

As one adjusting himself to a couch, Draccus lay back down across Moloch's two arms, which held him as they had the children in an attitude of parental tenderness. The idol's arms were still extended out level as the centurion lay there.

The four men at the chains began to pull. But the chains seemed to be caught. The hands, the forearms, the arms did not lift. They remained immovable. The four men pulling, called out to the five priests as if in surprise and concern: "The chains will not yield to our strength. The god will not comply."

The five priests spoke to the high pontiff: "The chains are fast. Moloch will not receive the Roman."

The high pontiff held out both hands toward the people and spoke to them in announcement and rebuke: "The Roman is unacceptable to Moloch as a sacrifice. The god is offended by this offering of an alien. Let the man go free."

The soldiers assisted him from the arms onto the platform. He stood there for a moment less in relief than in bewilderment.

"Come to us, Draccus," I called, "to me and to Anak!" He made his way down from the platform and through the crowd to where we stood. The people pressed back from him as he passed as from one contaminated. Old Anak held up a leg, I reached down my hand to clasp the centurion's, and he sprang up behind me.

"The unclean Roman!" shouted the populace. "Away with the unclean Roman!"

At this moment I felt a tug at my foot and looked down into the face of the Spaniard. His appearance was ill-timed and embarrassing, for everybody was looking at us on account of the outcries against Draccus. Gisbo was looking most intently of all, not at Draccus but at the Spaniard.

"The letter," said the Spaniard, "I have the letter for Hannibal."

"Not now," I said, for I saw Gisbo starting toward us. "Later at the elephant stables. Not now. Gisbo is coming."

"Gisbo!" he cried, and quit the elephant's side and pressed back through the crowd and was soon out of sight.

"The chains are fast. Moloch will not receive the Roman"

"Who was the Spaniard?" demanded Gisbo, coming up. "Who was the Spaniard addressing you and what did he say?"

"He said he used to know Scarbas. He was asking about Scarbas."

"What else?" His breath came fast, and his erect, rigid body, ordinarily under complete control, was shaking. He was gripped by some emotion, the nature of which I could not tell, whether suspense or anger or fear. In his upset condition he crowded closer to the elephant than he had ever been before and was less aware of him. Two or three times the elephant's trunk had collided with him. It happened again just before he started to leave me. He hit the trunk a hard blow near the tip, and another, and a third, in a kind of frenzy. Old Anak brought his trunk against Gisbo's side and knocked him to the pavement, and, to my horror there in the public square, was lifting one great foot to plant it on Gisbo's fallen body.

"Anak!" I shouted, and just in time to arrest that trampling.

"The elephant is a killer," yelled the crowd. "He is not safe to be on the streets of Carthage! Away with the dangerous elephant! Away with the unclean Roman!"

Three policemen came up, one of them declaring bluntly: "The killer elephant is under arrest and must be taken at once from the square."

Morbal was not far behind them. He came up puffing and announced himself: "Officers, I am Morbal, chief elephant keeper of Carthage. Here are my credentials. I will have my trained men take the animal to the elephant stables and will keep him in confinement there until formal orders are issued."

By this time Mago had also appeared and I appealed to him.

"Let him be taken now," Mago advised. "I will see the Suffetes tomorrow and get him released. The people are indignant and it is best to get him out of sight. Turn him over to Morbal's men to be taken to the stables and let Draccus go with him."

The next day he was not released, nor the next. Mago went to the Suffetes as he said he would but Gisbo had been there before him. They declared the elephant to be dangerous and he was to be detained in Carthage. He would be kept in the stables for a while. Then, if Morbal did not pronounce him cured, he would be executed.

"I know how you feel, Agenor," said Mago. "But it can't be helped. Nothing more can be done about it."

About a week later Morbal showed me the order he had received from the Suffetes:

To Morbal, Head Elephant Keeper, Greetings and Directions:

Furnish, as soon as possible for the army of Hannibal in Italy, to be delivered to him at Capua by the fleet of Admiral Bomilcar, forty elephants. Ten of these are to be of the largest size, but specific exception is made of the animal called Bostar. Twenty are to be of the middle size. Ten are to be of the smaller size, but none under thirty years of age.

By Order of the Suffetes of Carthage
On Decree of the Senate

Supplementary to Above: Owing to the detention in Carthage of the animal called Anak, on grounds of being dangerous, it is ordered that the animal called Bostar be sent in his place, over and above the forty as hereinbefore specified.

The Suffetes
For the Senate

"Morbal," I asked, "are you going with the elephants and have charge of them under Hannibal?"

"No, no, Agenor. I cannot be spared from the big herd here."

"But these just eat and do nothing. The ones there fight. They're more important."

My estimate of values nettled him a little. "I tell you I can't be spared," he repeated.

"Will Carthalo go, then?"

"I need him. He can't be spared either."

I didn't press the matter further because a vast buoyancy sprang up within me. Could it be that Hannibal meant to put me in charge of the whole forty-one and use the old drivers?

I did not have to travel about on foot. Bostar was turned over to me at once. But I still left the wide money belt around the prodigious waist of Old Anak for safekeeping, knowing that no thief could get at it there.

Misdes, whom I saw in the Square of Kinisdo, told me I was to leave in a week for Capua—at two hours after nightfall on Friday evening. Mago was being sent to Spain to raise the troops there. Gisbo and I would be the first ones to depart, in a forty-oar ship, taking a portion of the money voted by the Senate, and towing Bostar in a flatboat. Misdes would come later with Admiral Bomilcar's main fleet.

This made it necessary for me to act without further delay on plans I had turned over repeatedly in my mind.

"Carthalo," I said that evening, "Old Anak is being detained unjustly. He has never shown hostility toward anyone except Gisbo and always with good cause toward him. You, as a trained elephant man, know he is not dangerous."

"No, not now, Agenor. Not at all now, I should say. But, tell me, did anything ever happen to his right tusk?"

"Two things in the Alps. A big stone fell on it. And he had

to dig his tusks in the ice to keep from sliding over a precipice. Why do you ask?"

"Haven't you noticed how he spares that tusk when he can and shakes his head when he accidentally jars it? An abscess might be forming at the roots. It's something to be aware of."

"But he isn't dangerous now?"

"No, not in my opinion."

"Well, Carthalo, since that is so, I want you to take a hundred gold pieces to enable you to retire to a farm on the Bagradas River when you grow old. There are fifty elephant keepers. Give each of them two pieces so all will be involved and none can report. I will leave at two hours after nightfall on Friday evening, just a week from today. Is Morbal likely to be around the stables at that hour?"

"Not one chance in a hundred. He quits work early and is seldom here anymore in the evenings."

"Very well. Two of your men will bring Old Anak to the dock about five or ten minutes before time to leave. We don't want to have him around any longer beforehand than is necessary on account of the danger of his being recognized. I will be waiting. Paint a long scar on his flank like the one on Bostar. Have your men address him as Bostar. Bring him to me, put him on the flatboat, say good-by to him, all as if he is Bostar. I will do the rest."

"But Morbal in the morning? He will soon discover that Old Anak has been taken in place of Bostar. What then?"

"Declare that with bold cunning I passed him off to everybody as Bostar, with no one dreaming of such a thing. Or give Morbal some other plausible explanation. The fifty keepers will confirm whatever you tell him."

"What if he reports it to the authorities, and they send out a fast ship to bring you back?"

"He's not likely to go that far. He's very fond of Bostar and will be glad not to lose him; he doesn't care for Old Anak and will consider him a good riddance."

"It can be arranged," said Carthalo.

We shook hands upon it, but to bind things a little tighter and avoid later compunctions, I took him with me to the money belt and counted out his hundred gold pieces, adding ten more for good measure.

Though I had gone much about the town, I hadn't seen the Spaniard since the day of the sacrifice. I had often thought of him and often wondered why he never brought the letter. The mention of Gisbo seemed to have frightened him permanently and entirely away. But two evenings later, while I was visiting with ten or fifteen of the drivers, the man at the gate brought word that a Spaniard wanted to see me.

As I approached him, he stood nervously darting swift looks behind him every second or so. "The letter," he said, with panting breath. "I cannot talk now. I cannot tarry." He put the document into my hands and, without another word, took to his heels.

The envelope was sealed. Its superscription said: "To Hannibal, to be opened by him alone. In care of Agenor of the Elephants."

I went to Old Anak's stall, unlaced the money belt, and placed the letter inside the buckskin pouch.

The next morning the body of the dead Spaniard, with a spear through it, was found on the Mappals Road out toward the catacombs.

EIGHTEEN

Draccus and I, along with kidnapped Anak, were snugly aboard the raft, or flatboat, when Gisbo arrived, almost on the dot of two hours after nightfall, not more than two minutes before the small ship was due to depart. Everything so far had gone off without a hitch, but we couldn't help feeling a little nervous and uneasy, especially lest Gisbo should make a close inspection.

So we had lost no time in having our substitute tusker lie down on a soft pallet of straw after he was loaded.

Gisbo, in high good humor and accompanied by a group of aristocratic friends seeing him off, passed by us and merely said: "Agenor, your new elephant—what's his name, oh, yes, Bostar—has already gone to bed, I see."

He stepped from the dock onto the deck of the small ship, whose oarsmen were ready to row and whose captain immediately began to call the roll.

"First mate and crew."

"First mate, cook, two sailors, and forty oarsmen, all here, sir."

"General Gisbo."

"Here, captain."

He raised his voice a little: "Agenor of Hannibal's army."

227

"Present on the flatboat, sir."

"Draccus, the Roman, of Hannibal's army."

"Hic sum." The words slipped out as the reflex of old Roman roll calls. Immediately he added in Carthaginian: "Present, sir."

"Bostar, the elephant."

"Here, sir," I answered.

Gisbo asked the captain about the treasure voted by the Senate. "We were to take a twentieth at this time. It should be two million silver pieces."

"That is the amount, sir, carefully stowed away."

As we got out of the smooth harbor into the undulating sea, I leaned over the rear bulwark of the raft, with my back to Draccus and the elephant, and contemplated that whole peninsula of lamplit city from which the fresh rowers were rapidly pushing us—mighty and magnificent Carthage with seven hundred thousand souls and I, Agenor, with only one feeble soul. It gave me a feeling of humility and unimportance. Cities were powerful and splendid, and armies, but individual man was small and weak and plaintive. And then, in quick denial of these reflections, I thought of Hannibal, greater than cities, greater than armies, having within himself a majesty beyond that of multitudes.

Draccus came up and touched one of my elbows there upon the bulwark. "Agenor, sir, you had better speak to him. He wants to get up. Old Anak wants—"

"Ssh! By the dust of the dunes," I whispered in alarm, "never say that word, Draccus, never. Say Bostar, nothing but Bostar."

"But, Agenor, sir," he whispered back, "he doesn't pay any attention. How are we going to manage?"

"By guiding his trunk, by showing him, by the staff. We

have to. Watch your tongue, Draccus. Don't ever make that slip again."

In the days that followed, Old Anak must have thought it strange that his name had died so utterly upon our lips. He must have thought us slightly demented, the way we kept calling him Bostar. I know he was homesick for the old familiar address in rebuke, endearment, and command. As far as he was concerned, our interminable "Bostars" fell upon empty air. We were often put to extremities to get his attention and obedience.

It was about three hundred and fifty miles to Capua, Hannibal's new headquarters, on the same side of Italy as Rome and a hundred miles southeast of it. Our route was to be past the western end of Sicily.

While there was no room in the ship for so huge a passenger as the elephant, sufficient space was there for Draccus and me. We mainly preferred the raft. I could indulge this preference as I pleased, but not Draccus.

At daylight the first morning, the ship's captain called out: "The Roman is wanted. He will be cook's assistant in the galley."

"*Coquus non sum,*" said Draccus to me. "I am no cook."

"You don't have to be a cook to be a cook's assistant," I replied.

Two members of the crew rowed a small boat back to us, Draccus got in, and I saw little of him the rest of the voyage during the daytime. He was allowed to sleep on the raft, but he was so dog-tired by bedtime that he fell off into a toiler's slumber and into Roman dreams without much time for conversation. I spent part of my time on the ship, part on the raft.

The flatboat was attached to the ship by a towrope as big

as my wrist and about sixty feet long. It was this separation
that made the small boat necessary as a means of transportation
back and forth between the two.

Gisbo continued in the most obliging attitude of friendship
toward me. I realized this was due to his belief that Old Anak
was left behind and gone for good from the Carthaginian
army. This had been the barrier between us and now it was
removed. I think he had come to accept at nearly full value
my assurances that the Spaniard's conversation had been about
Scarbas and nothing else of importance. Still, he had some
lingering doubts on the subject. Or, rather, he wished to probe
me to the bottom as to what I might know about the man or
have learned from him.

One early afternoon he got in the small boat all by himself
and came back to me. He began to talk divertingly on the
amount of red color one saw in Carthage, and hadn't I
noticed it, from the red chariot wheels to the red flamingoes
in the lake—why, his own red cloak which made him so conspicuous in Italy rendered him almost unnoticeable in such a
scarlet-loving town. From this beginning, he gradually worked
the subject around to the Spaniard.

He had first spoken from the small boat, which he held
alongside with his hand. He now tied the boat up and boarded
the raft, standing in the gateway of the gunwale at the forward end. Then he leaned up against the elephant's shoulder
in a relaxed way, with his feet crossed. He threw his arm over
the elephant's trunk. He did all this, of course, thinking it was
Bostar and so having no fear of him or prejudice against him.
His fine garments and white hands didn't mind the contact
here. His delicate nostrils were not offended.

I sensed uneasily the danger of this familiarity. Though well meant, it exposed Gisbo no less to any actual resentment Old Anak might feel toward one who had irritated and struck him so frequently in the past.

"You have a wonderful elephant here, Agenor," he said. "I understand he was the most gigantic among the three hundred at Carthage, and I can't well see how any living thing can grow to greater bigness. A supreme replacement, Agenor, of the other one and not savage like him."

All this time he was leaning against the elephant, hugging his trunk with his arm and tracing his fingers along the creases of his hide. It was a new spectacle to me, as you can imagine, to see Gisbo making a toy and a plaything out of an elephant.

He now did something which filled me with misgivings and alarm but against which I dared not cry out. He took hold of the right tusk with a grip of his right hand and began to shake it, as one might do with the horn of an ox, and I suppose for the same reason, to see whether by this handle he could move the whole head.

Though Gisbo was playful and innocent, it meant exactly the same to Old Anak. This irritating man was at it again and in a very tender spot, about which I myself might not have known except for Carthalo.

The elephant let out a trumpet of pain and resentment and hit his tormentor across the chest with his trunk. He brought this back against Gisbo's side. Through the front opening of the bulwarks, Gisbo toppled over into the water as I cried out: "No, Anak, no! Anak, stop!"

And Gisbo, catching hold of the big towrope in his fall, heard the true name I uttered in command and restraint. In my excitement I had betrayed the elephant.

"Anak!" he exclaimed in fierce condemnation. "It is Anak,

you young cur! You brought that accursed elephant! You brought him by fraud! You wicked young whelp, you exposed me to his savagery! You exposed me to his foulness!"

His indignation and anger at me and my trickery were greater than his humiliation at being thrown into the water and his discomfort at being wet.

"Untie the boat and shove it to me!" he ordered. I did so. He climbed in, all dripping, rowed back to the ship, and changed his clothes.

What would be the outcome of this unfortunate occurrence, I could not conjecture. It weighed upon me heavily and ominously.

But there rose across the smooth sea a greater menace than the one from Gisbo.

A sudden storm came upon us late one afternoon as we were nearing Sicily but not yet in sight of its shores. All that had been so benignant and favorable was changed to distress for the small ship towing an elephant there in the Mediterranean. The mild breezes, the blue sky, the evenness where the forty oars dipped—these were transformed into a violent wind, a black, roily overhead, a great, boisterous sea. The lightning flashed like serpents' tongues, the thunder roared in prolonged reverberations, and the waves lifted us to high crests to lower us at once into deep ravines. Sometimes the ship would be upon one summit, the flatboat on the one behind, and the towrope would stretch taut across a chasm. The two waves spreading, would pull with such force that I looked to see the stern torn from the ship.

It was daytime and Draccus was not with me. As the elements raged so terribly I was alone with the elephant. He needed no urging to lie down. His bulk would slide as we were uptilted or hung sidewise upon the steeps of a wave. Now his back would strike against the bulwarks of the flatboat, now his projecting feet, his head, his rear, and the timbers would groan and crack so I was filled with trepidation that they would give way and boy and elephant would be pitched into the tumultuous sea.

For anchorage I clung to the money belt about Old Anak and crouched at his belly so his legs would protect me from the tremendous collisions with the bulwarks.

In the fury of sound and motion the captain was shouting at me across the sixty feet that separated us: "We must cut loose the raft. The towing in this storm will wreck us all. We will send the small boat. It is dangerous, but we will send it. We must cut free to protect the ship."

After all the things I had done to save Old Anak, was I to desert him now, and ever after, in my lonely hours and in my dreams, have visions of the fishes swimming through his skeleton in the bottom of the deep?

I believed the ship could live through it. The Carthaginians who had built the tough bulwarks of the flatboat and who had built the ship, had builded well and with a knowledge that such violence would assail their work. I believed the captain was timid, even that Gisbo was urging him to his final and irrevocable riddance of the elephant.

"No!" I shouted back. "I will not desert the elephant. If the ship can live at all, it can live by keeping the flatboat."

"You presumptuous cub," he yelled, "telling a sea captain what he can do or can't with a ship! The rowers are demanding it. And we cannot endanger the treasure of the army— two million silver pieces for an elephant."

This was the voice of the captain but the argument of Gisbo.

So I believed and demanded across the sixty feet of furious water: "You must continue the rowing."

"We are compelled to cut loose," declared the captain. "Without delay. We will send the boat."

"No!" I repeated. I thought my obstinacy would overcome their determination and that the captain would not dare, nor yet Gisbo, to maroon me there upon the wild, torn bosom of the stormy sea.

"We must cut loose the raft," insisted the captain. "And we will not leave you by your own willful desire in this danger. We will come and take you by force."

This was a contingency I hadn't counted on.

"Come, Agenor," Draccus appealed to me. "It is the only way."

To both of them I called back my loud and unchangeable refusal. Nevertheless, a practical thought was working in my head. The small boat! Having it, I could remain with Old Anak into the utmost duration of hope. If we couldn't ride out the storm together, I could take to the small boat in the last desperate moments and save myself.

To this thought and to the captain's ultimatum I fitted a proposal which I hurled across to him: "Leave me the small boat!"

The captain consulted with Gisbo. I could not hear what they said.

"Yes!" agreed the captain. "We will arrange it so. But we must hurry. The rowers complain; they clamor for relief; their strength is not equal to the resistance and jerks. Come for the boat. Come hand over hand along the towrope. No sailor will bring you the boat and return in this way. You must come and get it."

This struck me as a proposal of treachery. After they got me on the ship they would hold me there by force. I accused them of having this intention. The captain declared on his honor I would not be held. I believed Gisbo was advising him to let me have my way.

My two hands gripped the towrope. A wave slapped my face. Sometimes, in the passage across, there was a mountain of water in turmoil over my head. Sometimes I hung onto the rope in mid-air, dangling over a deep trough.

The captain made me sign a statement he had written in a shaky hand. His log book and papers would have to be in good order when he reported Agenor missing.

He went through an oral procedure in further protection of himself when he should stand before stern Admiral Bomilcar.

"Do you, Agenor of Hannibal's army, finally refuse to come?" he asked me.

"I refuse, sir," I said.

He asked the first mate, Gisbo, and Draccus if this refusal were given in their presence and each said this was so.

This formality and precautionary evidence angered the rowers, who uttered hoarse complaints with breath they ill could spare. "By the fires of Moloch, do not dally. Free us at once from that burden. Free us or we all perish." Their purple veins swelled along their hairy arms like welts as they pulled. When there was the counter force of a wave against the flat-boat, forty bodies tensed in unified exertion, forty blades bent under the strain, more strength came in the extremity of strength, but the ship stood stalled. "Hurry!" they urged. "The raft frustrates our toil."

But the captain made them wait while he added one more vocal affidavit: "Do you all three bear witness that upon your advice the captain gave the small boat to Agenor of Hannibal's army, at the boy's insistent request, for his safety, and as an alternative to forcing him from the raft?"

All three affirmed this. I got in the boat.

"*Vale,* Agenor! *"Vale!"* said Draccus.

I made my way across and with considerable difficulty transferred myself to the flatboat. I had scarcely completed the knot in fastening it up when the captain, at the stern of the ship, leaned over with a knife and severed the towrope.

The boy and the elephant were castaways upon the stormy sea—derelicts amidst forces so vast and malignant as to make the big elephant in the flatboat seem as puny as a fly upon a window sill.

More and ever more ridges intervened between us and the ship until it soon passed out of sight. We fared not worse, if anything better, from our well-ballasted craft's being able to adjust itself freely to the mighty and changing convolutions of the sea. Hour after hour we drifted and tossed. I lay down between his legs, holding onto the money belt. In endless succession came the rocking, the lifting and falling, the upending, the sidewise suspension on watery declivities. Waves rose up alongside, curled above us, fell dashing in our faces, and inundated the deck. Ever the noises assailed our ears, some short and quick, some drawn out, prolonged—the thunder rolling and rolling to burst in great claps, the heavings of the undulant sea, the wind with its violence fed from vast distances, the slap and swish of waves against the flatboat, and that cracking and straining of the bulwarks as Old Anak slid about.

In time I became aware of a slight cessation of the sound and tumult. I looked up, at the dark heavens into patches with stars shining through. The night gradually grew clear, the force of the wind abated, but not immediately did the sea recover from its mighty agitation.

The clouds had now moved entirely away from over the face of the moon. This showed me, and my ears confirmed it, a fresh danger terrible to recognize. There was land, there was Sicily. But it was not a flat coast to cause rejoicing. It was bluffs and headlands against which the surf rolled and dashed and thundered.

Under the moon, my eyes could make out nothing but a continuance of cliffs everywhere edging the sea. It meant certain destruction of the raft, certain death for the boy and the elephant.

I unlaced the money belt, took out the Spaniard's message, and put it in my pocket. The money could stay. I had no time to waste. When the body of the drowned elephant was driven in time upon some flat Sicilian beach, the natives would find this belt and have wealth for once in their meager lives.

"*Vale,* Anak! *Vale!*" I said, for that good-by seemed to me the most mournful, the most suitable that could be uttered at the parting of two friends, when either or both went forth into the unknown.

I began to untie the knot of the rope holding the small boat. I did not finish. The boat had been hammered to pieces against the side of the raft. I had been foolish and thoughtless in leaving it there, close up, at the front. I should have attached it at the stern with a long painter, using some of the towrope. The craft was completely wrecked and useless.

Out there, unchanged, were the bluffs and the pounding surf. Old Anak and I would take them together. For us, it was facing destruction inseparably now. For both alike, hope was at an end.

I put the Spaniard's letter back in the money belt. If the elephant were found beached somewhere along the coast, peradventure the sealed document would be saved and eventually reach Hannibal.

From doing this I looked toward the shore in surprise to see that we were being drawn in little if at all toward the rocks. We were moving along the shore rather than into it. The tide was apparently not yet running strongly at the flood. And the wind was blowing diagonally from the land. I bethought me of a way to use this latter fact. With much urging and prodding, I got Old Anak to his feet. His huge expanse would serve to some degree as a sail. I arranged him diagonally for the best effect of the offshore blowing.

The darkness had paled out into dawn when my straining eyes beheld the first long stretch of flat, wide beach. I made Old Anak lie down again. Within half an hour we waded out of the surf upon the dry shore of Sicily.

In the landing, Old Anak wrenched or jarred his right tusk again, either in being thrown head down into the sand or in some collision with the flatboat when he was pitched off in the first big roller on the shallows. He carried his head slightly toward the left side and pulled away if I reached out to take hold of the tusk.

A peasant's hut was a short distance down the beach. Standing in front of it and watching us, were a man, a woman, a boy about my size, and two girls of younger age. As we approached, the family huddled together in timidity and the man cried out, "Hannibal's elephant!"

They all fled into the house and barred the door, in front of which I stood calling out that we were friends but without response. I took ten gold pieces out of the money belt, went to a window, and tossed these in amidst the cowering family, saying: "I want food for the elephant and for myself. I have money. I will pay."

After a little delay, the man came out. Then the children ran to him and clung to his legs. In a short time they were no longer afraid.

There in Sicily I was liberal with gold, knowing the more of it I spent the happier General Samnis would be. I suppose such high wages were never paid in that district before or since. The man gathered in his relatives and neighbors, about fifteen men in all. They repaired the flatboat and towed Old Anak and me to Capua.

Near that place, one evening after everybody had given us up for dead, we appeared at an outer sentry post of Hannibal's camp. I asked to be taken at once to Hannibal.

NINETEEN

"W<small>HY, AGENOR</small>!" <small>EXCLAIMED HANNIBAL'S SERGEANT.</small> "<small>ARE YOU</small> real, or is it the ghost of a boy and the ghost of an elephant?"

"I must see the supreme commander," I replied.

"He is in his tent."

"Is he alone? I must see him alone."

"No one is with him."

Hannibal received me gladly: "Well, if it isn't Agenor, come back to us from the bottom of the sea!"

"Sir," I said, "I came as quickly as I could. I lost no time. I thought this might be important." And I handed him the water-stained but still sealed message which the Spaniard had given me.

He read it, put it down on his table in front of him, picked it up and read it again. His face looked stern and stormy. He got up and paced the tent floor that was thickly covered with rugs from some rich Roman's house in Campania. He sat down and beat his fingers upon the table. He looked at me.

"Agenor, did General Gisbo ever try to get rid of Old Anak?"

"Several times, sir."

"Why didn't you tell me?"

"I tried to tell you back there at the Trebia after Scarbas was killed. Do you remember, sir? You silenced me."

"So I did, but I wish you to tell me all now."

"At New Carthage, sir, General Gisbo irritated the elephant, wanting to make you think him dangerous so he would be left behind."

"Yes, I recall that evening after the debate."

"He tried to have Old Anak drowned while crossing the Rhone. That was what Gisbo made me promise not to tell. I had never kept anything back from Scarbas before. It made me feel very miserable and unclean. It was the first time, sir, I had ever felt that way on the inside."

"Dark and unworthy secrets, and not being aboveboard with those who trust you, always make you feel dirty on the inside, Agenor."

"I know, sir, and very wretched. The next time was in the Alps, when the big rocks tumbled down from the heights, but the rocks went over our heads—except one hit Old Anak's right tusk, which I think has an abscess starting at the roots now, and Carthalo thinks so."

"Oh, yes, Carthalo, Morbal's chief assistant. He was with Hasdrubal in Spain for about a year and did excellent work with the elephants there. Do you think, Agenor, that Carthalo would make a good head elephant man for the army, to handle the forty new ones we are getting?"

Plain was his meaning, plain especially to one who had been hugging dreams that a fifteen-year-old boy might become headkeeper. But I needed to be honest about Carthalo. "He knows elephants, sir. Just in a little while he found out that Old Anak had that sore tusk."

"We were speaking of the rocks," said Hannibal. "What made you think Gisbo had anything to do with them?"

"A Gaul who had been throwing them down was killed and tumbled down himself, right where we were, and on a finger, as he lay sprawling there, smashed and dead, was one of Gisbo's costly rings. Gisbo explained it later in a plausible way."

"Was the elephant let alone after that?"

"No, sir, there was the time when Gisbo and his horse went over the brink. I think he deliberately caused his horse to collide with Old Anak to start him slipping. But the elephant dug his tusks in the ice and stopped himself, though giving another awful wrench to his tusk."

"Was that all?"

"All for a while, sir. But, after the Battle of Trasymene, Gisbo was the one to suggest sending me as a spy to Rome. He believed I would never get back. You see, sir, he wanted riddance of me also because I knew about his spite against Old Anak and stood in his way. I was never able to put my finger on it exactly, nor was Scarbas, but I believe Old Anak knows some secret of Gisbo's."

"Yes, Agenor, a terrible secret of Gisbo's, but we will come to that later. Did that end Gisbo's efforts against Old Anak?"

"For a good while, sir. But on this trip to Carthage he was the one who spoke to the Suffetes, before General Mago could reach them, and caused Old Anak to be held there as dangerous, but I got him out anyway by bribing Carthalo and the drivers with the money General Samnis sent with me for just such things."

"And you found the Carthaginians responsive to bribes, Agenor?"

"Oh, yes, sir. General Samnis was wrong about the Romans but he was right about the Carthaginians. Even the high pontiff of Moloch. He was the worst of all. But he carried out his part, I'll say that for him."

"They generally do," observed Hannibal. "There is a kind of dark honor about it—a very strict code about staying bought, which is not always practiced by amateurs . . . I suppose Gisbo's seeing the Suffetes was his last act against Old Anak up to date?"

"Yes, sir, except I am sure he encouraged the captain to leave the elephant on the flatboat, and then, at my obstinacy, both of us."

"You were wrong in that situation, Agenor. It has turned out to advantage, and I rejoice that Old Anak was saved along with you. Several of your headstrong and individual performances have ended well. The danger is in your thinking they always will. Some day they are bound to get you and perchance others into a great deal of trouble."

"Yes, sir."

"The Spaniard in Carthage, the one who sent this letter, did you have a chance to talk with him?"

"Not in any proper sense, sir. Just a few words at three different times, but getting no information. Sight of him seemed to have a strange, disturbing effect on Gisbo, and the man fled once at the mere mention of Gisbo's name. He was found murdered on the Mappals Road the next morning after giving me the letter."

"Thank you, Agenor, for all you have told me. It will be helpful in what I am about to do. Don't leave. I want you to stay. I still need you. But promise not to say a word about the things you will hear in this tent."

"I promise, sir."

He summoned the sergeant: "Have General Gisbo brought here. Have him brought here at once. And send a man to General Samnis to get the little slip of paper which Scarbas left."

"Sergeant," I requested, "will you have Draccus fetched to get the elephant? He is tired and needs attention."

Hannibal turned to me while we waited: "Agenor, would you say I have reached the proper age to die?"

"The Romans, none others, would think so, sir. You are only thirty-one."

"You have it correctly, Agenor."

"There are three ages, sir, I never forget: yours, mine, Old Anak's—thirty-one, fifteen, eighty-nine."

"Eighty-nine! The gods are stingier in dealing out years to humans than to elephants. In Anak's span one could get through with his work. But thirty-one! Yet at thirty-three, Alexander had conquered the earth. If I were snuffed out to-morrow, Agenor, would aught of me echo down the world, do you think? Given two more years to equal Alexander's, with proud Rome under my feet, would the tongues of generations pronounce three names—Alexander, Pyrrhus, Hannibal, or perchance Hannibal, Alexander, Pyrrhus? But tomorrow, Agenor, I am thinking of tomorrow; if then, would his name be only a whisper, faint and brief, upon the lips of men?"

Neither the cause nor the meaning of these dismal reflections was anywise clear to me. I had no chance to attempt an answer, for General Gisbo was announced and was brought immediately in by the sergeant.

He gave a little start when he saw me sitting there in the tent, but he said never a word. He stood straight and tall in

front of the table and addressed the supreme commander: "Sir,
you summoned me?"

Hannibal spoke to him bluntly: "Sit down, Gisbo. I have
a letter for you to hear." And he began to read:

To Hannibal—

Hearken to the truth from Sanchez, the Spaniard. It is everywhere said and everywhere believed that a Spanish slave killed
Hasdrubal, the supreme commander, five years ago. This man
was accused, arrested, condemned, executed. But he was innocent.

From Sanchez, the Spaniard, receive now the true account. Hasdrubal was boar hunting in the Spanish forest, he and his Spanish
slave alone, riding the big elephant Anak. Hasdrubal felled a boar.
He left the slave to watch it while he rode to camp to send carriers
out. There the man remained, there he was found. But they said
he had returned after killing his master a mile away. He and he
alone had ridden forth with Hasdrubal. Who else was there to do
it? Yet there was another. Sanchez saw. The elephant saw.

Listen to the grim truth which Sanchez tells. Upon that day I also
hunted in the Spanish forest. I was about to step out into a rocky
clearing when I drew back and remained motionless and concealed. There across the open space Hasdrubal was riding the
elephant on the way to camp. Gisbo on his horse came up from
behind and cast his spear, straight and sure, through Hasdrubal's
body. He fell to the ground. The elephant stood with his head
over his dead master—and looked at the murderer as if identifying
him and fastening him in his remembrance forever. Then he
trumpeted loud and accusingly. Whereupon Gisbo raced away
upon his horse. The ground was stony and left no hoofprints.

Naught but truth comes from Sanchez, the Spaniard. I left the
scene as fast as my legs would carry me, since to be caught there
would couple me with the crime. After two miles, it must have
been, two miles of my rapidest running, I came out upon a trail,

to see Gisbo ahead, riding slowly now. As I emerged from the bordering brush, the rattle of this attracted his tense and guilty hearing. He questioned me whence I came, and made me walk beside his horse, and turned me over to soldiers to be confined.

Believe the truth which Sanchez writes. At nightfall I was sent away with other friends of the slave, all for being members of a conspiracy. This was ordered by Gisbo, in pretended outrage at the Hasdrubal murder. I, an educated man, became a slave in a silver mine. For nearly five years I worked under harsh overseers, until a few months since. But always I stole a little silver and concealed it. With this I made my escape. I joined a ship as an oarsman and came to Carthage, where I deserted.

This true record from Sanchez, the Spaniard, may never be made known. Gisbo recognized me in Carthage, in the Square of Kharmoun, on the day of the sacrifices to Moloch. He has since had me watched and followed. I may not be able to deliver this message to Hannibal's boy at the elephant stables.

Sanchez, the Spaniard, attests the truth of all he has said. Gisbo killed Hasdrubal, the supreme commander. My own eyes beheld it, and the eyes of the elephant. He was never sure that I saw. He knew unforgettably that the elephant did. He sent me to the silver mines, suspicious that I had seen, because I was running from the direction of the murder—where the big elephant had looked at him as if identifying him and fastening him in his remembrance forever.

Sanchez, the Spaniard

Meanwhile, the sergeant had brought in and put upon the table the small slip of paper which General Samnis had sent.

Hannibal now picked it up. "Here is something else," he said. "We found it in the pocket of dead Scarbas back there on the Trebia. I will read it also:

Gisbo

Old Anak

H——

That last name was never finished. In the mind of Scarbas some discovery was struggling to come out. You had set him to guessing hard, Gisbo, by your rancor toward the elephant. He had probed and probed into what was behind it. Now he was nearly sure, nearly but not quite sure, being a man who all his life had relied on definite facts. His fingers hesitated, like his mind, and wrote H and stopped. He did not have final proof yet. The factual and honest Scarbas did not finish writing the name which he strongly suspected, which was circumstantially evident, but which he was not certain of beyond peradventure. That name, Gisbo, belonged to the third of those there in the Spanish forest on that dark and criminal day five years ago. It was the name of Hasdrubal."

"It could not possibly have been Hamilcar, or Hannibal, or Hanno?" cynically inquired Gisbo. "There is no absence of Carthaginian names beginning with H."

"We will let it pass for the moment," said Hannibal. "Repeat to him what you told me, Agenor, in detail, fully."

I did so.

"Now," said Hannibal, "we have the testimony of the Spaniard, the testimony of Scarbas, the testimony of Agenor. The elephant is dumb and cannot speak, but we have his testimony from your malicious relationships with him. I now call upon you, Gisbo, to give the remaining testimony. You are the fifth who knows and can tell, more fully than all the rest."

"I killed him," said Gisbo. "I killed Hasdrubal."

The unhesitant calmness with which he confessed it, surprised Hannibal and it stunned me. Hannibal jumped to his feet and I thought for a moment he would slay Gisbo on the spot. But he sat down again and remained briefly silent until he collected himself.

"He was your friend. He thought you were his. Why?"

"My friend, yes. I was fond of him. I did not kill him for personal reasons but for the welfare of Carthage. You need not be told, Hannibal, that the Aristocratic Party, my party, has been against your father Hamilcar, against your brother-in-law Hasdrubal, against you. They wanted Carthage to be at peace. They wanted to carry on commerce and trade. They saw your family as rash and trouble-making demagogues, leading the country into unnecessary wars. They thought if Hasdrubal were killed, you would be too young—you were only twenty-six—to be made supreme commander. One of themselves would be elected. They intended it would be me. They intended it would be Gisbo. Then there would be peace with Rome. That is why I killed Hasdrubal. You, Hannibal, ought to be able to understand such reasons."

"I understand only that in cold blood you killed Hasdrubal, my brother-in-law, a man I loved, the supreme commander of the Carthaginians. But continue. Why did you pursue the elephant with your enmity?"

"To kill Hasdrubal seemed a duty and a desirable thing. I planned it coolly, carried it out coolly. Then, after the deed was accomplished, I failed to become supreme commander. The memory of my deed destroyed my peace. And every time I saw the elephant I thought of him as the only living thing that had witnessed my act."

"What of the Spaniard?"

"I did not know of a certainty about him. It was only on

the chance of his having been in the neighborhood that I put him out of the way as a slave in the silver mine. I did not consider him seriously or let him trouble my thoughts until I saw him in Carthage. Then I had him followed and killed along the Mappals Road, but too late."

"I understand," observed Hannibal. "All the time it was the elephant you feared? It is most curious. Why did you think any more of him than of the rocks, the watching trees, some other dumb brutes, your horse?"

"Because he seemed so vividly human, because he trumpeted accusingly, as the Spaniard said, and gave me that terrible look as if to remember me always for inescapable revenge. Except for that awful gaze, that awful gaze of judgment, I don't think I would have ever lost my coolness. I had heard tales of how an elephant never forgets a wrong. My intellect told me that in any case it is a dumb brute. It cannot reason in the way of understanding a crime. It certainly cannot report. I knew this intellectually, yet emotionally I carried with me the heavy uneasiness that Old Anak was always looking at me as the killer of Hasdrubal, always recollecting that day in the Spanish forest, always meditating my death with his tusks through me or under his ponderous and pitiless feet. I attributed to him human traits."

"Elephants don't remember in that way," I put in with that ever ready tongue of mine.

"I know, Agenor, and I knew all the time in cold logic, but I couldn't control that obsession which took hold of my senses. By imputing to Old Anak such remembrance, such reasoning, such revenge, I began to irritate and strike him. Then he retaliated to cause the very thing which was at first only in my inflamed imagination."

"And this," asked Hannibal, "made you try several times to get rid of him?"

"Yes, sir, in all the ways Agenor has described. When these clashes did not outlaw him as savage, Agenor became suspicious, which, in turn, made me try to get rid of him too. So one thing has grown out of another in my phobia of Old Anak as my Nemesis. If I had simply left the elephant alone, nothing would have happened."

"Nothing," I chimed in again.

"Is that all?" inquired Hannibal.

"All, sir. And what action do you mean to take? Haven't I served you ably as one of your generals? Hasn't the Purple Band under me done its part fully in every battle?"

"Yes," said Hannibal.

"Have I ever been disloyal to you or to the Carthaginian army, that is, in any important way, outside of these morbid vagaries concerning the elephant?"

"No," said Hannibal.

"Then should it not be overlooked? It was a political offense. It turned out for the welfare of Carthage. It made you supreme commander. It brought us here to conquer Rome. I was but an instrument of destiny. What is one man's life in the welfare of a nation? We recently killed sixty thousand from noon to dusk."

"Proceed," directed Hannibal. "If you have aught else to say, say it, before I pronounce sentence upon you."

"It is in your power to have me executed, Hannibal. But in doing so you will satisfy a doubtful justice and lose the leader of the Purple Band. You, the army, the conquest of Rome, all need my assistance. You have had it in the past, as

you acknowledge. You will continue to have it. Hasdrubal died
for Carthage. How he died should be forgotten."

"But we won't forget it," declared Hannibal. "Tomorrow—
tomorrow at noon—either you die or I do. Prepare for a duel
with me tomorrow."

"Don't think, Hannibal, that I am a suppliant for my life.
You have seen me in enough danger to know that."

"I know," agreed Hannibal.

"This duel is ill-considered. Better to have me executed out-
right. The Carthaginian army will lose the greatest commander
it ever had, the one man who can conquer Rome. It is not to
myself I refer, but to you—for in a duel, Hannibal, I will
surely kill you."

"It is a chance I must take."

"You, Hannibal, have lived in rude camps ever since you
were nine, handling swords roughly. I have been trained to the
sword all my life, as gentlemen are trained. There is a difference. I like not the prospect of killing the greatest general on
earth today. This is not a mature decision. It is prodigally
wasteful of leadership."

"You are some years older than I am, Gisbo."

"Of no importance. I will surely kill you."

"I think it will be the other way," said Hannibal. "But let's
not argue it here. It will all be determined tomorrow at
noon."

"If that is your will, so be it."

"One thing," said Hannibal, "you must do before then—
now. You must write out a confession as the murderer of
Hasdrubal, just the bare facts, leaving out the matter about the
elephant. I will keep it tonight. Tomorrow, before we begin

with the swords, I will give it to you and you can put it in your pocket. If you kill me, you will have it and can destroy it. If I kill you, I will take it from your pocket after you are dead. I will also write out a statement to protect you, in case I fall—that it was in an honorable duel and you were blameless. You will have an equal chance with the other generals of being elected supreme commander. You must swear that no prejudice will ever attach to the boy Agenor for knowing all that he does and he must swear never to breathe a word regarding the matter."

These papers were drawn up and these oaths were taken.

"How the Romans will rejoice," said Gisbo at the last. "How they will rejoice when they know that Hannibal is dead."

"I am not dead yet," replied Hannibal.

When I got to the tent, Draccus was eagerly waiting for me. "Old Anak is in a bad condition, Agenor, sir, come quick! I can't do anything with him. He is very savage and won't let me go near him. It's his injured tusk."

When I approached the elephant, he struck at me with his trunk. He would not allow the tusk to be handled. We soaked cloths in hot water, dropped these at the base of the tusk by means of a stick at first, and finally quieted him.

As we left him, bugles were sounding sleep-time in different parts of the camp. In view of what was appointed for the morrow, the notes fell upon my ears with special sadness and significance.

TWENTY

"It is time to bring the elephant to the supreme commander's tent," Hannibal's sergeant came and told me the next morning. The summons found me ready enough. I had been up since daybreak, my mind made wakeful by the dark events set for this day and by misgivings about Old Anak. The elephant was still listless but gave no evidence of being any longer in pain. I would not now have to tell Hannibal that he was too sick, and too unmanageable in his illness, to take along to the place of the duel. He was needed for a double reason—so that he who had witnessed the assassin's deed in Spain might witness its sequel, and to carry the accoutrements.

I helped the sergeant prepare the baggage and load it. My skin was chilled and moistened by the nature of the three grim parcels that so surely divined the long wakeless silence for a great general or for the greatest general. There were two Carthaginian long-bladed swords, exactly alike. We sheathed them in their scabbards, wrapped them up together, and tied them on. There was a pickaxe and a spade, which we rolled up in a covering to disguise them as we rode through camp. Then the sergeant brought out of the tent a big piece of white woolen cloth, much larger than a blanket. It was a Roman toga from some rich Campanian house, never used, fresh from the

weaver's, and giving off the pleasant odor of new woolen goods.
We folded, wrapped and tied this into a neat bundle.

Such were the things which Old Anak carried—two
weapons to kill with, two implements to dig a grave with, and
a shroud to wind a dead man in.

I climbed up to the neck of Old Anak. Hannibal mounted
his bay horse. From toe to top he was freshly uniformed.
Ordinarily I would have inspected this with delight. It now
made my heart sink. A man may meet life in old clothes but
he dresses up to meet death. The third member of our party
did not keep us waiting beyond the precise moment appointed.

Gisbo came riding up on his white horse whose brushed coat
shone in the morning sun. He was cheerful and smiling, and
it seemed to me he had never looked so handsome before. I
was as glad to note his magnificence as I was cast down to note
Hannibal's, and for the same reason in reverse. He wore his
finest red cloak. On his head was a burnished helmet, topped
by a scarlet plume. On his left fingers were all his costly
rings, with three additional ones now for the battles of Trebia,
Lake Trasymene, and Cannae.

"I am ready, sir," he announced.

They went ahead, the shining white horse and the shining
bay side by side. These two great Carthaginians seemed like
a pair of happy friends riding forth together upon a holiday.
They were talking but I could not catch their words. I, Agenor,
with my own spirit heavy within me like lead, followed some
distance behind on the elephant, toward whatever lonely tryst
had been chosen for this stern pilgrimage.

It was not long before we came to the foot of a high mound
or hill or flat-crowned butte, standing in isolation. The men
directed their horses up this, in single file now along a narrow

trail, Hannibal in front. I followed them to the top, at slower speed than theirs, fearful that the bordering bushes might freshly injure the tender tusk.

From an open summit area, I gazed out over the rich Campanian plains that had given us groaning carts of booty. I looked back at the camp of the Carthaginians, from which, at this distance, the tumult reached my ears only in snatches and faintly. I looked still farther away in the other direction at the Roman camp, whence no noises came but where I could make out indistinctly the blended movements of masses of men and the dust of their marching.

Hannibal and Gisbo sat upon their horses for a little while to watch one camp and then the other. Gisbo pointed toward the Romans: "That camp over there will rejoice at the boon I am compelled to confer upon them this day. How long will it be before their spies report that Hannibal is missing?"

Hannibal answered not at all. He dismounted from his horse, led him over to the edge of the summit, and tethered him to a sapling. Gisbo rode at his heels to a small tree near by and similarly tied up his horse. They walked back together to where I had halted Old Anak, in the open center of the hilltop.

"We'll unload the things," said Hannibal.

Anak kneeled. Hannibal took the package of swords and laid it down where we were. Then he lifted up the tools and carried them over to the base of a tree at the rim of the clearing. Gisbo followed with the bundle of cloth.

"What do I have here?" he inquired.

"A winding-sheet."

"Your own, my great commander. And what do you carry?"

"A pickaxe and a spade."

"To dig an alien pit for the greatest man in the world. But

it would be a pleasant spot, this one we are soon to turn into a cemetery, if it were not Roman soil, offering doubtful sanctity for supreme Carthaginian dust."

Gisbo's constantly taking it for granted that Hannibal was to be the victim of the duel, built up my despair but it did not cause Hannibal to weaken in his resolution. It was Gisbo himself I was to see blench a little as his old phobia returned briefly to clutch him.

"Isn't the elephant going to be removed like the horses?" he asked. "Is the beast to remain here close at hand to watch us?"

"Yes," replied Hannibal. "He will be here as in the Spanish forest. He saw the crime. Let him see the retribution."

Hannibal took out of his pocket Gisbo's confession and gave it to him. Before handing him another slip of paper, he read it aloud:

> This is to certify that General Gisbo killed Hannibal in honorable personal combat and is nowise blamable.
>
> Hannibal
> Witness—Agenor

"Do you, Agenor, hand us the weapons," directed Hannibal. "Give them to us crossed, with the hilts extended from you."

I remounted the elephant, to remain only far enough off not to interfere with the movements of the swordsmen. These, still grandly cloaked and helmeted, ceremoniously took their places in front of each other, though only a boy and an elephant were there to see. The combat about to begin here on the high butte top was all unbeknown to the two big armies, the Carthaginian and the Roman, that lay out there in opposite directions within the sweep of my eyes.

They stood face to face, four cubits apart, each holding the sword to the other in salute.

"There is still time to withdraw, my great commander," said Gisbo.

"Are you ready?" asked Hannibal.

"Ready, sir," said Gisbo.

And upon the instant the two men stood at guard.

I had seen the elephant drivers at their rough swordsmanship to while away the time, but never had I seen anything like this before, in skill or at such high stakes, where the greatest life in the world depended on the movement of a blade.

The action began, and for all my heavy dread of the outcome I could not help responding to the fascination of it all, as I saw the sharp points ever frustrated in going home to their targets, as I saw a danger appear and in a flash miscarry. The blade of one or the other would be turned aside with the sharp clang of metal against metal. As I watched, I could not find what I sought with my eyes—evidence that Hannibal would surely win. Quick he was, and marvelously dexterous, and his great mind was as fast as it was great. But Gisbo was swift, resilient, and efficient in all his rapid energies, unerring in every motion, never wasteful of it. His weapon outspeeded my eyes as he handled it now with the nails of his fingers up, now with them down, as his sword hand alternated from prone to supine in the torsions of his supple wrist. And I will ever remember the grace of him in advances and retreats, in thrusts and lunges. In the latter, time after time, I saw his left leg reaching diagonally out, his extended left arm above it, his right knee straight above his instep. In desperate attacks I would observe him so, firm-footed, poised and balanced, yet easy and immediately ready to change.

There came to me a moment of thanksgiving. The point of Hannibal's sword traveled straight and swift toward Gisbo's heart. Gisbo had not time for retreat or body evasion. Hannibal's thrust could not fail of its target. But Gisbo, in a double circle of the hilt, now with hand prone, now supine, met the blade with his own, once and a second time, and he beat aside the cold death that was entering his heart. This instantaneous motion I recognized as the universal parry practiced in the elephant stables clumsily, and never like this, and known to those awkward swordsmen as the Sicilian Girdle.

Following this, they stood briefly in attitudes of inactive threat, each pair of right-angled feet little more than a half-cubit apart, lower legs rising from the ground as upright as stakes, arms and swords held straight toward each other's breasts. At once they began to maneuver for position. They took lateral steps to the right and left, advanced and retreated, and made passes with the left foot forward of the right and the right past the left backward again, ever weaving in and out and dodging cuts and causing the swords to ring out sharply in collision.

Once more they faced each other dangerously, and this time it was Gisbo's advantage. In that fierce stroke, known as the Thrust of Antioch, his left foot sped past his right, and he aimed at Hannibal's left hip. Hannibal parried, and parried successfully, but Gisbo's right foot now went forward, and he pressed down Hannibal's sword between his own and the ground. Then he threw himself backward. As he did so, he brought his sword across Hannibal's face, and I thought those eyes would never see again. But the point only made a slash across his lower brow. This became at once a red straight line, and then the scarlet wetness began to obscure his vision so that ever and anon he gave a quick swipe with his left sleeve to clear it.

They now made a series of lateral steps. They came closer and ever closer to Old Anak, until his trunk could have reached out and encircled either of them. Once more Hannibal jumped to the right toward me. Gisbo, springing to the left, kept in front of him. Before I had time to back up the elephant out of the way, Hannibal, seizing a quick opportunity, brought his sword down to slash and unhinge Gisbo's left shoulder. Ready and rapid was the parry of Gisbo, but there was another, greater parry now. Hannibal's sword came down with all its might on the ivory tusk of Anak—the right, ulcerated tusk.

The elephant raised his head and bellowed in pain, and charged forward between the swordsmen, pushing them aside and interrupting their combat. He sped wildly on, without direction, uncontrollable, trumpeting in his torture.

"Anak!" I cried. "Anak, stop!" But my commands and cries had no effect. He shook his head and kept up the noises of his suffering and went about in a circle upon the summit of the butte. As he bore down uncheckably upon the horses, the two animals, the white and the bay, reared back in terror and broke their hitching reins and fled off the butte, down the slope, back toward the Carthaginian camp.

"Anak! Anak! Anak, stop!" I cried out repeatedly. Again and again I slashed his ear with the blade of the elephant staff. But he was completely out of control, unmanageable, hearing nothing, resenting everything, unaware of what he was doing. In his anguish Old Anak had gone mad.

Time after time I ripped at his ear, but he never ceased his aimless rushing. I was as helpless to guide him as to stop him—and he was now headed straight toward the two men who had re-engaged in fierce conflict, so taken up with the menace of each other that they knew naught of this terrible new one.

I remember it. I will never forget it. Hannibal stood there, pulled back as far as he could, but not far enough, in body evasion of the lunge of Gisbo.

"Admit you are conquered, Hannibal," said he. "Admit it so I can save you."

At this awful moment I found myself praying that Gisbo's sword would do its final work. Cleaner, more merciful this than the tusk of Anak—and Anak, with no human power to stop him, was bearing down upon Hannibal. In that fleeting instant, I thought how Anak had killed Scarbas. Now he was to kill the second of the two men I loved and he loved above all others.

In desperation I cried out, "Hannibal!" without respect, short, as quick as ever my tongue could say it. He may have thought it an exclamation from me because of the mortal point at his breast, or an urging for him to yield. Withal, to divert a moment's attention to a horrified boy would make him hostage to Gisbo's sword. If he were aware out of the tail of his eyes of the elephant's approach, this meant no more than that I was bringing him up again to watch. Whatever it was, he heeded me not at all, and stood there in the relentless route of the elephant, with Gisbo's blade tip at his breast above the heart.

"Let me save you, Hannibal," repeated Gisbo.

Hannibal said never a word in reply to the entreaty, but during the utterance of it sprang backward out of reach. And Gisbo, pursuing, took his place in the path of the oncoming elephant.

That ivory weapon, that piercing ivory weapon, spitted the left side of the swordsman. Gisbo was stuck through and lifted up by the diseased tusk of Anak. The fresh pain of this made the elephant scream out again. Simultaneously came the scream of Gisbo, aware in his final agony of the instrument of his fate!

"The elephant! My Nemesis! Death by the elephant was ordained."

Anak dashed on with uplifted head, still bearing Gisbo, now speechless and dead. I jumped from his neck to the ground as he went. With his burden, he rushed wildly off the hilltop, down the slope. He lowered his head and shook it and left the body of Gisbo lying there. He went on and on, tossing his head, and bellowing in his torment, on toward the distant Roman camp. Into that terror-stricken camp in a little while would come a mad elephant. The last act in the life of Old Anak would be to kill more Romans before they could kill him.

In silence we walked down the slope to where Gisbo's body was. Hannibal reached under the red cloak into the dead man's pocket to remove the confession and the slip of paper. He took off his helmet then, and I did likewise. There we stood bareheaded above Gisbo.

"He was a great general, Agenor," said Hannibal.

We looked up to gaze at the still fleeing Anak, very black in the Campanian landscape and growing smaller and still headed toward the enemy camp to do his final work of Roman destruction.

We waited upon the hilltop.

"Shall I begin to dig?" I asked.

"No, Agenor," Hannibal said. "Some men will soon be here. Our returned horses will cause them to come."

It was as he said. A squad of Numidian cavalry arrived with two extra horses. We continued to wait until they buried Gisbo there on the Roman hill, with all the costly rings upon his fingers, and with himself and his red cloak protected for a little while from the moldering earth by the white Roman toga wound about him. Hannibal told the Numidians and the army later that Old Anak had gone mad from an ulcerated tusk, had gored the great General Gisbo to death, and then had fled to the Roman camp.

Hannibal and I now rode side by side on the two extra horses. There was no speech between us until we approached the Carthaginian camp and saw a great column of Numidian horsemen arriving and heard the shouts that welcomed them. Then Hannibal spoke: "The fleet has come from Carthage. Admiral Bomilcar has brought the new troops."

At the end of the long column of cavalry was a long line of elephants. I counted them. There were forty. As they passed, the veteran, welcoming soldiers broke out into the chorus of their old, familiar song:

> His elephants large,
> With tusks they charge,
> They gore to death
> And tramp out breath—
> When Hannibal conquers Rome.

"Am I going to be the assistant in charge of them," I asked, "like I was with Scarbas? If you get Carthalo, can I be his assistant?"

"No," said Hannibal. "You will return with Admiral Bomilcar when he goes back to Carthage with the ships. Misdes has probably arrived with the new soldiers and elephants. He was to arrange for you to enter Hippomedon's School of Rhetoric."

"And I must do that, sir? Can't I wait another year?"

"You have already waited one year. You must do it now, Agenor."

"Will you promise me, then, to free Draccus and let him go back home?"

"We don't free Romans as a rule. But we will him. I promise."

I did not protest against my fate because I knew there was no need to, but I felt utterly desolate, utterly desolate and alone. Gone were the elephants, the bugles, the battles, the glory! Gone the radiant presence of Hannibal, the companionship of Draccus. Scarbas was in his grave, and I was now bereft of Anak forevermore. Behind was life and the enchantment of life. Before was only a dreary rhetoric school.

Ah, if this forlorn lad only had a father to whom he could run! What matter if he were but an ordinary man, one of poor estate, just so his arms were warm and enfolding and comforting and understanding. Strange that a Carthaginian orphan boy should think of a Roman to fill this great need at this urgent hour. I entered our tent and went up to Draccus and he held me tight.

"It is good-by, Draccus," I said, "it is good-by to everything."

TWENTY-ONE

Not at once but slowly did Hippomedon and his assistant Greeks shape Agenor of the Elephants into Agenor the Rhetorician.

All the sights and sounds where the great Hannibal was, flashing and in melody, came often to my eyes and ears from the page of the book in front of me. But Hippomedon had taken in wistful boys before, and ever as he put knowledge into their heads had removed the wild longings from their hearts. "Is Agenor woolgathering again?" he would ask, and upon the page whence the magic had come, would reappear Greek words and dull, deep learning.

For fourteen years longer Hannibal made the Romans tremble, losing no battle yet losing the war. He was to ride around the city walls with his cavalry as the terrorized inhabitants cried out, "Hannibal at the gates!" But he only threw his spear at one, and went sorrowfully away, never entering and knowing now he would never enter.

The younger Scipio, he who had saved his father at Ticinus, brought a big army to Africa, and encamped threateningly at Zama, a short distance from Carthage. The Senate summoned their great commander home. When he had leaned against Little Enoch's leg at New Carthage, he was twenty-nine years old. Now he was forty-five. When I had looked down at his young head there in the torchlight, his hair was coal black. Now, as he stepped from the ship, I saw it was graying at the temples. Here at the Carthage wharf my own age was the same as his had been on that May evening in Spain.

Hannibal met his first defeat in the hot African sands in the Battle of Zama. Thereby mighty Carthage began to fade. Thereby Rome began gathering up the nations of the world into her vast bosom.

Eighty elephants perished at Zama, making a total of a hundred and fifty-seven in three herds that had given up their lives in Hannibal's wars against Rome. By the severe terms of peace, Carthage surrendered all her war tuskers and promised to train no others. So thenceforward the stables were empty under the triple walls. Carthalo bought his farm on the Bagradus River and I used to visit him there. Morbal, increasingly old and inactive, went back to the stables once a week, and hobbled on his cane past the deserted stalls, thence sadly home. He died within a year.

"Agenor in his studies does not have the magnificence of Gillimas and Misdes before him," Hippomedon had to say disappointedly to the end. Nevertheless, I turned out to be a more successful lawyer than either of them. I suppose I had learned an outlook from Hannibal that cannot be taught in rhetoric schools. In any event, I had many rich clients, among them General Samnis, now become one of the great merchants and shippers of Carthage and ever complaining of the high taxes. "Agenor," he would ask mournfully, "you will visit General Samnis, will you not, when he is in the almshouse out at the isthmus?"

Both of Hannibal's brothers had been killed in the wars.

General Hanno, General Barmocarus, and General Maharbal lived in the fashionable suburb of Megara, where Hannibal also had his home, occupying his father Hamilcar's big residence of spotted-yellow Numidian marble. On occasional evenings, they met and talked of the old days, and at such times General Samnis, Gillimas, Misdes and I were there too. It was like a fresh wind blowing upon my spirit to go from a busy legal day on Kinisdo Square, where I was a man of dignity and importance, into this atmosphere where I was only Agenor of the Elephants again.

When Hannibal was elected Suffete, he made me his secretary. Sometimes I would go into his office to find him gazing out of the window over the blue Mediterranean toward Rome. "Hannibal is woolgathering again," I would chide him, using Hippomedon's remedy in reverse, to cure regrets and vanished dreams.

He put into effect many important reforms. Carthage began to be rich and flourishing again and offered to settle its tribute to Rome in one huge payment. The Romans became jealous and uneasy, egged on by redheaded, bilious-looking Cato the Censor. This man never made a speech without declaring at the end of it: *"Delenda est Carthago!* Carthage must be destroyed!"

At the time I was Hannibal's secretary I received the following letter:

Agenor the Rhetorician
Care of the Suffete Hannibal
Carthage

To Agenor Greetings and Affection:

This is Draccus, Agenor, sir, addressing you from the Balearics, the home of Yud and Dor. My two sons, Sempronius and Titus, have been urging me to write you. They want you to visit us and tell them all about elephants, particularly where they can buy a Little Enoch capable of becoming an Old Anak. They have already saved up ten *dinarii* apiece. How much more it will take, is one of the matters upon which they require your advice.

For a while they had ambitions to be slingers, but the necessary practice has discouraged them. Yud died a year since and Dor is very lonesome. He undertook to train the boys but soon became disgusted with their wayward zeal, pointing out that a slinger cannot be made by a little practice on Tuesday morning and a little more on Thursday afternoon. You have to be hitting something with a sling all the time. They told him they had their lessons to get and other things to do. He on his part advised them to give it up and they on theirs decided that to be like Agenor was much better anyway. The work would be less and the end more glorious.

Word came to us that one of Hannibal's acts as Suffete was to destroy the idol of Moloch and to have the black building torn down stone by stone. I need not tell you that I heard this from travelers with pleasure.

All who arrive here in ships from your country speak of Agenor as a great lawyer, the leading one in Carthage, and this makes me proud. Sempronius and Titus boast to the Balearic boys that they have a Carthaginian like-a-brother. It is thus they claim this fraternal relationship: "If he was like a son to you, father, then he is like a brother to us."

I think often of Agenor with the ready tongue but with marvelous grace in his heart for a captive Roman. Come to visit us of a sureness. Please give my respects and kind remembrances to the Suffete Hannibal.

Cornelius Draccus
Governor of the Balearic Islands

I do not put down here the large number of personal details contained in my reply to Draccus. Of my long letter to him I give only one paragraph, for which I had Hannibal's consent:

When you return to Italy, go to the Trebia battleground. Beginning where the Trebia River empties into the Po, walk along it to the seventh eastward bend. Then pace off four hundred cubits straight east. There you will find three graves, which, if they have remained undisturbed, would now appear as nothing more than three depressions in the level plain. These burials were kept secret from you at the time. The one on the south is the grave of Little Enoch. The one in the center is the grave of Scarbas. The one on the north contains upwards of five thousand pounds of ivory, sixty-nine tusks of the elephants who died after the battle in the snow and the cold. Go, if it please you, and dig up the tusks and let these be an endowment to Sempronius and Titus in Carthaginian gratitude to a captive Roman in whom Agenor, an orphan boy, found a father. If the Roman Government does not object, it is requested that enough of the funds from the sale of the ivory be used to place a simple stone over the center grave, with these words chiseled thereon:

Here lies Scarbas
A brave Carthaginian

This might be allowed on the basis of showing Roman magnanimity and bravery. There cannot be brave soldiers on one side unless they fight brave ones on the other . . .

Agenor

Cato the Censor kept saying, *"Delenda est Carthago!"* Greater and ever greater grew Roman fear of the reviving wealth and power of Carthage. In the eighth year after peace, three Roman commissioners came to Carthage. Hannibal knew they would ask for him. He knew this time the Senate would not and could not refuse to give him up.

So he took all his money, and it was much, and arranged for a ship to carry him away secretly in the night. As he prepared to go, I did likewise.

"Agenor, I cannot permit it," he said. "You have a distinguished career ahead of you in Carthage. You must not throw away everything to follow a lonely exile in his wanderings."

"In all things else I obey you, sir," I replied. "But not in this. I go."

First we voyaged to Tyre, thence to the King of Syria at Antioch. Hannibal almost persuaded this monarch of a mighty kingdom to send him to Italy with many ships, a herd of elephants, and a large army. His eyes, so long brooding, became alive and eager. "Agenor," he cried out as he studied his maps, "though the troops will be Asiatics, it will be no less Hannibal at the Roman gates."

But the king blew hot and cold. In the end his vacillations and uncertainties proved his ruin. Rome defeated him and made him a vassal and Hannibal fled, I with him.

We sought sanctuary in Crete. From here had long come the world's greatest bowmen, but we liked not the race when we tried to live among them. They had heard that Hannibal brought with him much wealth. To secure this was their main concern.

The King of Bithynia offered asylum and thither we went. The king, proud to have so renowned a guest, provided us with a spacious palace. In this, Hannibal contrived seven secret outlets. These were not known to the king, only to Hannibal, the workmen, and me.

To us here came a courier from Carthage, bringing many letters. One of these was from Gillimas. It gave word of my recent election as one of the two Suffetes of Carthage. Gillimas glowingly told of all the fine speeches that had been made about me. When an orator addressed the Aristocrats, he dwelt on my distinction as a lawyer. When he spoke to the educated groups, he recited my brilliant record at Hippomedon's School of Rhetoric. When he appealed to the ex-soldiers, he described my single-handed capture of Draccus and the fifteen others. When he electioneered the throngs of common men, he pictured me as an humble elephant boy. "Truly, Agenor," he concluded, "thou wert all things to all men, and won by a big majority. You must be here within two months to assume office. I will come to be with Hannibal in your stead."

I told Hannibal that I would not go.

"But you will," he declared. "You must. Let Gillimas come if you rhetoricians feel a duty to look after me. It is a great, a supreme honor. You cannot refuse it."

"I would only the more vividly see Carthage drink the cup of humiliation, only the more clearly see her moving toward eclipse and doom. To your ears as to mine have come the revengeful Roman threats that they intend some day to level Carthage to the ground, and run a plow over it, and plant salt in the furrows."

"Agenor, you talk like the boy who too soon left the tied debate. Accept not doom until you hear its actual trumpet. You must go. Besides, you can help me much more as Suffete than by staying here with me. We can perchance arrange things."

This was in the Year of the World 3822. Hannibal was now sixty-five, and I forty-nine. His hair was still thick, but it was very gray.

My ship was to arrive in two weeks. Ahead of it came another, bearing an embassy from Rome to the King of Bithynia. Chief of these Romans was Flaminius. At nightfall four days later there was a pounding on the regular front portal and Roman words crying out for us to open.

"They have come for me," said Hannibal. "Let us flee by one of the secret outlets. At once, Agenor, to number five in the south rear corner."

We hurried there, I ahead. I lifted the shutter from the little slit to see if the coast was clear. There stood four soldiers. To the six others in succession we ran and six times I called out, "It is guarded!"

"We are trapped," said Hannibal. "The king has made the workmen tell of the outlets and their location, and has betrayed us to the Romans to curry their favor. There is now no escape—but one."

We returned to his own private chamber and halted before its door. With his right thumb and forefinger, he pulled the ring from the third finger of his left hand. He held it out to me with the words, "Unscrew the gem to remove it."

"O Hannibal, I cannot," I cried.

"I will do it, Agenor. As the last of many favors, will you fetch a cup of water for your commander?"

I brought it and he emptied into it the contents of the vial. He held the cup in his left hand, steady and unshaking. And no less steady were his eyes and voice as he looked at me and spoke:

"They are pounding on the portal and will soon break it down. There is no time to lose. Take your ship as you intended, be a worthy Suffete, help Carthage all you may, save her if you can. I go now to free the Romans of their long fear of Hannibal. Good-by, Agenor."

He opened the door and went in and closed it and I continued to stand without. In a little while there was the sound of the front portal being broken down. Flaminius, in his white toga, preceded by a squad of soldiers, approached me. He asked where Hannibal was and I made a gesture toward the door. The soldiers went ahead, he followed, and I stepped back two paces so I could not see within.

Flaminius soon came out of the room and announced to me, not joyously, not sadly, rather as one cheated: "Hannibal is dead."